'Zafón combines sincere engagement with genre tradition, with clever touches of the literary post-modern . . . This is explicitly, and joyously, a book about books, about what can be learned from them and what is lost when they are lost'   Steven Poole, *Guardian*

'*The Prisoner of Heaven* is the third part of the story and, like the first, is narrated by Daniel Sempere. But it too contains stories within stories, and the real narrative here belongs to the irrepressible Fermín Romero de Torres . . . Zafón's characters and dialogue are as lively and full-blooded as ever'   Stephanie Merritt, *Observer*

Praise for *The Angel's Game*

'*The Angel's Game* weaves the conventions of Wilkie Collins and Dickens into something original and surprisingly moving'
Stephanie Merritt, *Observer*

'Beyond plentiful shocks and thrills, Zafón niftily treads the fine line between a story of paranormal events and one of psychological delusion'   Boyd Tonkin, *Independent*

'The gothic landscape of the Cemetery of Forgotten Books – the winding streets of Barcelona's old quarter – haunt a novel about books and writing and secrets. Wonderful'
Kate Mosse, *The Times*

'The prose is intelligent but unpretentious, and the author is clear in his intentions to provide a rollicking, fun read . . . the novel's themes address the power of narrative, and many sharp lines pertain to storytelling . . . hugely enjoyable'

*ph*

'A heady brew of detective thriller; supernatural horror tale, magical realist fable and heartbreaking love story'

*Daily Mail*

'His narrative style embraces relentless pace and fantastical and magical diversions . . . Zafón is the tempter'    *Guardian*

Praise for *The Shadow of the Wind*

'If you thought the gothic novel died with the nineteenth century, this will change your mind . . . in Zafón's hands, every scene seems to come from an early Orson Wells movie . . . one gorgeous read'    Stephen King

'Zafón's book is tremendously enjoyable . . . his story is impressively well-rounded. Humour, horror, politics and romance are skilfully deployed and the overall effect is hugely satisfying'    *Sunday Telegraph*

'Walk down any street in Zafón's Barcelona and you'll glimpse the shades of the past and the secrets of the present, inscribed alike in the city's material fabric and the lives of its citizens'    Michael Kerrigan, *Guardian*

'*The Shadow of the Wind* is a triumph of the storyteller's art. I couldn't put it down. Enchanting, hilarious and heartbreaking, this book will change your life'    *Daily Telegraph*

'Gripping and instantly atmospheric, this literary mystery opens in the Cemetery of Forgotten Books, a maze-like library of obscure tomes hidden away in Barcelona's Old City, where the hero, Daniel, is taken as a boy . . . But he little realises the evil which it will unleash and the devastating impact it will have on his life'

*You* magazine (*Mail on Sunday*)

'Everything about *The Shadow of the Wind* is smooth. The language purrs along, while the plot twists and unravels with a languid grace . . . Zafón's novel is atmospheric, beguiling and thoroughly readable' *Observer*

'Gabriel García Márquez meets Umberto Eco meets Jorge Luis Borges . . . Ruiz Zafón gives us a panoply of alluring and savage personages and stories. His novel eddies in currents of passion, revenge and mysteries whose layers peel away onion-like yet persist in growing back . . . we are taken on a wild ride that executes its hairpin bends with breathtaking lurches' *New York Times*

'One of those rare novels that combine brilliant plotting with sublime writing. It's about Barcelona again, and word of mouth alone is sure to make it a bestseller'

James Daunt, *Sunday Times*

Carlos Ruiz Zafón is the author of seven novels, including the international phenomenon *The Shadow of the Wind*, and *The Angel's Game*. His work has been published in more than forty-five different languages, has sold over thirty million copies, and has been honoured with numerous international awards. He divides his time between Barcelona, Spain, and Los Angeles, California.

www.carlosruizzafon.co.uk

BY CARLOS RUIZ ZAFÓN

*The Prince of Mist*
*The Midnight Palace*
*The Watcher in the Shadows*
*Marina*

The Cemetery of Forgotten Books
*The Shadow of the Wind*
*The Angel's Game*
*The Prisoner of Heaven*

*The*

# PRISONER
*of* HEAVEN

CARLOS RUIZ ZAFÓN

*Translated from the Spanish by Lucia Graves*

WEIDENFELD & NICOLSON

A W&N PAPERBACK

First published in Great Britain in 2012
by Weidenfeld & Nicolson
This paperback edition published in 2013
by Weidenfeld & Nicolson,
an imprint of the Orion Publishing Group Ltd
Carmelite House, 50 Victoria Embankment
London EC4Y 0DZ

An Hachette UK company

12 14 16 18 20 19 17 15 13

First published in Spain as *El Prisioner del Cielo*

Copyright © Shadow Factory, S.L. 2011
Translation © Lucia Graves 2012
Photographs © Mark Rusher

Extract from *The Barcelona of Carlos Ruiz Zafón*
© Sergio Vila-Sanjuán, 2008

ISBN 978-1-780-22285-1

Printed and bound in Great Britain by Clays Ltd, St Ives plc

MIX
Paper from
responsible sources
FSC
www.fsc.org    FSC® C104740

www.orionbooks.co.uk

## THE CEMETERY OF FORGOTTEN BOOKS

*The Prisoner of Heaven* is part of a cycle of novels set in the literary universe of the Cemetery of Forgotten Books of which *The Shadow of the Wind* and *The Angel's Game* are the two first instalments. Although each work within the cycle presents an independent, self-contained tale, they are all connected through characters and storylines, creating thematic and narrative links.

Each individual instalment in the Cemetery of Forgotten Books series can be read in any order, enabling the reader to explore the labyrinth of stories along different paths which, when woven together, lead into the heart of the narrative.

*The Prisoner of Heaven*

I have always known that one day I would return to these streets to tell the story of the man who lost his soul and his name among the shadows of a Barcelona trapped in a time of ashes and silence. These are pages written in the flames of the city of the damned, words etched in fire on the memory of the one who returned from among the dead with a promise nailed to his heart and a curse upon his head. The curtain rises, the audience falls silent and before the shadow lingering over their destiny descends upon the set, a chorus of pure souls takes the stage with a comedy in their hands and the blessed innocence of those who, believing the third act to be the last, wish to spin a Christmas story – unaware that once the last page is turned, the poison of its words will drag them slowly but inexorably towards the heart of darkness.

Julián Carax
*The Prisoner of Heaven*
(Éditions de la Lumière, Paris, 1992)

# Part One

## *A Christmas Story*

# 1

*Barcelona, December 1957*

THAT YEAR AT CHRISTMAS TIME, EVERY MORNING DAWNED laced with frost under leaden skies. A bluish hue tinged the city and people walked by, wrapped up to their ears and drawing lines of vapour with their breath in the cold air. Very few stopped to gaze at the shop window of Sempere & Sons; fewer still ventured inside to ask for that lost book that had been waiting for them all their lives and whose sale, poetic fancies aside, would have contributed to shoring up the bookshop's ailing finances.

'I think today will be the day. Today our luck will change,' I proclaimed on the wings of the first coffee of the day, pure optimism in a liquid state.

My father, who had been battling with the ledger since eight o'clock that morning, twiddling his pencil and rubber, looked up from the counter and eyed the procession of elusive clients disappearing down the street.

'May heaven hear you, Daniel, because at this rate, if we don't make up our losses over the Christmas season, we won't even be able to pay the electricity bill in January. We're going to have to do something.'

'Fermín had an idea yesterday,' I offered. 'He thinks it's a brilliant plan that'll save the bookshop from imminent bankruptcy.'

'Lord help us.'

I quoted Fermín, word for word:

'*Perhaps if by chance I was seen arranging the shop window in my underpants, some lady in need of strong literary emotions would be drawn in and inspired to part with a bit of hard cash. According to expert opinion, the future of literature depends on women and as God is my witness the female is yet to be born who can resist the primal allure of this stupendous physique,*' I recited.

I heard my father's pencil fall to the floor behind me and I turned round.

'So saith Fermín,' I added.

I thought my father would smile at Fermín's plea, but when I noticed that he remained silent, I sneaked a glance at him. Not only did Sempere senior not appear to find the suggestion the least bit funny, but he had adopted a pensive expression, as if he were seriously considering it.

'Well, well . . . perhaps Fermín has unexpectedly hit the nail on the head,' he murmured.

I looked at him in disbelief. Maybe the customer drought that had struck in the last few weeks was finally affecting my father's good judgement.

'Don't tell me you're going to allow him to wander around the bookshop in his Y-fronts.'

'No, of course not. It's about the shop window. Now that you've mentioned it, it's given me an idea . . . We may still be in time to save our Christmas after all.'

He disappeared into the back room, then emerged sporting his official winter uniform: the same coat, scarf and hat I remembered him wearing since I was a child. Bea suspected that my father hadn't bought any new clothes since 1942, and everything seemed to indicate that my wife was right. As he slipped on his gloves, my father smiled absently, his eyes twinkling with almost childlike excitement, a look that only momentous tasks managed to bring out in him.

'I'll leave you on your own for a while,' he announced. 'I'm going out to do an errand.'

'May I ask where you're going?'

My father winked at me.

'It's a surprise. You'll see.'

I followed him to the door and saw him set off at a brisk pace towards Puerta del Ángel, one more figure in the grey tide of pedestrians advancing through another long winter of shadows and ashes.

# 2

Making the most of the fact that i'd been left alone, I decided to turn on the radio and enjoy a bit of music while I reorganised the collections on the shelves to my liking. My father argued that to have the radio on when there were customers in the shop was in bad taste, and if I turned it on when Fermín was around, he'd start to hum on the back of any melody, or even worse, given a chance he'd start swaying to what he called 'sensual Caribbean rhythms' and after a few minutes he'd get on my nerves. Taking those practical difficulties into account, I'd come to the conclusion that I should limit my enjoyment of the radio waves to the rare moments when there was nobody else in the shop but me and thousands of books.

That morning, Radio Barcelona was broadcasting a rare recording of a fabulous Louis Armstrong concert – made when the trumpeter and his band had played at the Hotel Windsor Palace on Avenida Diagonal, three Christmases earlier. During the publicity breaks, the presenter insisted on labelling that music as *chass*, with the warning that some of its suggestive syncopations might not be suitable for pious Spanish listeners brought up on the popular *tonadillas* and boleros that ruled the airwaves.

Fermín was in the habit of saying that if Don Isaac Albéniz had been born black, jazz would have been invented in the village of Camprodón, near the Pyrenees. That glorious sound, he said, was one of the precious few true achievements of the twentieth century along with the pointed bras worn by his adored Kim Novak in some of the films we saw at the Fémina Cinema matinees. I wasn't going to argue with that. I let the remainder of the morning drift by between the alchemy of the music and the perfume of books, savouring the satisfaction that comes from a simple task well done.

Fermín had taken the morning off to finalise preparations for his wedding with Bernarda, due to take place at the beginning of February, or so he said. The first time he'd brought up the subject, barely two weeks earlier, we'd all told him he was rushing into it and that too much haste would lead him nowhere fast. My father tried to persuade him to postpone the event for at least two or three months, arguing that weddings were always best in the summer when the weather was good. But Fermín had insisted on sticking to his date, alleging that, being a specimen weathered in the harsh, dry airs of the Extremadura hills, he was prone to break into profuse perspiration during the Mediterranean summer, a semi-tropical affair in his estimation, and didn't deem it appropriate to celebrate his nuptials flashing sweat stains the size of pancakes under his armpits.

I was beginning to think that something odd must be happening to Fermín Romero de Torres – proud standard-bearer of civil resistance against the Holy Mother Church, banks and good manners in that pious 1950s Spain so given to religious services and propaganda newsreels – for him to display such urgency for tying the knot. In his pre-matrimonial zeal he'd even befriended Don Jacobo, the new parish priest at the church of Santa Ana, who was blessed with a relaxed ideology and the manners of a retired boxer. Fermín had infected him with his boundless passion for dominoes, and together they staged epic matches at the Bar Admiral on Sundays after mass. Don Jacobo would laugh his head off when my friend asked him, between glasses of fine liqueurs, if he had it from a higher source that nuns actually had thighs, and if that were the case, were they as soft and nibbly as he'd been suspecting since adolescence?

'You'll manage to get that priest excommunicated,' my father scolded him. 'Nuns are not to be looked at, or touched.'

'But the reverend is almost more of a rogue than I am,' Fermín protested. 'If it weren't for the uniform . . .'

I was recalling that conversation and humming to the sound of Maestro Armstrong's trumpet when I heard the soft tinkle of the doorbell and looked up, expecting to see my father returning from his secret mission, or Fermín ready to start the afternoon shift.

'Good morning,' came a deep, broken voice from the doorway.

# 3

Cast against the light from the street, the silhouette resembled a tree trunk lashed by the wind. The visitor sported a dark, old-fashioned suit and presented a grim figure as he leaned on his walking stick. He took one step forward, limping visibly. The light from the small lamp on the counter revealed a face lined by age and the unmistakable trace of misfortune. The man stared at me for a few moments, sizing me up unhurriedly. He had the cold eyes of a bird of prey, patient and calculating.

'Are you Señor Sempere?'

'I'm Daniel. Señor Sempere is my father, but he's not in right now. Is there anything I can help you with?'

The visitor ignored my question and began to wander around the bookshop examining everything in detail with almost covetous interest. The limp affecting him suggested that the wounds concealed beneath those clothes must have been quite severe.

'Souvenirs from the war,' said the stranger, as if he'd read my thoughts.

I kept my eyes on him, following his inspection tour through the bookshop, suspecting where he was going to drop anchor. Just as I'd imagined, he stopped in front of the ebony and glass cabinet, a relic dating back to the shop's origin in 1888 when Great-grandfather Sempere, then a young man recently arrived from his fortune-seeking adventures in the Americas, had borrowed some money to buy an old glove shop and turn it into a bookshop. That cabinet, crown jewel of the shop, was reserved for the most valuable items.

The visitor drew close enough to the cabinet for his breath to leave a trail on the glass. He pulled out a pair of spectacles, put them on and proceeded to study the contents. His expression made me think of a weasel examining freshly laid eggs in a chicken coop.

'Beautiful piece,' he murmured. 'Looks pricey.'

'A family heirloom. Its value is mostly sentimental,' I replied, feeling uncomfortable at the assessments of that peculiar customer, whose gaze seemed bent on costing even the air we were breathing.

After a while he put his spectacles away and spoke in a measured tone.

'I understand that a gentleman, well known for his wit, works for you.'

When I didn't reply immediately, he turned round and threw me a withering look.

'As you can see, I'm on my own. Perhaps, sir, if you would kindly tell me what book you're after, I could try to find you a copy, with pleasure.'

The stranger granted me a smile that was anything but friendly and then nodded.

'I see you have a copy of *The Count of Monte Cristo* in that cabinet.'

He wasn't the first customer to notice the book. I gave him the official sales patter we reserved for such occasions.

'The gentleman has a very good eye. It's a magnificent edition, numbered and with illustrations by Arthur Rackham. It belonged to the private library of an important collector in Madrid. A unique piece, and catalogued.'

The visitor listened without interest, focusing his attention on the consistency of the ebony shelves and making it clear that my words bored him.

'All books look the same to me, but I like the blue on that cover,' he replied in a scornful tone. 'I'll take it.'

Under other circumstances I would have jumped for joy at the thought of being able to sell what was probably the most expensive book in the entire shop, but the thought that it should end up in the hands of that character made my stomach turn. Something told me that if that volume left the bookshop, nobody would ever bother to read even the first paragraph.

'It's a very costly edition. If you like, sir, I can show you other editions of the same work in perfect condition and at much more reasonable prices.'

People with a meagre soul always try to make others feel small too, and the stranger, who could probably conceal his on the head of a pin, gave me his most disdainful look.

'And with blue covers too,' I added.

He ignored the impertinence of my irony.

'No, thank you. This is the one I want. I don't care about the price.'

I agreed reluctantly and walked over to the cabinet. As I pulled out the key and opened the glass door, I could feel the stranger's eyes piercing my back.

'Good things are always under lock and key,' he muttered under his breath.

I took the book and sighed.

'Is the gentleman a collector?'

'I suppose you could call me that. But not of books.'

I turned round with the book in my hand.

'And what do you collect, sir?'

Once again, the stranger ignored my question and stretched a hand out for the book. I had to resist the urge to put the volume back in the cabinet and turn the key. My father would never forgive me if I let such a sale go by when business was so bad.

'The price is three hundred and fifty pesetas,' I said before handing it to him, hoping the figure would make him change his mind.

He nodded without batting an eyelid and pulled out a one-thousand-peseta note from the pocket of a suit that cannot have been worth a *duro*. I wondered whether the note was forged.

'I'm afraid I don't have change for such a large note, sir.'

I would have asked him to wait a moment while I ran down to the nearest bank for change and, at the same time, to make sure it wasn't a fake, but I didn't want to leave him alone in the bookshop.

'Don't worry. It's genuine. Do you know how you can tell?'

The stranger raised the note against the light.

'Look at the watermarks. And these lines. The texture . . .'

'Is the gentleman an expert in forgeries?'

'In this world, everything is a fake, young man. Everything except money.'

He placed the note in my hand and closed my fist over it, patting my knuckles.

'Keep the change for my next visit,' he said. 'On account.'

'It's a lot of money, sir. Six hundred and fifty pesetas . . .'

'Loose change.'

'Let me give you a receipt then.'

'I trust you.'

The stranger examined the book without interest.

'By the way, it's a gift. I'm going to ask you to deliver it in person.'

For a moment, I hesitated.

'We don't normally do deliveries, but in this case we'll be happy to take care of your package, free of charge. May I ask whether the address is in Barcelona itself or . . .?'

'It's right here,' he said.

His icy look seemed to betray years of anger and resentment.

'Would you like to include a dedication, or add a personal note before I wrap the book up, sir?'

The visitor opened the book at the title page with some difficulty. I noticed then that his left hand was artificial, made of painted porcelain. He pulled out a fountain pen and wrote a few words. Then he gave the book back to me and turned to leave. I watched him as he hobbled towards the door.

'Would you be so kind as to give me the name and address where you would like us to deliver the book, sir?' I asked.

'It's all there,' he said, without turning his head.

I opened the book and looked for the page with the inscription the stranger had written out.

*For Fermín Romero de Torres,*
*who came back from among the dead*
*and holds the key to the future.*

13

Then I heard the tinkle of the doorbell and when I looked up, the stranger was gone.

I dashed over to the door and peered out into the street. The visitor was limping away, merging with the silhouettes that moved through the veil of blue mist sweeping up Calle Santa Ana. I was about to call him, but I bit my tongue. The easiest thing would have been to let him go and have done with it, but my instinct and my characteristic lack of prudence got the better of me.

# 4

I HUNG THE CLOSED SIGN ON THE DOOR AND LOCKED UP, determined to follow the stranger through the crowd. I knew that if my father returned and discovered that I had abandoned my post – on the one occasion when he'd left me alone and bang in the middle of that sales drought – I'd be in serious trouble. But I'd think of a convenient excuse along the way. Better to face my father's temper than be consumed by the anxiety left in me by that sinister character, and not know what was the true intent of his business with Fermín.

A professional bookseller has few opportunities to acquire the fine art of following a suspect in the field without being spotted. Unless a substantial number of his customers are prominent defaulters, such opportunities are only granted to him vicariously by the collection of crime stories and penny dreadfuls on his bookshelves. Clothes maketh not the man, but crime, or its presumption, maketh the detective, especially the amateur sleuth.

While I followed the stranger towards the Ramblas, I recalled the essentials, beginning by leaving a good fifty metres between us, camouflaging myself behind someone larger and always having a quick hideaway ready – a doorway or a shop – in case the subject I was tailing should stop and turn around without warning. When he reached the Ramblas the stranger crossed over to the central boulevard and began to walk down towards the port. The boulevard was festooned with traditional

Christmas decorations and more than one shop had decked its window with lights, stars and angels announcing a seasonal bonanza. If the regime's radio said better times were ahead, it must be true.

In those days, Christmas still retained a certain aura of magic and mystery. The powdery light of winter, the hopeful expressions of people who lived among shadows and silences, lent that setting a slight air of promise in which at least children and those who had learned the art of forgetting could still believe.

Perhaps that is why it became increasingly obvious to me that nobody seemed more out of place amid all that Christmas fantasy than the peculiar object of my investigation. He limped slowly, often stopping by one of the bird stalls or flower stands to admire parakeets and roses, as if he'd never before set eyes on one. A couple of times he walked over to the newspaper kiosks that dotted the Ramblas and amused himself, glancing at the covers of papers and magazines and idly twirling the postcard carousels. He acted as if he had never been there in his life, like a child or a tourist walking down the Ramblas for the first time – but then children and tourists often display an air of innocence that comes with not knowing one's whereabouts, whereas our man couldn't have looked less innocent even with the blessing of Baby Jesus, whose statue he passed when he reached the Church of Belén.

Then he stopped, apparently entranced by a cockatoo that was eyeballing him from one of the animal stalls opposite the entrance to Calle Puertaferrisa. Approaching the birdcage just as he'd approached the glass cabinet in the bookshop, the stranger started mumbling something to the cockatoo. The bird, a specimen with a large head, the body of a capon and luxurious plumage, survived the stranger's sulphuric breath and applied itself with great relish and concentration to what his visitor was reciting. In case there was any doubt, the bird nodded its head repeatedly and raised its feathery pink crest, visibly excited.

After a few minutes, the stranger, satisfied with his avian

exchange, resumed his itinerary. No more than thirty seconds later, as I walked past the bird stall, I noticed that a small hullabaloo had broken out. The shop assistant, plainly embarrassed, was hastily covering the cockatoo's cage with a hood because the bird kept repeating with exemplary elocution the refrain, *Franco, you prick, you can't lift your dick*. I was in no doubt at all about the source of the couplet. The stranger at least displayed a daring sense of humour and audacious political leanings, which in those days were as rare as skirts worn above the knee.

Distracted by the incident, I thought I'd lost sight of him, but soon I glimpsed his hunched figure standing in front of the window of the Bagués jewellery shop. I sidled over to one of the scriveners' booths bordering the entrance to the Palace of La Virreina and observed him carefully. His eyes shone like rubies, and the sight of gold and precious stones behind the bulletproof pane seemed to have awoken a lust in him that not even a row of chorus girls from La Criolla in its years of splendour could have aroused.

'A love letter, an application, a request to the distinguished official of your choice, a spontaneous "hope this letter finds you well" for the relatives in the country, young man?'

The scribe whose booth I had adopted as a hiding place was peering out like a father confessor and looked at me expectantly, hoping I'd make use of his services. The poster above the counter read:

## OSWALDO DARÍO DE MORTENSSEN
### MAN OF LETTERS AND FREE THINKER

*Writes love letters, petitions, wills, poems, praises,*
*greetings, pleas, obituaries, hymns, dissertations, applications*
*and all types of compositions in all classic styles and metrics*
*Ten céntimos per sentence (rhymes are extra)*
*Special prices for widows, disabled war veterans and minors.*

'What say you, young man? A love letter of the sort that makes girls of a courting age wet their petticoats with desire? I'll give you a special price.'

I showed him my wedding ring. Oswaldo, the scribe, shrugged his shoulders, unperturbed.

'These are modern times,' he argued. 'If you knew the number of married men and women who come by my booth . . .'

I read the notice again. There was something familiar about it, which I couldn't put my finger on.

'Your name rings a bell . . .'

'I've seen better times. Maybe from back then.'

'Is it your real name?'

'*Nom de plume.* An artist's name needs to match his mission. On my birth certificate I'm Jenaro Rebollo, but with a name like that, who is going to entrust their love letters to me . . .? What do you say to the day's offer? Are we to prepare a letter of passion and longing?'

'Some other time.'

The scribe nodded with resignation. He followed my eyes and frowned, intrigued.

'Watching the lame guy, aren't you?' he remarked casually.

'Do you know him?' I asked.

'For about a week now I've seen him walk past this place every day and stop right there, by the jeweller's shop window, where he stares open-mouthed as if what was on show were not rings and necklaces but Bella Dorita's bare derrière,' he explained.

'Have you ever spoken to him?'

'One of my colleagues copied out a letter for him the other day; he's missing some fingers, you see . . .'

'Which one of your colleagues was that?' I asked.

The scribe looked at me doubtfully, fearing the possible loss of a client if he replied.

'Luisito, the one over there, next to the music store, the one who looks like a seminarist.'

I offered him a few coins in gratitude but he refused them.

'I make a living with my pen, not with my tongue. There are plenty of the latter already in this courtyard. If you ever find yourself in need of grammatical rescue, you'll find me here.'

He handed me a card with the same wording as on his poster.

'Monday to Saturday, from eight to eight,' he specified. 'Oswaldo, soldier of the written word, at your service for any epistolary cause.'

I put the card away and thanked him for his help.

'Your bird's flying off.'

I turned and could see that the stranger was moving on again. I hastened after him, following him down the Ramblas as far as the entrance to the Boquería market, where he stopped to gaze at the sight of the stalls and people coming and going, loading or unloading fine delicacies. I saw him limp up to Bar Pinocho and climb on to one of the stools, with difficulty but with aplomb. For the next half-hour the stranger tried to polish off the treats which the youngest in the bar, Juanito, kept serving him, but I had a feeling that he wasn't really up to the challenge. He seemed to be eating more with his eyes, as if when he asked for tapas, which he barely sampled, he was recalling days of healthier appetites. Sometimes the palate does not savour so much as try to remember. Finally, resigned to the vicarious joy of watching others eating and licking their lips, the stranger paid his bill and continued on his voyage until he reached the entrance to Calle Hospital, where the peculiar arrangement of Barcelona's streets had conspired to place one of the great opera houses of the old world next to one of the most squalid red-light districts of the northern hemisphere.

# 5

At that time of the day the crews of a number of military and merchant ships docked in the port happened to be venturing up the Ramblas to satisfy cravings of various sorts. In view of the demand, the supply had already appeared on the corner: a rota of ladies for rent who looked as if they had clocked up quite a few miles and were ready to offer a very affordable minimum fare. I winced at the sight of tight skirts over varicose veins and purple patches that hurt just to look at them, at wrinkled faces and a general air of last-fare-before-retiring that inspired anything but lust. A sailor must have had to spend many months on the high seas to rise to the bait, I thought, but to my surprise the stranger stopped to flirt with a couple of those ladies of the long-gone springtime, as if he were bantering with the fresh beauties of the finest cabarets.

'Here, ma' love, let me take twenty years off you with my speciality rubdown,' I heard one of them say. She could easily have passed for the grandmother of Oswaldo the scribe.

You'll kill him with a rubdown, I thought. The stranger, with a prudent gesture, declined the invitation.

'Some other day, my darling,' he replied, stepping further into the Raval quarter.

I followed him for a hundred more metres or so, until I saw him stop in front of a narrow, dark doorway, nearly opposite the Hotel Europa. He disappeared into the building and I waited half a minute before going in after him.

Inside, a dark staircase seemed to trail off into the bowels of the building. The building itself looked as if it were listing to port, or perhaps were even on the point of sinking into the catacombs of the Raval district, judging from the stench of damp and a faulty sewerage system. On one side of the hallway stood some sort of porter's lodge where a greasy-looking individual in a sleeveless vest, with a toothpick between his lips and a transistor radio, cast me a look somewhere between inquisitive and plainly hostile.

'You're on your own?' he asked, vaguely intrigued.

It didn't take a genius to realise I was in the lobby of an establishment that rented out rooms by the hour and that the only discordant note about my visit was the fact that I wasn't holding the hand of one of the cut-price Venuses on patrol round the corner.

'If you like, I'll get a nice girl for you,' he offered, preparing a parcel with a towel, a bar of soap and what I guessed must be a rubber or some other prophylactic device to be used as a last resort.

'Actually, I just wanted to ask you a question,' I began.

The porter rolled his eyes.

'It's twenty pesetas for half an hour, and you provide the filly.'

'Tempting. Perhaps some other day. What I wanted to ask you was whether a gentleman has just gone upstairs, a couple of minutes ago. An older man. Not in the best shape. On his own. Filly-less.'

The porter frowned. I realised from his expression that he was instantly downgrading me from potential client to pesky fly.

'I haven't seen anyone. Go on, beat it before I call Tonet.'

I gathered Tonet could not be a very endearing character. I placed my few remaining coins on the counter and gave the porter a conciliatory smile. In a flash, the money vanished as if it were an insect and the porter's hands – with their plastic thimbles – the darting tongue of a chameleon.

'What do you want to know?'

'Does the man I described to you live here?'

'He's been renting a room for a week.'

'Do you know his name?'

'He paid a month in advance, so I didn't ask.'

'Do you know where he comes from, what he does for a living . . .?'

'This isn't a phone-in programme. People come here to fornicate and I don't ask any questions. And this one doesn't even fornicate. So you do the sums.'

I reconsidered the matter.

'All I know is that every now and then he goes out and then comes back. Sometimes he asks me to send up a bottle of wine, bread and a bit of honey. He pays well and doesn't say a word.'

'And you're sure you don't remember any names?'

He shook his head.

'All right. Thanks, and I'm sorry I bothered you.'

I was about to leave when the porter's voice called me back.

'Romero,' he said.

'Pardon?'

'I think he said he's called Romero, or something like that . . .'

'Romero de Torres?'

'That's it.'

'Fermín Romero de Torres?' I repeated, incredulous.

'That's the one. Wasn't there a bullfighter going by that name before the war?' asked the porter. 'I thought it sounded familiar . . .'

# 6

I MADE MY WAY BACK TO THE BOOKSHOP, MORE CONFUSED than before I left. As I walked past La Virreina Palace, Oswaldo, the scribe, raised a hand in greeting.

'Any luck?' he asked.

I mumbled a negative reply.

'Try Luisito, he might remember something.'

I gave Oswaldo a nod and went over to Luisito's booth. Luisito was cleaning his collection of nibs. When he saw me he smiled and asked me to sit down.

'What's it going to be? Pleasure or business?'

'Your colleague Oswaldo sent me.'

'Our mentor and master,' declared Luisito. 'A great man of letters, unrecognised by the corrupt establishment. And there he is, in the street, working with words at the service of the illiterate.'

'Oswaldo was saying that the other day you served an older man, lame and a bit clapped out, with one hand missing and some fingers of the other . . .'

'I remember him. I always remember one-handed men. Because of Cervantes – he lost a hand in the battle of Lepanto, you know?'

'I know. And could you tell me what business brought this man to you?'

Luisito stirred in his chair, uncomfortable at the turn the conversation was taking.

'Look, this is almost like a confessional. Professional confidentiality is paramount.'

'I understand that. The trouble is, this is a serious matter.'

'How serious?'

'Sufficiently serious to threaten the well-being of people who are very dear to me.'

'I see, but . . .'

Luisito craned his neck and tried to catch Oswaldo's eye at the other end of the courtyard. I saw Oswaldo nod and then Luisito relaxed.

'The gentleman brought a letter he'd written. He wanted it copied out in good handwriting, because with his hand . . .'

'And the letter was about . . .?'

'I barely remember, we write so many letters every day . . .'

'Make an effort, Luisito. For Cervantes' sake.'

'Well, although I may be confusing it with another letter I wrote for some other client, I believe it was something to do with a large sum of money the one-handed gentleman was hoping to receive or recover, or something like that. And something about a key.'

'A key.'

'Right. He didn't specify whether this was an Allen key, a piano key or a door key.'

Luisito smiled at me, visibly pleased with his own wit.

'Do you remember anything else?'

Luisito licked his lips thoughtfully.

'He said he found the city very changed.'

'In what way, changed?'

'I don't know. Changed. Without dead bodies in the streets.'

'Dead bodies in the streets? Is that what he said?'

'If I remember correctly . . .'

# 7

I THANKED LUISITO FOR THE INFORMATION AND HURRIED back, hoping I'd reach the shop before my father returned from his errand and my absence was detected. The CLOSED sign was still on the door. I opened it, unhooked the notice and took my place behind the counter, convinced that not a single customer had come by during the almost forty-five minutes I had been away.

As I wasn't busy, I started to think about what I was going to do with that copy of *The Count of Monte Cristo* and how I was going to broach the subject with Fermín when he arrived. I didn't want to alarm him unnecessarily, but the stranger's visit and my poor attempt at solving what he was up to had left me feeling uneasy. Normally, I would simply have told Fermín what had happened and left it at that, but I knew that on this occasion I had to be tactful. For some time now, Fermín had appeared crestfallen and in a filthy mood. I'd been trying to cheer him up but none of my feeble attempts seemed to make him smile.

'There's no need to clean the books so thoroughly, Fermín,' I would say. 'I've heard that very soon only *noir* will be fashionable.' I was alluding to the way the press was beginning to describe the new novels of crime and punishment that only trickled in occasionally and then in tame translations.

Far from smiling kindly at my poor jokes, Fermín would grab any opportunity to embark on one of his tirades in support of doom and gloom.

'The entire future looks *noir* anyway,' he would declare. 'If there's going to be a flavour in vogue in this age of butchery, it will be the stink of falsehood and crime disguised in a thousand euphemisms.'

Here we go, I thought. The Book of Revelation according to St Fermín Romero de Torres.

'Don't exaggerate, Fermín. You should get more sun and fresh air. The other day I read in the paper that vitamin D increases our faith in fellow humans.'

'Well, I also read in the paper that imported cigarettes make you taller and that banks around the world are deeply committed to eradicating poverty and disease on the planet in less than ten years,' he replied. 'So there you go.'

When Fermín embraced organised pessimism the best option was not to argue with him.

'Do you know, Daniel? Sometimes I think that Darwin made a mistake and that in fact man is descended from the pig, because eight out of every ten members of the human race are swine, and as crooked as a hog's tail.'

'Fermín, I prefer it when you go for the humanist and positive view of things, like the other day when you said that deep down nobody is bad, only frightened.'

'It must have been low blood sugar doing the talking. What rubbish.'

These days, the cheerful Fermín I liked to remember seemed to have beaten a retreat and been replaced by a man consumed by anxieties and stormy moods he did not wish to share. Sometimes, when he thought nobody could see him, he would shrink into a corner, anguish gnawing at his insides. He'd lost some weight, and considering that he was as thin as a rake at the best of times and his body seemed mostly composed of cartilage and attitude, his appearance was becoming worrisome. I'd mentioned it to him once or twice, but he denied there was any problem and dodged the issue with Byzantine excuses.

'It's nothing, Daniel. It's just that I now follow the football league, and every time Barça loses my blood pressure plummets. All I need is a bite of Manchego cheese and I'm as strong as an ox again.'

'Really? But you haven't been to a football match in your life.'

'That's what you think. When I was a kid everybody told me I had the legs to be a dancer or a football player.'

'Well, to me you look like a complete wreck, legs and all. Either you're ill or you're just not looking after yourself.'

For an answer he'd show me a couple of biceps the size of sugared almonds and grin as if he were a door-to-door toothpaste seller.

'Feel that! Tempered steel, like the Cid's sword.'

My father attributed Fermín's low form to nerves about the wedding and everything that came with it, from having to fraternise with the clergy to finding the right restaurant or café for the wedding banquet, but I suspected that his melancholy had much deeper roots. I was debating whether to tell Fermín what had happened that morning and show him the book, or wait for a better moment, when he dragged himself through the door with a look on his face that would have won top honours at a wake. When he saw me he smiled faintly and offered a military salute.

'Good to see you, Fermín. I was beginning to think you weren't going to come in today.'

'I'd rather be dead than idle. I was held up by Don Federico, the watchmaker. When I walked past his shop he filled me in on some gossip about the fact that someone had seen Señor Sempere walking down Calle Puertaferrisa this morning, looking very dapper and en route to an unknown destination. Don Federico and that hare-brained Merceditas wanted to know whether perhaps he'd taken a mistress – apparently, these days it gives you a certain credibility among the shopkeepers in the district and if the damsel is a cabaret singer, all the more so.'

'And what did you reply?'

'That your father, as an exemplary widower, has reverted to

a state of primal virginity, which has baffled the scientific community but earned him a fast-track application for sainthood at the archbishop's office. I don't discuss Señor Sempere's private life with friends or foes because it's nobody's business but his own. And whoever comes to me with such rubbish will get from me no more than a slap in the face and that's that.'

'You're a gentleman of the old school, Fermín.'

'The one who is of the old school is your father, Daniel. Between you and me, and this mustn't go beyond these four walls, it wouldn't be a bad thing if your father let down his hair every now and then. Ever since we started crossing this financial desert he has spent his entire time walled up in the storeroom with that Egyptian Book of the Dead.'

'It's the accounts book,' I corrected him.

'Whatever. In fact, for days now I've been thinking we should take him along to El Molino music hall and then out on the town. Even if our hero is as boring as a paella made of cabbage on that front, I'm sure a head-on collision with an elastic and decidedly buxom lass would shake up the marrow in his bones,' said Fermín.

'Look who's talking. The life and soul of the party. To be honest, you're the one I'm worried about,' I protested. 'For days you've been looking like a cockroach stuffed in a raincoat.'

'Since you mention it, that's an adroit comparison, if I may say so. For the cockroach may not have the swaggering good looks required by the frivolous norms of this daft society we've had the dubious fortune to live in, but both the underrated arthropod and yours truly are characterised by an unmatched instinct for survival, an overwhelming appetite and a leonine libido that won't relent even under extreme radiation levels.'

'It's impossible to argue with you, Fermín.'

'That's because of my natural flair for high dialectics, always ready to strike back at the slightest hint of inanity, dear friend. But your father is a tender, delicate flower and I think the time has come to take action before he turns into a complete fossil.'

'Take what action, Fermín?' my father's voice cut in behind us. 'Don't tell me you're going to set up a tea party with Rociíto.'

We turned round like two schoolboys caught in the act. My father, looking most unlike a tender flower, was watching us severely from the door.

# 8

'AND HOW ON EARTH DO YOU KNOW ABOUT ROCIÍTO?' mumbled Fermín in astonishment.

After savouring the fright he'd given us, my father smiled kindly and gave us a wink.

'I might be turning into a fossil, but my hearing is still pretty good. My hearing and my thinking. That's why I've decided that something had to be done to revitalise our business,' he announced. 'The cabaret outing can wait.'

Only then did we notice that my father was carrying two hefty bags and a large box wrapped in brown paper and tied with thick string.

'Don't tell me you've just robbed the local bank,' I said.

'I try to avoid banks as much as possible: as Fermín says, they're the ones who usually rob us. I've been to the Santa Lucía market.'

Fermín and I looked at each other in bewilderment.

'Aren't you going to help me? This weighs a ton.'

We proceeded to unload the contents of the bags onto the counter while my father unwrapped the box. The bags were packed with small objects, each one protected with more brown paper. Fermín unwrapped one of them and stared at it, perplexed.

'What's that?' I asked.

'I'm inclined to say it's an adult sumpter at a scale of one to one hundred,' Fermín suggested.

'A what?'

'Namely, a donkey or an ass, the delightful hoofed quadruped that with winning charm and zest peoples this uniquely Spanish landscape of ours. Only this is a miniature version, like the model trains they sell in Casa Palau,' Fermín explained.

'It's a clay donkey, a figure for the crib,' my father explained.

'What crib?'

My father opened the cardboard box and pulled out the enormous manger with lights he'd just bought and which, I guessed, he was planning to place in the shop window as a Christmas advertising gimmick. Meanwhile Fermín had already unwrapped a number of oxen, pigs, ducks, as well as three wise old kings riding camels, some palm trees, a St Joseph and a Virgin Mary.

'Succumbing to the tyranny of National-Catholic propaganda and its surreptitious indoctrination techniques through a display of Yuletide figures and tall stories does not sound to me like a solution,' Fermín declared.

'Don't talk rubbish, Fermín,' my father interjected. 'This is a lovely tradition, and people like to see nativity scenes during the Christmas season. The bookshop needed some of that colourful, happy spark that Christmas requires. Have a look at all the shops in the area and you'll see how, by comparison, we look like an undertaker's parlour. Go on, help me and we'll set it up in the shop window. And move to the second row all those books on physics and the history of Western philosophy, Fermín. They scare the seasonal customer away.'

'The end is near,' mumbled Fermín.

Between the three of us we managed to position the manger and set the little figures in place. Fermín collaborated unwillingly, frowning and searching for any excuse to express his objection.

'Señor Sempere, with all due respect, may I bring to your attention that this Baby Jesus is thrice the size of his putative father and hardly fits in the cradle?'

'It doesn't matter. They'd sold out of all the smaller ones.'

'Well, I think that next to the Virgin Mary he looks like one of those Japanese fighters with a weight-management problem, greased-back hair and swirly underpants tied up like a loincloth over their nether regions.'

'Sumo wrestlers, they're called,' I said.

'The very ones,' Fermín agreed.

My father sighed, shaking his head.

'Besides, look at those eyes. You'd think he was possessed.'

'Come on, Fermín, shut up and switch on the crib lights,' my father ordered, handing him the plug.

By performing one of his balancing acts Fermín managed to slip under the table that held the manger and reach the socket at one end of the counter.

'And there was light,' my father pronounced, gazing enthusiastically at the shining new Sempere & Sons nativity scene.

'Adapt or perish!' he added, pleased with himself.

'Perish,' mumbled Fermín under his breath.

Not a minute had passed after the official lighting-up when a lady, with three children in tow, stopped by the shop window to admire the crib and, after a moment's hesitation, ventured into the shop.

'Good afternoon,' she said. 'Do you have any storybooks about the lives of the saints?'

'Of course,' said my father. 'Allow me to show you the much-recommended collection *Little Jesus Light of My Life*, which I'm sure the children will love. Profusely illustrated and with a foreword by our beloved archbishop. Doesn't get any better.'

'Sounds lovely. The fact is, it's so hard to find books with a positive message these days, the sort that make you feel really good about yourself, instead of pushing all that violence and depravity so in vogue today.'

Fermín rolled his eyes. He was about to open his mouth when I stopped him and dragged him away from the customer.

'I know what you mean, madam,' my father agreed, looking at me out of the corner of his eye, and implying with his expression that I should keep Fermín bound and gagged because we weren't going to lose that sale for anything in the world.

I pushed Fermín into the back room and made sure the curtain was drawn so that my father could tackle the situation unhindered.

'Fermín, I don't know what's up with you. I realise you're not convinced by all this business of nativity scenes, and I respect that, but if an Infant Jesus the size of a steamroller and four clay piglets lift my father's spirits, and on top of that pull customers into the bookshop, I'm going to ask you to set the existentialist pulpit aside and look as if you're part of the choir, at least during business hours.'

Fermín sighed and nodded, looking abashed.

'Of course, Daniel,' he said. 'Forgive me. I'd be prepared to walk the road to Santiago dressed up as the tooth fairy if that were to please your father and save the bookshop.'

'All you need to do is tell him you think the crib idea is a good one, and play along with him.'

Fermín nodded.

'Consider it done. I'll apologise to Señor Sempere later for overstepping the mark, and as an act of contrition I'll contribute a little nativity figurine to prove that even large department stores can't beat me at Christmas spirit. I have a friend who had to go underground who makes those lovely traditional squatting figurines – the "crappers" – in the image of Franco, so realistic they give you goose pimples.'

'A lambkin or a King Balthazar will do.'

'Your wish is my command, Daniel. Now, if you don't object, I'll go and do something useful and start opening the boxes from the widow Recasen's lot. They've been here for a week gathering dust.'

'Shall I help you?'

'Don't worry. You get on with your stuff.'

I watched him make his way to the stockroom at the far end and put on his blue work overalls.

'Fermín,' I began.

He turned round obligingly. I paused for a moment.

'Something happened today that I need to tell you about.'

'Yes?'

'Actually, I'm not quite sure how to explain this. Someone came in and asked after you.'

'Was she pretty?' asked Fermín, trying to look jolly but unable to hide a flicker of anxiety in his eyes.

'It was a gentleman. In pretty bad shape and rather odd-looking, to tell you the truth.'

'Did he leave a name?' asked Fermín.

I shook my head.

'No. But he left this for you.'

Fermín frowned. I handed him the book the stranger had bought a couple of hours before. Fermín took it and stared at the cover without understanding.

'But isn't this the Dumas we had in the glass cabinet at three hundred and fifty?'

I nodded.

'Open it at the first page.'

Fermín did as I asked. When he read the dedication he suddenly went pale and gulped. He closed his eyes for a moment and then looked at me without saying a word, seeming to have aged five years in as many seconds.

'When he left the shop I followed him,' I said. 'For the past week he's been living in a seedy establishment where they rent rooms by the hour, on Calle Hospital, opposite the Hotel Europa, and from what I've been able to find out, he uses a false name – yours, in fact: Fermín Romero de Torres. I've discovered, through one of the scribes in La Virreina, that he had a letter copied out in which he referred to a large amount of money. Does any of this ring a bell?'

Fermín seemed to be curling up, as if every word I spoke were a blow raining down on him.

'Daniel, it's very important that you don't follow this individual

33

or speak to him again. Don't do anything. Keep well away from him. He's very dangerous.'

'Who is this man, Fermín?'

Fermín closed the book and hid it behind a pile of boxes on one of the shelves. He took a quick look in the direction of the shop and once he was sure my father was still busy with the customer and couldn't hear us, he drew closer to me and spoke in a very low voice.

'Please don't tell your father or anyone else about this.'

'Fermín . . .'

'Do me this favour. For the sake of our friendship.'

'But, Fermín . . .'

'Please, Daniel. Not here. Trust me.'

I agreed reluctantly and showed him the one-thousand-peseta note the stranger had paid me with. I didn't have to explain where it had come from.

'That money is cursed, Daniel. Give it to the Sisters of Charity or to some beggar in the street. Or, better still, burn it.'

Without another word he proceeded to remove his overalls and slip on his frayed raincoat and his beret. On that matchstick head of his the beret looked like one of Dali's melting clocks.

'Are you leaving already?'

'Tell your father something unexpected has cropped up. Will you?'

'Of course, but . . .'

'I can't explain this to you now, Daniel.'

He clutched his stomach with one hand as if his insides had got tied in a knot.

'Fermín, if you tell me about it I might be able to help . . .'

Fermín paused for a moment, but then shook his head and walked out into the hallway. I followed him as far as the main door and saw him set off in the rain, just a little man with the entire world on his shoulders, while the night, blacker than ever, stole down over Barcelona.

# 9

IT IS A SCIENTIFICALLY ACKNOWLEDGED FACT THAT ANY infant a few months old has an unerring instinct for sensing the exact moment in the early hours when his parents have managed to nod off, so he can raise the tone of his cries, thereby ensuring they don't get more than thirty minutes' sleep at a time.

That night, like almost all others, little Julián awoke around three in the morning and didn't hesitate to announce the fact at the top of his lungs. I opened my eyes and turned over. Next to me, Bea, gleaming in the half-light, slowly stirred, revealing the outline of her body under the sheets, and mumbled something. I resisted my natural impulse to kiss her on the neck and relieve her of that overlong, reinforced nightgown that my father-in-law, probably on purpose, had given her on her birthday. Try as I might, I couldn't get it to disappear in the laundry.

'I'll get up,' I whispered, kissing her on the forehead.

Bea replied by rolling over and covering her head with the pillow. I paused to admire the curve of her back and its enticing descent which no nightdress in the world could have obscured. I'd been married to that wonderful creature for almost two years and was still surprised to wake up by her side, feeling her warmth. I'd started to pull back the sheet and caress her velvety thigh when Bea's hand stuck its nails into my wrist.

'Not now, Daniel. The baby's crying.'

'I knew you were awake.'

'It's hard to get any sleep sharing a house with men who either can't stop crying or can't refrain from fondling your backside – they won't let you string together more than two hours' rest a night.'

'Well, it's your loss.'

I got up and walked down the corridor to Julián's room at the back. Shortly after the wedding, we'd moved into the attic apartment in the same building as the bookshop. Don Anacleto, the secondary-school teacher who had lived in it for twenty-five years, had decided to retire and return to his native Segovia to write spicy poems under the shade of the old Roman aqueduct and broaden his understanding of the art of roast suckling pig.

Little Julián welcomed me with loud, shrill crying that threatened to shatter my eardrums. I took him in my arms and after smelling his nappy and confirming that for once there were no nasty surprises, I did what every new father with any sense would do: whisper some silly nonsense and dance about the room with ridiculous little jumps. I was in the middle of doing just that when I realised Bea was staring at me disapprovingly from the doorway.

'Give him to me. You're going to unsettle him even more.'

'He's not complaining,' I protested, handing her the baby.

Bea took him in her arms and murmured a melody in his ear as she gently rocked him. Five seconds later Julián had stopped crying and was giving that enchanted half-smile his mother always managed to elicit from him.

'Go on,' said Bea, softly. 'I'll be along in a second.'

Having been thrown out of the room, my incompetence at handling babies at the crawling stage clearly proven, I went back to our bedroom and lay down, knowing I wouldn't be able to sleep a wink the rest of the night. A while later, Bea appeared round the door and lay down next to me with a sigh.

'I'm dead tired.'

I put my arms around her and we lay there quietly for a few minutes.

'I've been thinking,' said Bea.

Tremble, Daniel, I thought. Bea sat up and then crouched down on the bed, facing me.

'When Julián is a bit older and my mother is able to look after him for a few hours a day, I think I'm going to work.'

I nodded.

'Where?'

'In the bookshop.'

I thought it best to keep quiet.

'I think it would do you all good,' she added. 'Your father is getting too old to put in all those hours and, don't be offended, but I think I'm better at dealing with customers than you, not to mention Fermín, who recently seems to scare business away.'

'I won't argue with that.'

'What's the matter with him, anyway? The other day I bumped into Bernarda in the street and she burst out crying. I took her to one of the milk bars on Calle Petritxol and after I'd plied her with cups of hot chocolate and whipped cream she told me that Fermín is behaving really oddly. For some days now, it seems he's been refusing to fill in the parish church papers for the wedding. I have a feeling Fermín isn't getting married. Has he said anything to you?'

'Yes, I've noticed it too,' I lied. 'Perhaps Bernarda is pushing him too hard . . .'

Bea looked at me but didn't say anything.

'What?' I asked finally.

'Bernarda asked me not to tell anyone.'

'Not to tell what?'

Bea fixed her eyes on mine.

'She's late this month.'

'Late? She's got behind with her work?'

Bea looked at me as if I were stupid, and then the penny dropped.

'*Bernarda is pregnant?*'

'Don't speak so loudly, you'll wake Julián.'

'Is she pregnant or isn't she?' I repeated, in a tiny voice.

'Looks like it.'

'And does Fermín know?'

'She hasn't wanted to tell him yet. She's scared he'll make a quick exit.'

'Fermín would never do that.'

'All you men would do that, given a chance.'

I was surprised by the harshness of her tone, which she quickly sweetened with an unconvincingly meek smile.

'How little you know us.'

She sat up in the dark and without saying a word lifted off her nightdress and let it fall to one side of the bed. She let me gaze at her for a few seconds and then, slowly, leaned over me and licked my lips unhurriedly.

'How little I know you,' she whispered.

# 10

THE FOLLOWING DAY THE ATTRACTION OF THE ILLUMINATED manger was proving its worth, and I saw my father smile to himself for the first time in weeks as he entered a few sales in the ledger. From early morning some old customers who hadn't set foot in the bookshop for a while began to drop by, together with new readers who were visiting us for the first time. I let my father deal with them all with his expert hand and enjoyed watching him as he recommended titles, roused their curiosity and guessed at their tastes and interests. It promised to be a good day, the first in many weeks.

'Daniel, we should bring out the collections of illustrated children's classics. The Vértice editions, with the blue spines.'

'I think they're in the basement. Do you have the keys?'

'Bea asked me for them the other day. She wanted to take something down there – something to do with the baby. I don't remember her giving them back to me. Have a look in the drawer.'

'They're not here. I'll run up to the flat to look for them.'

I left my father serving a gentleman who had just come in, looking to buy a history of old Barcelona cafés, and went out through the back room to the staircase in the hallway. The flat Bea and I shared was high up and, apart from the extra light it provided, walking up and down those stairs invigorated both our spirits and our legs. On the way I came across Edelmira, a widow on the third floor who had once been a chorus girl and now made a living by painting Madonnas and saints in her home. Too many years on the stage of the Arnau Theatre had finished off her knees and now she had to hold on to the banisters with both hands to negotiate a simple flight of stairs. In spite of her problems, she always had a smile on her lips and something kind to say.

'How's your beautiful wife, Daniel?'

'Not as beautiful as you, Doña Edelmira. Shall I help you down?'

As usual, Edelmira refused my help and asked me to give her regards to Fermín, who always volunteered slightly flirtatious comments or cheeky propositions when he saw her go by.

When I opened the door of the apartment, it still smelled of Bea's perfume and that mixture of aromas given out by babies and their props. Bea usually got up early and took Julián out for a walk in the shiny new Jané pushchair Fermín had given us, which we all referred to as 'the Mercedes'.

'Bea?' I called out.

It was a small flat, and my voice echoed back even before I'd closed the door behind me. Bea had already left. I stepped into the dining room, trying to reconstruct my wife's train of thought and work out where she could have put the basement keys. Bea was far tidier and more methodical than me. I began by looking through the drawers in the dining-room sideboard where she usually kept receipts, unanswered letters and loose change. From there I moved on to side tables, fruit bowls and shelves.

The next stop was the glass cabinet in the kitchen, where Bea usually left notes and reminders. Finally, having had no luck so far, I ended up in the bedroom, standing in front of the bed and looking around me with a critical eye. Bea's clothes took up seventy-five per cent of the wardrobe, drawers and other storage areas in the bedroom. Her line of reasoning was that I always dressed the same, so I could easily make do with a corner of the cupboard. The arrangement of her drawers was far too sophisticated for me. I felt a sudden twinge of guilt as I went through my wife's private belongings, but after rummaging in vain through all the bits of furniture in sight, I still hadn't found the keys.

Let's re-enact the crime scene, I said to myself. I vaguely remembered that Bea had said something about taking down a box with summer clothes. That had been a couple of days ago. If I was right, that day Bea was wearing the grey coat I'd given her on our first wedding anniversary. I smiled at my powers of deduction and opened the wardrobe to search for the coat. There it was. If everything I'd learned reading Conan Doyle and his disciples was correct, my father's keys would be in one of the pockets of that coat. I thrust my hand into the right pocket and felt two coins and a couple of mints, the sort they give you at the chemist. I went on to inspect the other pocket and was pleased to confirm my thesis. My fingers felt the bunch of keys.

And something else.

There was a piece of paper in the pocket. I pulled out the keys and, after a moment's doubt, decided to take out the paper too. It was probably one of those lists of errands Bea would always make to avoid forgetting anything.

When I took a closer look I realised it was an envelope. A letter. It was addressed to her maiden name, Beatriz Aguilar, and the postmark dated it a week earlier. The letter had been sent to the home of Bea's parents, not to the flat in Santa Ana. I turned it over and when I read the name of the sender, the basement keys slipped out of my hand.

*Pablo Cascos Buendía*

Bewildered, I sat on the bed and stared at the envelope. Pablo Cascos Buendía had been Bea's fiancé when we started going out together. The son of a wealthy family who owned a number of shipyards and industries in El Ferrol, he had always rubbed me up the wrong way, and I could tell the feeling was mutual.

41

At that time, he had been doing his military service as a second lieutenant. But ever since Bea had written to him to break off their engagement I hadn't heard any more about him. Until now.

What was a letter from Bea's ex-fiancé, with a recent date stamped on it, doing in her pocket? The envelope was open, but I hesitated for a whole minute before pulling out the letter. Realising this was the first time I had spied behind Bea's back, I was on the point of replacing it and hurrying out of there. My moment of virtue lasted about ten seconds. Any trace of guilt and shame evaporated before I reached the end of the first paragraph.

Dear Beatriz,

I hope you're well and feeling happy in your new life in Barcelona. You haven't replied to any of the letters I've sent you these past months, and sometimes I wonder what I've done to make you ignore me. I realise that you're a married woman with a child and that perhaps it's wrong for me to write to you, but I confess that even after all this time I can't forget you, although I've tried and I'm not ashamed to admit that I'm still in love with you.

My life has also taken a new course. A year ago I started to work as head of sales for an important publishing firm. I know how much books mean to you, and working among them makes me feel closer to you. My office is in the Madrid branch, although I travel all over Spain for my work.

I never stop thinking about you, about the life we could have shared, the children we might have had together . . . I ask myself every day whether your husband knows how to make you happy and whether you didn't marry him through force of circumstance. I can't believe that the modest life he can offer you is what you want. I know you well. We were colleagues and friends, and there haven't been any secrets between us. Do you remember those afternoons we spent together on San Pol beach? Do you remember the plans, the dreams we shared, the promises we made to one another? I've never felt this way about anyone else. Since we broke off our engagement I've been out with a few girls, but now I know that none of them can compare with you. Every time I kiss other lips I think of yours, and every time I touch someone else's skin, it's your skin I feel.

In a month's time I'll be travelling to Barcelona to visit our offices there and hold a few meetings with the staff about a future restructuring of the firm. I could easily have solved these matters by letter and telephone. The real reason for my trip is none other than the hope of being able to see you again. I know you'll think I'm mad, but that would be better than thinking I'd forgotten you. I arrive on 20 January and will be staying at the Hotel Ritz on the Gran Vía. Please, I beg you, let's meet, even if only for a while. Let me tell you in person what is in my heart. I've made a reservation in the hotel restaurant for the 21st at 2 o'clock. I'll be there, waiting for you. If you come, you'll make me the happiest man in the world and I'll know that my dreams of regaining your love might still come true.

I love you, always,

PABLO

For a couple of seconds I sat there, on the bed I'd shared with Bea just a few hours earlier. I slipped the letter back in the envelope, and when I stood up I felt as if I'd just been punched in the stomach. I ran to the bathroom sink and threw up that morning's coffee. I let the cold water run and splashed my face. The eyes of a younger Daniel whose hands were shaking the first time he had caressed Bea gazed back at me from the mirror.

WHEN I RETURNED TO THE BOOKSHOP, MY FATHER SHOT me a questioning look and glanced at his wristwatch. I knew he must have been wondering where I'd been for the past half-hour, but he didn't say anything. I handed him the keys to the basement, avoiding his eyes.

'But weren't you going to go down to fetch the books?' he asked.

'Of course. Sorry. I'll go right away.'

My father looked at me askance.

'Are you all right, Daniel?'

I nodded, feigning surprise at the question. Before I'd given him a chance to ask me again, I headed off for the basement to collect the boxes he'd asked for. The way down was at the back of the building's entrance hall. A metal door with a padlock, set beneath the first flight of the main staircase, opened on to a spiral stairway descending into the dark and smelling of damp and dead flowers. A small row of light bulbs, flickering anaemically, hung from the ceiling, making the place look like an air-raid shelter. I started down the stairs and, when I reached the basement, groped about for the light switch.

A yellowish bulb lit up above my head, revealing the outline of what was really just a junk room with delusions of grandeur. Rusty old bicycles with no known owner, worthless paintings covered in cobwebs and cardboard boxes piled up on rotting wooden shelves created a tableau that did not invite one to hang around any longer than was strictly necessary. It wasn't until I gazed at the sight before me that I realised how strange it was that Bea should have wanted to come down here instead of asking me to do it. I scanned that maze of household junk and wondered how many more secrets she had hidden there.

When I realised what I was doing I sighed. The words from that letter were seeping into my mind like drops of acid. I made myself promise that I wouldn't start rummaging in boxes, searching for bundles of perfumed envelopes from that creep. I would have broken my promise seconds later had I not heard someone coming down the steps. I raised my head and saw Fermín at the foot of the staircase, staring at the scene with a look of disgust.

'Smells like a corpse and a half here. Are you sure someone hasn't left the embalmed body of Merceditas's mother, among crochet patterns, in one of these boxes?'

'Since you're down here, you can help me take up the boxes my father needs.'

Fermín rolled up his sleeves, ready to get started. I pointed at a couple of boxes with the Vértice label on them and we took one each.

'Daniel, you look even worse than me. Is anything wrong?'

'It must be the basement vapours.'

I left the box on the floor and sat on it.

'May I ask you a question, Fermín?'

Fermín also put his box down and used it as a stool. I looked at him, ready to speak, but unable to pull the words out of my mouth.

'Trouble in the boudoir?' he ventured.

I blushed when I realised how well my friend knew me.

'Something like that.'

'Señora Bea, blessed is she among womenfolk, is not in a mood for battle, or, on the contrary, she is all too willing, and you can barely offer the minimum services? Do bear in mind that when women have a baby, it's as if someone had dropped an atom bomb of hormones into their bloodstream. One of the great mysteries of nature is how they don't go crazy during the twenty seconds that follow the birth. I know all this because obstetrics, after free verse, is one of my hobbies.'

'No, it's not that. At least, as far as I know.'

Fermín gave me a puzzled look.

'I must ask you not to tell anyone what I'm about to tell you, Fermín.'

Fermín crossed himself solemnly.

'A short while ago, I accidentally discovered a letter in Bea's coat pocket.'

My pause didn't seem to impress him.

'And?'

'The letter was from her ex-fiancé.'

'Lieutenant Vapid? Hadn't he gone back to El Ferrol to play the lead in a spectacular career as a spoiled brat?'

'That's what I thought. But it seems that in his free time he writes love letters to my wife.'

Fermín jumped up.

'The son-of-a-bitch,' he muttered, even more furious than me.

I pulled the letter out of my pocket and handed it to him. Fermín sniffed the paper before opening it.

'Is it me, or does the swine send letters on perfumed paper?' he asked.

'It wouldn't surprise me. The man's like that. The best part comes afterwards. Read, read . . .'

Fermín read the letter, mumbling to himself and shaking his head.

'Not only is this specimen a disgusting piece of excrement, he's also as cloying as they come. This "kissing other lips" line should be enough to get him jailed for life.'

I put the letter away and looked down at the floor.

'Don't tell me you're suspicious of Señora Bea?' asked Fermín in disbelief.

'No, of course not.'

'You liar.'

I stood up and began to pace around the basement.

'And what would you do if you found a letter like that one in Bernarda's pocket?'

Fermín took his time to consider the matter.

'What I would do is trust the mother of my child.'

'Trust her?'

Fermín nodded.

'Don't take it badly, Daniel, but you have the basic problem of all men who marry a real looker. Señora Bea, who is and always will be a saint as far as I'm concerned, is, in the popular parlance, such a tasty dish you'd want to lick the plate clean. As a result, it's only to be expected that dedicated sleazy types, full-time losers, poolside gigolos and all the half-arsed posers in town should go after her. With or without a husband and child: the simian stuck in a suit we all too kindly call *Homo sapiens* doesn't give a damn about that. You may not have noticed, but I'd bet my silk undies that your saintly wife attracts more flies than a pot of honey in a barn. That cretin is just like one of those scavenger birds, throwing stones to see if he hits something. Trust me, a woman with her head and petticoat both firmly in place can see that type coming from afar.'

'Are you sure?'

'Absolutely. Do you really think that if Doña Beatriz wanted to cheat on you she'd have to wait for a slobbering halfwit to sweet-talk her into it with his reheated boleros? I wouldn't wonder that at least ten suitors put in an appearance every time she goes out, showing off her good looks and her baby. Believe me, I know what I'm talking about.'

'Quite frankly, I'm not sure whether all this is much comfort.'

'Look, what you need to do is put that letter back in the coat pocket where you found it and forget all about it. And don't even think of mentioning the matter to your wife.'

'Is that what you would do?'

47

'What I'd do is go and find that numbskull and land him such a glorious kick in the balls they'd have to surgically remove them from the back of his neck, and all he'd want to do then is join a Carthusian monastery. But that's me.'

I felt the anguish spreading inside me like a drop of oil on clear water.

'I'm not sure you've helped me much, Fermín.'

He shrugged his shoulders, picked up the box and vanished up the stairs.

WE SPENT THE REST of the morning working in the bookshop. After mulling over the business of the letter in my head for a couple of hours, I came to the conclusion that Fermín was right. What I couldn't quite work out was whether he was right about trusting her and keeping quiet, or about going out to get that moron and give him a genital makeover. The calendar on the counter said 20 December. I had a month to decide.

The day's business picked up little by little, with modest but steady sales. Fermín didn't miss a single chance to praise my father for the glorious crib, and for his brilliant idea of buying that Baby Jesus reminiscent of a Basque weightlifter.

'Seeing such dazzling salesmanship on display I'll leave the floor to the master and retire to the back room to sort out the collection the widow left with us the other day.'

I took the opportunity to follow Fermín and draw the curtain behind us. Fermín looked at me, slightly alarmed, but I gave him a friendly smile.

'I'll help you if you like.'

'As you wish, Daniel.'

For a few minutes we began to unpack the boxes of books and classify them in piles by genre, condition and size. Fermín didn't open his lips and avoided my eyes.

'Fermín . . .'

'I've already told you not to worry about that business of the letter. Your wife is not a trollop, and if she ever wants to dump

48

you – and pray heaven that will never happen – she'll tell you face to face without the need for soap-opera shenanigans.'

'Got the message, Fermín. But that's not it.'

Fermín looked up, distressed, knowing what was coming.

'I've been thinking that today, after we close, we could go out, grab a bite and have some man-talk, you know, just you and me,' I began. 'To talk about our stuff. About yesterday's visitor. And about whatever it is that's worrying you, which I have an inkling might be connected.'

Fermín left the book he was cleaning on the table. He gazed at me in dismay and sighed.

'I'm in a real mess, Daniel,' he mumbled at last. 'A mess I don't know how to get out of.'

I put my hand on his shoulder. Under the overalls all I could feel was skin and bone.

'Then let me help you. Two heads are always better than one.'

He seemed at a loss.

'Surely we've got out of worse situations, you and I,' I insisted.

He smiled sadly, not too convinced by my forecast.

'You're a good friend, Daniel.'

Not half as good as he deserved, I thought.

# 12

Back then Fermín still lived in the same old *pensión* on Calle Joaquín Costa, where I had it on good authority that the rest of the lodgers, in secret collaboration with Rociíto and her sisters-in-arms, were preparing a stag night for him that would go down in history. Fermín was already waiting for me by the front door when I went by to pick him up just after nine.

'To be honest, I'm not that hungry,' he announced when he saw me.

'Pity, because I thought we could go down to Can Lluís,' I proposed. 'They're serving chickpea stew and baby lamb chops tonight . . .'

'Well, let's not make hasty decisions here,' Fermín reconsidered. 'A good repast is like a lass in bloom: not to appreciate it is the business of fools.'

With that pearl from the eminent Don Fermín Romero de Torres's stockpile of aphorisms, we ambled down towards what was one of my friend's favourite restaurants in the whole of Barcelona and much of the known world. Can Lluís was located at 49 Calle de la Cera, on the threshold of the Raval quarter. Behind its modest appearance, Can Lluís conveyed an intimate atmosphere steeped in the mysteries of old Barcelona, offering exquisite food and impeccable service at prices that even Fermín, or I, could afford. On weekdays, it attracted a bohemian community, in which people from the theatre, literary types and other creatures high and low rubbed shoulders and toasted each other.

When we walked in we spied one of the bookshop's regular customers, Professor Alburquerque, a fine reviewer and local savant who taught at the arts faculty and made Can Lluís his second home. He was enjoying dinner at the bar and leafing through a newspaper.

'Long time no see, Professor,' I said as I walked past him. 'You must pay us a visit some time and replenish your stock. A man can't live on obituaries from *La Vanguardia.*'

'I wish I could. It's those damned dissertations. Having to read the inane babble written by the spoiled rich kids who come through university these days is beginning to give me bouts of dyslexia.'

At that point, one of the waiters served him his pudding, a plump crème caramel wobbling under a surge of burned sugar tears and smelling of the finest vanilla.

'Your lordship will get over it after a couple of spoonfuls of this marvel,' said Fermín. 'Goodness me: it jiggles just like the formidable bust of Doña Margarita Xirgu.'

The learned professor gazed at his pudding in the light of those considerations and agreed, spellbound. We left the wise man enjoying the sugary charms of the famous stage diva and took shelter at a corner table at the back of the dining room, where we were soon served a sumptuous meal. Fermín devoured it with the appetite of a retreating army.

'I thought you weren't hungry,' I let drop.

'Hard muscle burns a lot of calories,' Fermín explained, mopping his plate with the last piece of bread in the basket, although I thought it was just his anxiety doing all the eating.

Pere, the waiter who was serving us, came over to see how everything was going and when he saw Fermín's ravaged plate, he handed him the dessert menu.

'A little dessert to finish off the job, maestro?'

'Come to think of it, I wouldn't say no to a couple of those home-made crème caramels I saw earlier, if possible with a bright red cherry on top of each one,' said Fermín.

Pere assented. He told us that when the owner heard how Fermín had expounded on the consistency and the metaphorical attractions of that recipe, he'd decided to rechristen the crème caramels '*margaritas*'.

'I'm fine with an espresso,' I said.

'The boss says coffee and dessert are on the house,' said Pere.

We raised our wine glasses in the direction of the owner, who was standing behind the bar chatting with Professor Alburquerque.

'Good people,' mumbled Fermín. 'Sometimes one forgets that not everyone in this world is a bastard.'

I was surprised at the bitterness of his tone.

'Why do you say that, Fermín?'

My friend shrugged his shoulders. Shortly after, the crème caramels arrived, swaying temptingly, topped with shiny cherries.

'May I remind you that in a few weeks' time you're getting married, and your *margarita* days will be over?' I joked.

'Poor me,' said Fermín. 'I'm afraid I'm all bark and no bite. I'm not the man I used to be.'

'None of us are what we once were.'

Fermín started on the crème caramels, savouring every mouthful.

'I don't know where I've read that deep down we've never been who we think we once were, and we only remember what never happened . . .' said Fermín.

'That's the beginning of a novel by Julián Carax,' I replied.

'True. Where might our friend Carax be? Don't you ever wonder?'

'Every single day.'

Fermín smiled, remembering our past adventures. Then he pointed to my chest and gave me a questioning look.

'Does it still hurt?'

I undid a couple of buttons on my shirt and showed him the scar Inspector Fumero's bullet had left when it went through my chest that faraway day, in the ruins of the Angel of Mist.

'Every now and then.'

'Scars never go away, do they?'

'They come and go, I believe. Fermín: look into my eyes.'

Fermín's evasive eyes looked straight into mine.

'Are you going to tell me what's going on?'

For a couple of seconds Fermín hesitated.

'Did you know that Bernarda is expecting?' he asked.

'No,' I lied. 'Is that what's worrying you?'

Fermín shook his head as he finished up his second crème caramel with the teaspoon, sipping the remains of the syrup.

'She hasn't wanted to tell me yet, poor thing, because she's worried. But she's going to make me the happiest man in the world.'

I looked at him carefully.

'To be honest, right now, you don't exactly look the picture of happiness. Is it because of the wedding? Are you worried about having to go through a church wedding and all that?'

'No, Daniel. I'm actually quite excited about it, even if there are priests involved. I could marry Bernarda every day of the week.'

'Then what?'

'Do you know the first thing they ask you when you want to get married?'

'Your name,' I said, without thinking.

Fermín nodded his head slowly. It hadn't occurred to me to think about that until then. Suddenly I understood the dilemma my good friend was facing.

'Do you remember what I told you years ago, Daniel?'

I remembered it perfectly. During the civil war, and thanks to the nefarious dealings of Inspector Fumero who, before joining the fascists, acted as a hired thug for the communists, my friend had landed himself in prison, where he'd been on the verge of losing his mind and his life. When he managed to get out, alive by some sheer miracle, he decided to adopt a new identity and erase his past. He was at death's door when he borrowed a name he saw on an old poster in the Arenas bullring. That is how

Fermín Romero de Torres was born, a man who invented his life story day after day.

'That's why you didn't want to fill in those papers in the parish church,' I said. 'Because you can't use the name Fermín Romero de Torres.'

Fermín nodded.

'Look, I'm sure we can find a way of getting you new documentation. Do you remember Lieutenant Palacios, the one who left the police force? He teaches physical education at a school in the Bonanova area, but sometimes he drops by the bookshop. Well, one day, talking about this and that, he told me there was a whole underground market of new identities for people who were returning to Spain after spending years away. He said he knows someone with a workshop near the old Royal Shipyards who has contacts in the police force and for a hundred pesetas can supply people with a new identity card and get it registered in the ministry.'

'I know. His name was Heredia. Quite an artist.'

'Was?'

'He turned up floating in the port a couple of months ago. They said he'd fallen off a pleasure boat while he was sailing towards the breakwater. With his hands tied behind his back. Fascist humour.'

'You knew him?'

'We met now and then.'

'Then you do have documents that certify you are Fermín Romero de Torres . . .'

'Heredia managed to get them for me in 1939, towards the end of the war. It was easier then – Barcelona was a madhouse – and when people realised the ship was sinking they'd even sell you their coat of arms for a couple of *duros*.'

'Then why can't you use your name?'

'Because Fermín Romero de Torres died in 1940. Those were bad times, Daniel, far worse than these. He didn't even last a year, poor bastard.'

'He died? Where? How?'

'In the prison of Montjuïc Castle. In cell number thirteen.'

I remembered the dedication the stranger had left for Fermín in the copy of *The Count of Monte Cristo.*

*For Fermín Romero de Torres,*
*who came back from among the dead*
*and holds the key to the future.*

13

'That night I only told you a small part of the story, Daniel.'

'I thought you trusted me.'

'I would trust you with my life. If I only told you part of it, it was to protect you.'

'Protect me? From what?'

Fermín looked down, devastated.

'From the truth, Daniel . . . from the truth.'

# Part Two
## *From Among the Dead*

# 1

*Barcelona, 1939*

NEW PRISONERS WERE BROUGHT IN BY NIGHT, IN CARS OR black vans that set off from the police station on Vía Layetana and crossed the city silently, nobody noticing or wishing to notice them. The vehicles of the political police drove up the old road scaling the slopes of Montjuïc and more than one prisoner would relate how, the moment they glimpsed the castle on top of the hill silhouetted against black clouds that crept in from the sea, they felt certain they would never get out of that place alive.

The fortress was anchored at the highest point of the rocky mountain, suspended between the sea to the east, Barcelona's carpet of shadows to the north and, to the south, the endless city of the dead – the old Montjuïc Cemetery whose stench rose up among the boulders and filtered through cracks in the stone and through the bars of the cells. In times past, the castle had been used for bombarding the city below, but only a few months after the fall of Barcelona, in January, and the final defeat in April, death came to dwell there in silence and Barcelonians, trapped in the longest night of their history, preferred not to look skywards and recognise the prison's outline crowning the hill.

Upon arrival, prisoners brought in by the political police were assigned a number, usually that of the cell they were going to occupy and where they were likely to die. For most tenants, as some of the jailers liked to refer to them, the journey to the

59

castle was only one-way. On the night tenant number 13 arrived in Montjuïc it was raining hard. Thin veins of black water bled down the stone walls and the air reeked of excavated earth. Two police officers escorted him to a room containing only a metal table and a chair. A naked bulb hung from the ceiling and flickered every time the generator's flow diminished. He stood there waiting in his soaking clothes for almost half an hour, watched by a guard with a rifle.

At last he heard footsteps, the door opened and in came a man who couldn't have been a day over thirty. He wore a freshly ironed wool suit and smelled of eau de cologne. He had none of the martial looks of a professional soldier or police officer: his features were soft and his expression seemed pleasant. To the prisoner he came across as someone affecting the manners of a wealthy young man, giving off a condescending air of superiority in a setting that was beneath him. His most striking feature were his eyes. Blue, penetrating and sharp, alive with greed and suspicion. Only his eyes, behind that veneer of studied elegance and kind demeanour, betrayed his true nature.

Two round lenses augmented them, and his pomaded hair, combed back, lent him a vaguely affected look that didn't match the sinister decor. The man sat down on the chair behind the desk and opened a folder he was carrying. After a quick inspection of its contents, he joined his hands, placed his fingertips under his chin and sat scrutinising the prisoner, who finally spoke up.

'Excuse me, but I think there has been a mistake . . .'

The blow on the prisoner's stomach with the rifle butt knocked the wind out of him and he fell, curled up into a ball.

'You only speak when the governor asks you a question,' the guard told him.

'On your feet,' commanded the governor in a quavering voice, still unused to giving orders.

The prisoner managed to stand up and face the governor's uncomfortable gaze.

'Name?'

'Fermín Romero de Torres.'

The prisoner noticed disdain and indifference in those blue eyes.

'What sort of name is that? Do you think I'm a fool? Come on: name, the real one.'

The prisoner, a small, frail man, held out his papers for the governor. The guard snatched them from him and took them over to the table. The governor had a quick look at them, then clicked his tongue and smiled.

'Another Heredia job . . .' he murmured before throwing the documents into the wastepaper basket. 'These papers are no good. Are you going to tell me your name, or do we have to get serious?'

Tenant number 13 tried to utter a few words, but his lips trembled and all he managed to do was stammer something incomprehensible.

'Don't be afraid, my good man, nobody's going to bite you. What have you been told? There are plenty of fucking reds out there who like to spread slander around, but here, if people collaborate, they get treated well, like Spaniards. Come on, clothes off.'

The new tenant seemed to hesitate for a moment. The governor looked down, as if the whole situation was making him feel uncomfortable and only the prisoner's stubbornness was keeping him there. A second later, the guard dealt him another blow with the rifle butt, this time in the kidneys, and knocked him down again.

'You heard the governor. Strip down. We don't have all night.'

Tenant number 13 managed to get up on his knees and remove his dirty, bloodstained clothes. Once he was completely naked, the guard stuck the rifle barrel under a shoulder and forced him to stand up. The governor looked up from the desk and grimaced with disgust when he saw the burns covering his torso, buttocks and much of his thighs.

'It looks like our champion is an old acquaintance of Fumero's,' the guard remarked.

'Keep your mouth shut,' ordered the governor without much conviction.

He looked at the prisoner with impatience and realised he was crying.

'Come on, stop crying and tell me your name.'

The prisoner whispered his name again.

'Fermín Romero de Torres . . .'

The governor sighed wearily.

'Look, I'm beginning to lose my patience. I want to help you, and I don't really feel like having to call Inspector Fumero and tell him you're here . . .'

The prisoner started to whimper like a wounded dog and was shaking so violently that the governor, who clearly found the scene distasteful and wanted to put an end to the matter as soon as possible, exchanged a glance with the guard and, without saying a word, wrote the name the prisoner had given him in the register, swearing under his breath.

'Bloody war,' he muttered to himself when they took the prisoner to his cell, dragging him naked through the flooded tunnels.

# 2

THE CELL WAS A DARK, DAMP RECTANGLE. COLD AIR BLEW in through a small hole drilled in the rock. The walls were covered with crudely etched marks and messages left by previous tenants. Some had written their names, a date, or left some other proof of their existence. One of them had busied himself scratching crucifixes in the dark, but heaven did not seem to have noticed them. The iron bars securing the cell were rusty and left a film of brown on one's hands.

Huddled up on the ramshackle bunk, Fermín tried to cover his nakedness with a bit of ragged cloth which, he imagined, served as blanket, mattress and pillow. The half-light was tinged with a coppery hue, like the breath of a dying candle. After a while, his eyes became accustomed to the gloom and his ears sharpened, allowing him to pick up the sound of slight movements through a litany of dripping leaks and echoes carried by the draught that seeped in from outside.

Fermín had been sitting there for half an hour when he noticed a shape in the dark, at the other end of the cell. He stood up and stepped slowly towards it: it was a dirty canvas bag. The cold and the damp had started to get into his bones and, although the smell from that bundle, spattered with dark stains, did not augur well, Fermín thought that perhaps it contained the prisoner's uniform nobody had bothered to give him and, with a bit of luck, a blanket to protect him from the bitter cold. He knelt down and untied the knot closing one end of the bag.

When he drew the canvas aside, the dim light from the oil lamps flickering in the corridor revealed what at first he took to be the face of a doll, one of those dummies tailors place in their shop windows to show off their suits. The stench and his nausea made him realise it was no dummy. Covering his nose and mouth with one hand, he pulled the rest of the canvas to one side, then stepped backwards until he collided with the wall of the cell.

The corpse seemed to be that of an adult anywhere between forty and seventy-five years of age, who couldn't have weighed more than fifty kilos. A tangle of white hair and a beard covered much of his face and skeletal torso. His bony hands, with long, twisted nails, looked like the claws of a bird. His eyes were open, the corneas shrivelled up like overripe fruit. His mouth was open too, with his tongue, black and swollen, wedged between rotten teeth.

'Take his clothes off before they come and fetch him,' came a voice from the cell on the other side of the corridor. 'You won't get anything else to wear until next month.'

Fermín peered into the shadows and spied two shining eyes observing him from the bunk in the other cell.

'Don't be afraid, the poor soul can't hurt anyone any more,' the voice assured him.

Fermín nodded and walked over to the sack again, wondering how he was going to carry out the operation.

'My sincerest apologies,' he mumbled to the deceased. 'May God rest your soul.'

'He was an atheist,' the voice from the opposite cell informed him.

Fermín gave another nod and decided to skip the formalities. The cold permeating the cell was so intense it cut through one's bones, and any courtesy seemed redundant. Holding his breath, he set to work. The clothes smelled the same as the dead man. Rigor mortis had begun to spread through the body and the task of undressing the corpse turned out to be much harder than he'd anticipated. Once the deceased's best clothes had been plucked off, Fermín covered him again with the sack and closed it with a reef knot that even the great Houdini would have been unable to tackle. At last, dressed in a ragged and foul-smelling prison uniform, Fermín huddled up again on the bed, wondering how many prisoners had worn it before him.

'Much appreciated,' he said finally.

'You're very welcome,' said the voice on the other side of the corridor.

'Fermín Romero de Torres, at your service.'

'David Martín.'

Fermín frowned. The name sounded familiar. For five long minutes he shuffled through distant memories and echoes from the past and then, suddenly, it came to him. He remembered whole afternoons spent in a corner of the library on Calle del Carmen, devouring a series of books with racy covers and titles.

'Martín the author? Of *City of the Damned*?'

A sigh in the shadows.

'Nobody appreciates pen names any more.'

'Please excuse my indiscretion. It's just that I had an almost scholarly devotion to your work. That's why I know you were the person writing the novels of the immortal Ignatius B. Samson . . .'

'At your service.'

'Well, Señor Martín, it's an honour to meet you, even if it is in these wretched circumstances, because I've been a great admirer of yours for years and . . .'

'Are you two lovebirds going to shut up? Some people here are trying to sleep,' roared a bitter voice that seemed to come from the next-door cell.

'There goes old Sourpuss,' a second voice cut in, coming from further down the corridor. 'Pay no attention to him, Martín. If you fall asleep here you just get eaten alive by bedbugs, starting with your privates. Go on, Martín, why don't you tell us a story? One about Chloé . . .'

'Sure, so you can jerk off like a monkey,' answered the hostile voice.

'Fermín, my friend,' Martín announced from his cell. 'Let me introduce you to Number Twelve, who finds something wrong in everything, and I mean *everything*, and Number Fifteen, insomniac, educated and the cell block's official ideologue. The rest don't speak much, especially Number Fourteen.'

'I speak when I have something to say,' snapped a deep, icy voice Fermín assumed must belong to Number 14. 'If we all followed suit, we'd get some peace at night.'

Fermín took in this peculiar community.

'Good evening, everyone. My name is Fermín Romero de Torres and it's a pleasure to make all your acquaintances.'

'The pleasure is entirely yours,' said Number 15.

'Welcome, and I hope your stay is brief,' offered Number 14.

Fermín glanced again at the sack housing the corpse and gulped.

'That was Lucio, the former Number Thirteen,' Martín explained. 'We don't know anything about him because the poor fellow was mute. A bullet blew off his larynx at the battle of the Ebro.'

'A shame he was the only one,' remarked Number 15.

'What did he die of?' asked Fermín.

'In this place one just dies from being here,' answered Number 12. 'It doesn't take much more.'

# 3

ROUTINE HELPED. ONCE A DAY, FOR AN HOUR, THE INMATES from the first two cell blocks were taken to the yard within the moat to get a bit of sun, rain, or whatever the weather brought with it. The menu consisted of a half-full bowl of some cold, greasy, greyish gruel of indeterminate provenance and rancid taste which, after a few days, and with hunger cramps in one's stomach, eventually became odourless and thus easier to get down. It was doled out halfway through the afternoon, and in time prisoners came to look forward to its arrival.

Once a month prisoners handed in their dirty clothes and were given another set which had supposedly been plunged into boiling water for a minute, although the bugs didn't seem to have noticed it. On Sundays inmates were advised to attend mass. Nobody dared miss it, because the priest took a roll call and if there was any name missing he'd write it down. Two absences meant a week of fasting. Three, a month's holiday in one of the solitary confinement cells in the tower.

The cell blocks, courtyard and any other areas through which the prisoners moved were heavily guarded. A body of sentries armed with rifles and guns patrolled the prison and, when the inmates were out of their cells, it was impossible for them to look in any direction and not see at least a dozen of those guards, alert, their weapons at the ready. They were joined by the less threatening jailers, none of whom looked like soldiers; the general feeling among the prisoners was that they were a bunch of unfortunate souls who had been unable to find a better job in those hard times.

Every block of cells had a jailer assigned to it. Armed with a bundle of keys, he worked twelve-hour shifts sitting on a chair at the end of the corridor. Most of the jailers avoided fraternising with the prisoners and didn't give them a word or a look beyond what was strictly necessary. The only one who seemed to be an exception was a poor devil nicknamed Bebo, who had lost an eye in an air raid when he worked as a nightwatchman in a factory in Pueblo Seco.

It was rumoured that Bebo had a twin brother jailed in Valencia, and perhaps this was why he showed some kindness towards the prisoners. When nobody was watching, he would occasionally slip them some drinking water, a bit of dry bread or whatever he could scrounge from the hoard the guards amassed out of packages sent by the prisoners' families. Bebo liked to drag his chair near David Martín's cell and listen to the stories the writer sometimes told the other inmates. In that particular hell, Bebo was the closest thing to an angel.

NORMALLY, AFTER SUNDAY MASS, the governor addressed a few edifying words to the prisoners. All they knew about him was that his name was Mauricio Valls and that before the war he'd been an aspiring writer who worked as secretary and errand-boy for a well-known local author, a long-standing rival of the ill-fated Don Pedro Vidal. In his spare time Valls penned bad translations of Greek and Latin classics and, with the help of a couple of kindred souls, edited a cultural pamphlet with high pretensions and low circulation. They also organised literary gatherings in which a whole battalion of like-minded luminaries deplored the state of things, forecasting that if one day they were able to call the shots, the world would rise to Olympian heights.

His life seemed destined for the bitter, grey existence of mediocrities whom God, in his infinite cruelty, has endowed with delusions of grandeur and a boundless ambition far exceeding their talents. The war, however, had recast his destiny as it had that of so many others, and his luck had changed when, in a situation somewhere between chance and fortune-hunting, Mauricio Valls, until then enamoured only of his own prodigious talent and exquisite refinement, wedded the daughter of a tycoon whose far-reaching enterprises supported much of General Franco's budget and his troops.

The bride, eight years his senior, had been confined to a wheelchair since the age of thirteen, consumed by a congenital illness that mercilessly devoured her muscles and her life. No man had ever looked into her eyes or held her hand to tell her she was beautiful and ask what her name was. Mauricio, who like all untalented men of letters was, deep down, as practical as he was conceited, was the first and last to do so, and a year later the couple married in Seville, with General Queipo de Llano and other luminaries of the state apparatus in attendance.

'Valls, you'll go far,' Serrano Súñer himself predicted during a private audience in Madrid to which Valls had gone to plead for the post of director of the National Library.

'Spain is living through difficult moments, and every well-born Spaniard must put his shoulder to the wheel and help contain the hordes of Marxists attempting to corrupt our spiritual resolve,' the Caudillo's brother-in-law announced, looking resplendent in his pantomime-admiral's uniform.

'You can count on me, Your Excellency,' Valls offered. 'For whatever is needed.'

'Whatever is needed' turned out to be the post of director, not of the wondrous National Library in Madrid as he would have wished, but of a prison with a dismal reputation, perched on a clifftop overlooking the city of Barcelona. The list of close friends and protégés requiring plum posts was exceedingly lengthy and Valls, despite all his endeavours, only made the bottom third of the queue.

'Be patient, Valls. Your efforts will be rewarded.'

That is how Mauricio Valls learned his first lesson in the complex national art of elbowing ahead after any change of regime: thousands of supporters had joined the ranks and the competition was fierce.

# 4

THAT, AT LEAST, WAS THE STORY. THIS UNCONFIRMED catalogue of suspicions, accusations and third-hand rumours reached the ears of the prisoners – and of whoever would listen – thanks to the shady machinations of the previous governor. He had been unceremoniously removed from office after only two weeks in charge and was poisoned with resentment against that upstart Valls, who had robbed him of the post he'd been fighting for throughout the entire war. As luck would have it, the outgoing governor had no family connections and carried with him the fateful precedent of having been caught, when inebriated, uttering humorous asides about the Generalissimo of all Spains and his remarkable likeness to Dopey. Before being installed as deputy governor of a Ceuta prison, he had put all his efforts into badmouthing Don Mauricio Valls to the four winds.

What was uncontested was that nobody could refer to Valls by any name other than 'the governor'. The official version, which he himself put about and authorised, was that he, Don Mauricio, was a man of letters, of recognised achievement and cultured intellect, blessed with a fine erudition acquired during the years he'd studied in Paris. Beyond his temporary position in the penitentiary sector of the regime, his future and his mission lay in educating the ordinary people of a decimated Spain, teaching them how to think with the help of a select circle of sympathisers.

His lectures often included lengthy quotes from his own writings, poems or educational articles which he published regularly in the national press on literature, philosophy and the much-needed renaissance of thought in the Western world. If the prisoners applauded enthusiastically at the end of these masterly sessions, the governor would make a magnanimous gesture and order the jailers to give out cigarettes, candles or some other luxury confiscated from the batch of donations and parcels sent to the prisoners by their families. The more desirable items had been previously expropriated by the guards, who took them home or sometimes even sold them to the inmates. It was better than nothing.

Those who died from natural or loosely attributed causes – on average between five and ten a week – were collected at midnight, except at weekends or on religious holidays, when the body would remain in the cell until the Monday or the next working day, usually keeping a new tenant company. When prisoners called out to announce that one of their companions had passed away, a jailer would walk over, check the body for pulse or breath and then put it into one of the canvas sacks used for this purpose. Once the sack had been tied, it remained in the cell until the undertakers from the neighbouring Montjuïc Cemetery came by to collect it. Nobody knew what they did with them and when the prisoners asked Bebo about it, he refused to answer, lowering his eyes.

Once a fortnight a summary trial took place and those condemned were shot at dawn. Sometimes, owing to the bad state of the rifles or the ammunition, the execution squad didn't manage to pierce a vital organ and the agonised cries from the wounded who had fallen into the moat rang out for hours. Occasionally an explosion was heard and the shouts would suddenly cease. The theory circulating among the prisoners was that one of the officers finished them off with a grenade, but nobody was sure whether that was strictly accurate.

Another rumour making the rounds was that on Friday

mornings the governor received visits in his office from wives, daughters, fiancées, or even aunts and grandmothers of the prisoners. Having removed his wedding ring, which he hid in the top drawer of his desk, he listened to their requests, considered their pleas, offered a handkerchief for their tears and accepted gifts and favours of another kind, after promising them better diets and treatment for their loved ones, or the review of dubious sentences, which regrettably were never addressed.

On selected occasions, Mauricio Valls served them teacakes and a glass of muscatel, and if, despite the hard times and poor nutrition, they were still attractive enough to pinch he would read them some of his writings and confess that his marriage to an ailing spouse was a trial of sanctity imposed upon his manhood. He'd then go on about how much he deplored his job as a jailer and how he considered it humiliating for a man of such high culture and refinement to be confined to that shameful post, when his natural destiny was to be a part of the country's higher echelons.

The advice from the more experienced prisoners was not to mention, and if possible not even think about, the governor. Most of them preferred to talk about the families they had left behind and the life they remembered. Some had photographs of girlfriends or wives which they treasured and would defend with their lives if anyone tried to snatch them away. More than one prisoner had told Fermín that the first three months were the worst. Afterwards, once you lost all hope, time began to go faster and the senseless days deadened your soul.

# 5

On Sundays, after Mass and the governor's speech, some of the prisoners would gather in a sunny corner of the courtyard to share a cigarette or two and listen to the stories David Martín would tell them, when his mind was clear. Fermín, who knew them all because he'd read the entire *City of the Damned* series, would join the group and let his imagination fly. But often Martín didn't seem to be fit enough even to tell them the time of day, so the others would leave him alone while he wandered around talking to himself. Fermín observed him closely, following him at times, because there was something about that poor devil that broke his heart. Using all his cunning and wily tricks, Fermín would try to obtain cigarettes for him, or even a few lumps of sugar, which Martín loved.

'You're a good man, Fermín. Try not to let it show,' the writer would tell him.

Martín always carried an old photograph on him, which he liked to gaze at for long spells. It showed a man dressed in white, holding the hand of a girl of about eight. They were both watching the sunset from the end of a wooden jetty that stretched out over a beach, like a gangway suspended over crystalline waters. Usually, when Fermín asked him about the photograph, Martín didn't reply. He would just smile, before putting the picture back in his pocket.

'Who is the girl in the photograph, Señor Martín?'

'I'm not sure, Fermín. Sometimes my memory lets me down. Doesn't that happen to you?'

'Of course. It happens to everyone.'

It was rumoured that Martín was not altogether in his right mind, but soon after Fermín started to befriend him he realised that the poor man was far worse than the rest of the prisoners assumed. There were moments when he proved more lucid than anyone, but often he didn't seem to understand where he was and he spoke about people and places that obviously existed only in his imagination or memory.

Often Fermín would wake up in the early hours and hear Martín talking in his cell. If he drew stealthily up to the bars and listened carefully, he could hear him clearly arguing with someone he called 'Señor Corelli' who, judging by the words he exchanged with him, appeared to be a notoriously sinister character.

On one of those nights, Fermín lit the remains of his last candle and raised it in the direction of the opposite cell. He wanted to make sure Martín really was alone and that both voices, his own and the other voice belonging to the person called Corelli, were coming from the same lips. Martín was walking in circles round his cell, and when their eyes met, Fermín realised that his prison mate couldn't see him. He was behaving as if those walls didn't exist and his conversation with that strange man was taking place far from there.

'Pay no attention to him,' murmured Number 12 from the shadows. 'He does that every night. He's off his trolley. Lucky him.'

The following morning, when Fermín asked him about the man called Corelli and his midnight conversations, Martín looked at him in surprise and gave him a puzzled smile. On another occasion, when Fermín was so cold he couldn't sleep, he walked over to the bars again and listened to Martín talking to one of his invisible friends. That night Fermín dared to interrupt him.

'Martín? It's me. Fermín, your neighbour across the landing. Are you all right?'

Martín walked over to the bars of his cell and Fermín could see his face was covered in tears.

'Señor Martín? Who is Isabella? You were talking about her a moment ago.'

Martín stared at him.

'Isabella is the only good thing remaining in this shitty world,' he replied after a while, with unusual bitterness. 'If it weren't for her, we might as well set fire to the whole thing and let it burn until even the ashes have blown away.'

'I'm sorry, Martín. I didn't mean to bother you.'

Martín withdrew into the shadows. The following day he was found shivering in a pool of his own blood. Seeing that Bebo had fallen asleep in his chair, he'd managed to slit his wrists by scratching them against the stone. When they took him away on a stretcher he was so pale Fermín thought he would never see him again.

'Don't worry about your friend, Fermín,' said Number 15. 'If that was anyone else, he'd go straight into the canvas sack, but the governor won't let Martín die. Nobody knows why.'

David Martín's cell was empty for five weeks. When Bebo brought him back, carrying him like a child, dressed in white pyjamas, Martín's arms were bandaged up to his elbows. He didn't remember anyone and spent the first night talking to himself and laughing. Bebo placed his chair facing Martín's bars and kept a close eye on him all night, handing him sugar lumps he'd stolen from the officers' room and hidden in his pockets.

'Señor Martín, please don't speak like that. God will punish you,' the jailer whispered to him between one sugar lump and the next.

IN THE REAL WORLD, Number 12 had been Dr Román Sanahuja, head of General Medicine at Barcelona's Hospital Clínico, an honourable man, cured of ideological delusions, whose conscience and refusal to denounce his friends had sent him to the castle. As a rule, no prisoner's line of work was recognised within those walls. Unless such a line could reel in some benefit for the governor. In Dr Sanahuja's case, his usefulness was soon established.

'Unfortunately I don't have adequate medical resources at my disposal,' the governor had explained to him. 'Quite frankly, the regime has other worries and doesn't give a toss if you all rot in your cells from gangrene. After much battling I've got them to supply me with a badly equipped medicine cabinet and a washed-up quack who wouldn't even be accepted as a janitor in a veterinary clinic, I'm sure. But that's what there is. I know for a fact that before succumbing to the error of neutrality, you were a doctor of some renown. For reasons that are not of your concern, I have a vested interest in ensuring our mutual friend David Martín does not leave us prematurely. If you agree to collaborate and help keep him in reasonably good health, considering the circumstances, I can assure you I will make your stay in this place more agreeable and will personally see that your case is re-examined with a view to shortening your sentence.'

Dr Sanahuja nodded.

'It has come to my notice that some of the prisoners regard Martín as being rather soft in the head, as you would say. Is that so?' asked the governor.

'I'm not a psychiatrist, but in my humble opinion, I believe Martín is clearly unbalanced.'

The governor weighed up that remark.

'And, according to your expert medical opinion, how long would you say he could last?' he asked. 'Alive, I mean.'

'I don't know. Conditions in this prison are unhealthy and . . .'

The governor cut him off with a bored expression.

'And sane? How long do you think Martín can remain in possession of his mental faculties?'

'Not long, I think.'

'I see.'

The governor offered him a cigarette, which the doctor refused.

'You like him, don't you?'

'I hardly know him,' replied the doctor. 'He seems a decent enough man.'

The governor smiled.

'And an execrable writer. Possibly the worst this country has ever had.'

'You're the recognised authority on all matters literary, Governor. I know nothing about the subject.'

The governor gave him an icy look.

'I've sent men into solitary confinement for three months for less impertinent remarks. Few survive, and those who do come back in a worse state than your friend Martín. Don't make the fatal mistake of assuming that your qualifications grant you any privileges. Your records say you have a wife and three daughters out there. Your luck, as well as that of your family, depends on how useful you make yourself to me. Am I getting this across clearly?'

Dr Sanahuja swallowed hard.

'Yes, Governor.'

'Thank you, *Doctor*.'

FROM TIME TO TIME, the governor would ask Sanahuja to take a look at Martín. It was no secret that the governor didn't trust the resident prison doctor, a dishonest charlatan who seemed to have forgotten the notion of preventive care from signing so many death certificates. The governor dismissed him shortly afterwards.

'How would you describe the patient's general state, Doctor?'

'Weak.'

'I see. What about his demons, so to speak? Is he still talking to himself and imagining things?'

'There's no noticeable change in that regard.'

'I'll take that as a yes. I read an excellent article in the *ABC* by my good friend Sebastián Jurado, in which he talks about schizophrenia, the poets' illness.'

'I'm not qualified to make such a diagnosis.'

'But you are, I hope, qualified to keep him alive, aren't you?'

'I'm doing my best with what I've got.'

'Your best may not be good enough. Consider the plight of your daughters. So young and vulnerable. So unprotected and with all those callous swine and reds still hiding out there.'

As the months went by, Dr Sanahuja became quite fond of Martín and one day, while sharing cigarette stubs, he told Fermín what he knew about the man whom some, because of his ravings and his status as the prison's resident lunatic, had jokingly nicknamed 'the Prisoner of Heaven'.

# 6

'TRUTH BE TOLD, I THINK THAT BY THE TIME THEY BROUGHT David Martín here he'd already been ill for some time. Have you ever heard of schizophrenia, Fermín? It's one of the governor's favourite new words.'

'It's what we civilians like to refer to as "being off one's rocker".'

'It's no joke, Fermín. It's a very serious illness. Not my speciality, but I've seen a few cases and the patients often hear voices, or they see and remember people and events that have never taken place . . . The mind slowly deteriorates and the patient can no longer distinguish between reality and fiction.'

'Like seventy per cent of Spaniards . . . And do you think poor Martín suffers from this illness, Doctor?'

'I'm not sure. As I said, I'm not a specialist, but I'd say he shows some of the most common symptoms.'

'Perhaps in this case his illness is a blessing . . .'

'It's never a blessing, Fermín.'

'And does he know that he is, shall we say, affected?'

'Madmen always think it's the others who are mad.'

'That's what I was saying about seventy per cent of Spaniards . . .'

A guard was watching them from the top of a sentry box, as if he were trying to read their lips.

'Lower your voice or we'll get into trouble.'

The doctor signalled to Fermín to turn around and walk towards the other end of the courtyard.

'In times like these, even walls have ears,' said the doctor.

'All we need now is for the walls to grow half a brain between the ears and we might get out of this mess,' answered Fermín.

'Do you know what Martín said to me the first time I was told by the governor to give him a medical examination?

'"Doctor, I think I've discovered the only way of getting out of this prison."

'"How?"

'"Dead."

'"Can't you think of a more practical way?"

'"Have you read The Count of Monte Cristo, Doctor?"

'"As a kid. I barely remember it."

'"Well, reread it. It's all there."

'I didn't want to tell him the governor had ordered all books by Dumas to be removed from the prison library, together with anything by Dickens, Galdós and many other authors whose works he considered rubbish for entertaining the uncultured masses. He replaced them with a collection of some of his own unpublished novels and short stories, together with books by friends of his, bound in leather by Valentí, a prisoner with a graphic arts background. Once Valentí had handed in his work, the governor let him die of exposure, forcing him to spend five nights out in the yard, in the rain, in the middle of January, just because he'd joked about the elegance of the governor's prose. Valentí managed to leave this place through Martín's method: dead.

'After I'd been here for some time, listening to conversations among the jailers, I realised that David Martín had come to the prison at the request of the governor himself. He was being held at La Modelo Prison, accused of a string of crimes which I don't think anyone really believed he'd committed. Among other things, they said he'd killed his mentor and best friend in a fit of jealousy – a wealthy man called Pedro Vidal, a writer like him – as well as Vidal's wife, Cristina. People also said he'd cold-bloodedly murdered a number of policemen and someone else, I can't remember who. These days they accuse so many people of so many things, you just don't know what to make of it. I find it hard to believe that Martín is a murderer, but it's also true that during the war years I saw so many people on either side remove their mask and show who they really were, that anything seems possible. Everyone casts the stone and then points a finger at his neighbour.'

'If I were to tell you . . .' remarked Fermín.

'The fact is that the father of this Vidal character is a powerful industrialist, stinking rich. They say he was one of the key bankers on the national side. Why is it that all wars are won by bankers? Anyway, this magnate, Vidal, personally asked the Ministry of Justice to find Martín and make sure he rotted in prison because of what he'd done to his son and his daughter-in-law. Apparently, Martín had fled the country and been on the run for almost three years when they found him near the border. He couldn't have been in his right mind to return to Spain where they were waiting to crucify him – at least, that's what I think. And to make matters worse, this happened during the final days of the war, when thousands of people were crossing over in the opposite direction.'

'Sometimes one just gets tired of fleeing,' said Fermín. 'The world's very small when you don't have anywhere to go.'

'I suppose that's what Martín must have thought. I don't know how he managed to cross the border, but some Puigcerdà locals notified the Civil Guards after they'd seen him wandering around the town for days, dressed in rags and talking to himself. Then some shepherds said they'd seen him on the Bolvir road, a couple of kilometres from Puigcerdà, near a large old house called La Torre del Remei, which in wartime had been turned into a hospital for wounded soldiers. It was run by a group of women who probably felt sorry for Martín and, taking him for a soldier, offered him shelter and food. When the Civil Guards got there he'd already left, but that night they caught him walking over the frozen lake, attempting to make a hole in the ice with a stone. At first they thought he was trying to commit suicide, so they took him to Villa San Antonio, the sanatorium. Apparently one of the doctors there recognised him – don't ask me how – and as soon as his name reached the military headquarters he was transferred to Barcelona.'

'The lion's den.'

'You can say that again. It seems the trial barely lasted two days. The list of accusations against him was endless and although there was hardly any evidence or proof of any sort to sustain them, for some strange reason the public prosecutor managed to produce a good number of witnesses. Dozens of people filed through court, showing such zealous hatred for Martín that even the judge was surprised – no doubt they had all been given handouts by the elder Vidal. Among them were old colleagues of Martín's from the years when he worked for a minor newspaper called *The Voice of Industry*. Coffee-shop intellectuals, poor devils and envious pricks of all sorts came out of the woodwork to swear that Martín was guilty of everything he was accused of, and more. You know how things work here. On the judge's orders, and Vidal senior's advice, all his works were confiscated and burned, being considered subversive material, immoral and contrary to decent behaviour. When Martín declared in the trial that the only decent behaviour he defended was reading, and anything else was the reader's business, the judge added another ten years to the sentence he'd already given him. It seems that instead of keeping his mouth shut during the trial Martín replied to everything he was asked without mincing his words, and ended up digging his own grave.'

'Everything can be forgiven in this world, save telling the truth.'

'The fact is, he was given a life sentence. *The Voice of Industry*, owned by Vidal senior, published a long piece listing all his crimes, and to cap it all, an editorial. Guess who signed it.'

'Our illustrious prison governor, Don Mauricio Valls.'

'The very one. He described him as "the worst writer in history" and was delighted that his books had been destroyed because they were "an affront to humanity and good taste".

'That's exactly what they said about the Palau de la Música auditorium,' Fermín pointed out. 'We're so fortunate in this country to be blessed with the very cream of the international intellectual community. Unamuno was right when he said: let others do the inventing, we'll provide the opinions.'

'Innocent or not, after witnessing his public humiliation and the burning of every single page he'd ever written, Martín ended up in a cell in La Modelo Prison, where he probably would have died in a matter of weeks if it hadn't been for the fact that our governor, who had been following the case with great interest and for some strange reason was obsessed with Martín, was given access to his file and then asked for his transfer to this place. Martín told me that the day he arrived here, Valls had him brought into his office and fired off one of his lectures.

'"*Martín, you're a convicted criminal and probably a fanatical subversive, but something binds us together. We're both men of letters, and although you spent your failed career writing rubbish for the ignorant masses who lack all intellectual guidance, I think you may be able to help me and thus redeem your errors. I have a collection of novels and poems I've been working on for the past few years. They're of an extraordinarily high literary standard. So much so, I very much fear that in this illiterate country there could be no more than three hundred readers capable of understanding and appreciating their worth. That is why I've been thinking that perhaps, because of the way you have prostituted your writings, and your closeness to the common man who reads potboilers in trams, you might help me make some small changes that will draw my work nearer to the lamentable levels of Spanish readers. If you agree to collaborate, I can assure you that I'll make your existence far more pleasant. I could even get your case reopened. Your little friend . . . What's her name? Ah, yes, Isabella. A beauty, if you will allow me the comment. Anyhow, your girlfriend came to see me and told me she's hired a young lawyer, someone called Brians, and has managed to raise enough money for your defence. Let's not kid ourselves: we both know there were no grounds for your case and you were sentenced thanks to dubious witnesses. You seem to make enemies with incredible ease, even among people I'm sure you don't even know exist. Don't make the mistake of making another enemy of me, Martín. I'm not one of those poor devils. Here, between these walls, to put it plainly, I am God."*

'I don't know whether Martín accepted the governor's proposal or not, but I have a feeling he did, because he's still alive and clearly our particular God is still interested in keeping it that way, at least for the moment. He's even provided Martín with paper and the writing tools he has in his cell, I suppose so that he can rewrite our governor's great works and enable him to enter the Hall of Fame, achieving the literary glory he so craves. Personally, I don't know what to think. My impression is that poor Martín is in no fit state to rewrite even his own name. He seems to spend most of his time trapped in a sort of purgatory he's been building in his own head, where remorse and pain are eating him alive. Although my field is general medicine and I'm not qualified to give a diagnosis . . .'

# 7

THE GOOD DOCTOR'S STORY KINDLED FERMÍN'S INTEREST. True to his unconditional support of lost causes, he decided to do a little investigation on his own, hoping to discover more about Martín and, at the same time, perfect the idea of the escape *via mortis*, in the style of Monsieur Alexandre Dumas. The more he turned the matter over in his mind, the more he thought that, at least in this particular, the Prisoner of Heaven was not as nuts as they all made him out to be. Whenever they were allowed out into the yard, Fermín would contrive to go up to Martín and engage in conversation with him.

'Fermín, you and I are beginning to look like a couple. Every time I turn around, there you are.'

'I'm sorry, Señor Martín, it's just that I'm intrigued about something.'

'And what is it, exactly, that intrigues you so, pray tell?'

'Well, to put it bluntly, I can't for the life of me fathom how a decent fellow like you has consented to help that conceited, repugnant meatball of a governor in his rapacious attempts to pass himself off as chief literary lion.'

'Direct, aren't you? There don't seem to be any secrets in this place.'

'It's just that I have a natural flair for the art of detection and the finer investigative pursuits.'

'In which case you surely must also have surmised that I'm not a decent fellow, but a criminal.'

'That seems to have been the judge's estimation.'

'Backed up by an army and a half of witnesses who testified under oath.'

'Incidentally, all on a crook's payroll and chronically constipated with envy and petty chicanery, if I may say so.'

'You may, but it hardly changes anything. Tell me, Fermín, is there anything about me you don't know?'

'Heaps of things. But the one issue that really sticks in my gullet is why you are in business with that self-absorbed dunce. People like him are the gangrene of this country.'

'There are people like him everywhere, Fermín. Nobody holds the patent.'

'But only here do we take them seriously.'

'Perhaps, but don't judge him so hastily. In this whole farce, the governor is a far more complex character than it would appear. This self-absorbed dunce, as you so generously call him, is, for starters, a very powerful man.'

'God, according to him.'

'Within this particular purgatory, that may not be too far off the mark.'

Fermín screwed up his nose. He didn't like what he was hearing. It almost sounded as if Martín had been sipping the wine of his own downfall.

'Has he threatened you? Is that it? What more can he do to you?'

'To me? Nothing, except make me laugh. But to others, outside this place, he can do a lot of harm.'

Fermín kept quiet for a long while.

'You must forgive me, Señor Martín. I didn't mean to offend you. I hadn't thought of that.'

'You don't offend me, Fermín. On the contrary. I think you hold a far too generous view of my circumstances. Your trust says much more about yourself than about me.'

'It's that young miss, isn't it? Isabella.'

'It's a missus.'

'I didn't know you were married.'

'I'm not. Isabella isn't my wife. Or my lover, if that's what you're thinking.'

Fermín kept silent. He didn't want to doubt Martín's words, but just hearing him talk about that girl – whether she was single or married – he was quite convinced that she was the person poor Martín loved most in the world, probably the only thing that kept him alive in that well of misery. And the saddest thing was that he didn't even seem to realise it.

'Isabella and her husband run a bookshop, a place that has always held a very special meaning for me, ever since I was a child. The governor told me that if I didn't do what he was asking, he'd make sure they were accused of selling subversive material. They'd have their business seized and then they'd be sent to prison and their son, who isn't even three years old, would be taken from them.'

'That fucking son-of-a-bitch,' Fermín muttered.

'No, Fermín,' said Martín. 'This isn't your war. It's mine. It's what I deserve for having done what I've done.'

'You haven't done anything, Martín.'

'You don't know me well enough, Fermín. Not that you need to. What you must concentrate on is getting out of here.'

'Glad you bring that up, since that's the other thing I wanted to ask you. I hear you're developing an experimental method for getting out of this chamber pot. If you need a skinny guinea pig – but one that is bursting with enthusiasm – consider me at your service.'

Martín observed him thoughtfully.

'Have you read Dumas?'

'From cover to cover.'

'You look the type. If that's the case, you'll have an inkling of what's coming. Listen well.'

# 8

FERMÍN HAD BEEN IN CAPTIVITY FOR SIX MONTHS WHEN a series of circumstances substantially changed the course of his life. The first of these was that during that period, when the regime still believed that Hitler, Mussolini and Co. were going to win the war and that Europe would soon parade the same colours as the Generalissimo's underpants, an unhindered wave of thugs, informers and newly appointed commissars drove up the number of imprisoned, arrested, prosecuted or 'disappeared' citizens to an all-time high.

THE COUNTRY'S JAILS COULDN'T cope with the influx. The military authorities had instructed the Montjuïc prison management to double or even treble their intake and thus absorb part of the torrent of convicts flooding that defeated, miserable Barcelona of 1940. To that effect, in his flowery Sunday speech, the governor informed the prisoners that from then on they would share their cells. Dr Sanahuja was moved into Martín's cell, presumably to keep an eye on him and protect him from his suicidal fits. Fermín had to share cell 13 with his grumpy old next-door neighbour, Number 14. All the prisoners in the block were coupled together in order to make room for the new arrivals who were driven up every night in vans from La Modelo or the Campo de la Bota prisons.

'Don't pull that face. I like it even less than you do,' Number 14 informed his new companion when he moved in.

'Let me warn you that unbridled hostility gives me insidious bouts of gas,' Fermín threatened. 'So drop the Buffalo Bill act. Make an effort to behave and try to piss facing the wall and without splashing, or one of these days you'll wake up sprouting mushrooms.'

Ex-Number 14 spent five days without speaking to Fermín. Finally, surrendering in the face of the sulphuric flatulence Fermín offered him in the middle of the night, he switched strategy.

'I did warn you,' said Fermín.

'All right. I give in. My name is Sebastián Salgado, a trade unionist by profession. Let's shake hands and be friends, but, please, I beg you, stop farting like that, because I'm beginning to hallucinate and in my dreams I see Comrade Joseph Stalin doing the charleston.'

Fermín shook Salgado's hand and noticed that he was missing his little finger and his ring finger.

'Fermín Romero de Torres, pleased to make your acquaintance at last. Member of the secret service in the Caribbean sector of the Catalan Government, now in the clandestine reserve. But my true vocation is bibliographer and lover of literature.'

Salgado looked at his new comrade-in-arms and rolled his eyes.

'And they say Martín is mad.'

'A madman is one who considers himself sane and thinks that fools don't belong in his rank.'

Salgado nodded, defeated.

THE SECOND CIRCUMSTANCE OCCURRED a few days later, when a couple of guards turned up at dusk to fetch him. Bebo opened their cell, trying to hide his concern.

'You, Skinny Arse, get up,' one of the guards muttered.

For a moment Salgado thought his prayers had been answered and Fermín was being taken away to be shot.

'Be brave, Fermín.' He smiled encouragingly. 'Off to die for God and country, what could be more beautiful?'

The two guards grabbed Fermín, shackled his hands and feet, and dragged him away among the anguished looks of the entire block and Salgado's roars of laughter.

'You're not farting your way out of this one, that's for sure,' laughed his companion.

# 9

FERMÍN WAS LED THROUGH A MAZE OF TUNNELS UNTIL they reached a long corridor with a heavy wooden door visible at one end. He felt queasy, convinced that his miserable life was now over and that Inspector Fumero would be waiting behind that door with a welding torch and the night off. To his surprise, when he reached the door one of the guards removed his shackles while the other one rapped gently.

'Come in,' answered a familiar voice.

That is how Fermín found himself in the governor's office, a room luxuriously decorated with fancy furniture and carpets presumably stolen from some ritzy mansion in the Bonanova area. The scene was rounded off with a Spanish flag – eagle, coat of arms and inscription – a portrait of the Caudillo with more retouching than a publicity shot of Marlene Dietrich and the governor himself, Don Mauricio Valls, smiling behind his desk, enjoying an imported cigarette and a glass of brandy.

'Sit down. Don't be afraid,' he invited.

Fermín noticed a tray next to him, with a plateful of actual red meat grilled to perfection, sautéed fresh peas and steaming mashed potatoes that smelled of hot butter and spices.

'It's not a mirage,' said the governor softly. 'It's your dinner. I hope you brought an appetite.'

Fermín, who hadn't seen anything like it since 1936, threw himself on the food before the vision evaporated. The governor watched him wolf it down with a mild expression of disgust and disdain behind his fixed smile, smoking and smoothing his slicked-back hair every other minute. When Fermín had licked his plate clean as a mirror, Valls told the guards to leave. On his own, the governor seemed far more sinister than with an armed escort.

'Fermín, isn't it?' he asked casually.

Fermín nodded.

'You'll wonder why I've summoned you.'

Fermín shrank in his chair.

'Nothing that need worry you. On the contrary. I've made you come because I want to improve your living conditions and, who knows, perhaps review your sentence: we both know that the charges brought against you didn't hold water. That's the problem with times like ours; a lot of things get stirred up and sometimes it's the innocent who suffer. Such is the price of our national renaissance. Over and above such considerations, I want you to understand that I'm on your side. I'm a bit of a prisoner here myself. I'm sure we both want to get out as soon as possible, and I thought we could help one another. Cigarette?'

Fermín accepted timidly.

'If you don't mind, I'll save it for later.'

'Of course. As you please. Here, have the whole packet.'

Fermín slid it into his pocket. The governor leaned over the table, smiling. There's a snake just like that in the zoo, thought Fermín, but that one only eats mice.

'So, how do you like your new cellmate?'

'Salgado? A true humanitarian.'

'I don't know whether you're aware that before we put him inside, this swine was an assassin for hire working for the communists.'

Fermín shook his head.

'He told me he was a trade unionist.'

Valls laughed softly.

'In May 1938, all on his own, he slipped into the home of the Vilajoana family on Paseo de la Bonanova and did away with them all, including their five children, the four maids and the eighty-six-year-old grandmother. Do you know who the Vilajoanas were?'

'Well, actually . . .'

'Jewellers. At the time of the crime there were jewels and cash in the house to the value of sixty-five thousand pesetas. Do you know where this money is now?'

'I don't know.'

'You don't know, and nobody knows. The only person who knows is Comrade Salgado, who decided not to hand it over to the proletariat but to hide it, so he could live in grand style after the war. Which is something he'll never do because we'll keep him here until he sings like a canary or until your friend Fumero slices what's left of him into little cutlets.'

Fermín nodded, putting two and two together.

'I'd noticed he is missing a couple of fingers on his left hand and he walks in a funny way.'

'One of these days you must ask him to pull his trousers down and you'll see he's also missing some other key equipment he's lost along the way because of his stubborn refusal to cooperate.'

Fermín gulped.

'I want you to know that I find such atrocities repugnant. That's one of the two reasons why you're here, and why I've ordered Salgado to be moved to your cell. Because I believe that when people talk they get to understand one another. I want you to discover where he's hidden the stash from the Vilajoanas, and from all the other thefts and crimes he's committed in the last few years, and I want you to tell me.'

Fermín felt his heart fall to the ground.

'And the other reason?'

'The second reason is that I've noticed that you have recently become pals with David Martín. Which is fine by me. Friendship is a virtue that ennobles humans and helps rehabilitate prisoners. I'm not sure if you know that Martín is a writer of sorts.'

94

'I've heard something.'

The governor threw him an icy glance but kept up his friendly smile.

'Martín isn't a bad person, really, but he's mistaken about a lot of things. One of them is this naive notion that he has to protect the weak and the innocent and such.'

'How extravagant of him.'

'Indeed. That's why I thought that perhaps it would be good if you keep close to him, with your eyes and ears well open, and tell me what he tells you, what he thinks and feels . . . I'm sure there must be something he's mentioned to you that has caught your attention.'

'Come to think of it, Governor, he's recently been complaining quite a lot about a spot in his groin where his underpants rub against him.'

The governor sighed and muttered something under his breath, visibly tired from having to feign so much politeness with such an undesirable specimen.

'Look here, you imbecile, we can do this the easy way or the hard way. I'm trying to be reasonable, but all I have to do is to pick up the phone and your friend Fumero will be here in half an hour. I've been told that lately, as well as the welding torch, he keeps a cabinetmaker's toolbox in one of the basement cells with which he works wonders. Am I making myself clear?'

Fermín clasped his hands to hide his trembling.

'Beautifully. Forgive me, Governor. I hadn't eaten beef for so long that the protein must have gone straight to my head. It won't happen again.'

The governor resumed his smile and continued as if nothing had happened.

'In particular, I'm interested in finding out whether he's ever mentioned a cemetery of forgotten books, or dead books, or something along those lines. Think carefully before you answer. Has Martín ever talked to you about such a place?'

Fermín shook his head.

'I swear, sir, I've never in my life heard Señor Martín, or anyone else, mention that place . . .'

The governor winked at him.

'I believe you. And that's why I know that if he does mention it, you'll tell me. And if he doesn't, you'll bring up the subject and find out where it is.'

Fermín nodded repeatedly.

'And one more thing. If Martín talks to you about a job I've asked him to do for me, convince him that in his own best interests, and in particular those of a certain young lady he holds in very high esteem, as well as the husband and child of the latter, he'd better get cracking and write his best work.'

'Do you mean Señora Isabella?' Fermín asked.

'Ah, I see he's mentioned her to you . . . You should see her,' said the governor while he wiped his glasses with a handkerchief. 'Young, really young, with that firm schoolgirl flesh . . . You don't know how often she's been sitting here, right where you are now, pleading for that poor wretch Martín. I won't tell you what she's offered me because I'm a gentleman but, between you and me, the devotion this girl feels for Martín is very telling. If I had to make a bet, I'd say that kid, Daniel, isn't her husband's but Martín's. He might have abysmal taste when it comes to literature but an exquisite eye for sluts.'

The governor stopped when he noticed that the prisoner was giving him an impenetrable look which he didn't appreciate.

'What are you staring at?' he challenged him.

He banged the table with his knuckles and instantly the door behind Fermín opened. The two guards grabbed him by his arms, hauling him up from his chair until his feet were dangling in the air.

'Remember what I've told you,' said the governor. 'In four weeks' time I want you in that chair again. If you bring me results, I can assure you your stay here will change for the better. If not, I'll book you into the basement cell with Fumero and his toys. Are we clear?'

'Crystal.'

Then, with a bored expression, the governor signalled to his men to take the prisoner away and downed his glass of brandy, sick and tired of having to talk to those uncultured yokels, day in, day out.

# 10

*Barcelona, 1957*

'DANIEL, YOU'VE GONE PALE,' MURMURED FERMÍN, ROUSING me from my trance.

The dining room in Can Lluís, the streets we had walked down to get there, had all disappeared. All I could see before me was that office in Montjuïc Castle and the face of that man talking about my mother with words and insinuations that seared my very soul. At the same time, something cold and sharp moved inside me, an anger I had never known before. For a split second what I most yearned for in the world was to have that son-of-a-bitch before me so I could wring his neck and watch him until the veins in his eyes burst.

'DANIEL . . .'

I closed my eyes and took a deep breath. When I opened them again I was back in Can Lluís, and Fermín Romero de Torres was looking at me, completely vanquished.

'Forgive me, Daniel,' he said.

My mouth was dry. I poured myself a glass of water and drank it down, waiting for words to come to my lips.

'There's nothing to forgive, Fermín. Nothing of what you've told me is your fault.'

'For a start, it's my fault for having to tell you,' he said, in such a soft voice it was barely audible.

I saw him lower his eyes, as if he didn't dare look me in the face. He seemed so overcome with pain from remembering that episode and having to reveal the truth to me that I felt ashamed of my own bitterness.

'Fermín, look at me.'

Fermín managed to look at me out of the corner of his eye and I smiled at him.

'I want you to know that I'm grateful to you for having told me the truth and that I understand why you preferred not to tell me anything about this years ago.'

Fermín nodded weakly but something in his eyes made me realise that my words were no comfort to him at all. On the contrary. We sat in silence for a few moments.

'There's more, isn't there?' I asked at last.

Fermín nodded.

'And what follows is worse?'

Fermín nodded again.

'Much worse.'

I looked away and smiled at Professor Alburquerque, who was now leaving, not without raising a hand in farewell.

'Well then, why don't we ask for another bottle of water and you tell me the rest?'

'Better if it's wine,' Fermín considered. 'The strong stuff.'

# 11

*Barcelona, 1940*

A WEEK AFTER THE MEETING BETWEEN FERMÍN AND THE prison governor, a couple of individuals nobody in the cell block had ever set eyes on before – though they reeked of the political branch from a mile off – handcuffed Salgado and took him away without saying a word.

'Bebo, do you know where they're taking him?' asked Number 19.

The jailer shook his head, but the look in his eyes suggested that he'd heard something and preferred not to discuss the matter. With nothing else to talk about, Salgado's absence immediately became a subject for debate and speculation among the prisoners, who came up with all sorts of theories.

*'That guy was a mole, put in here by the* Nacionales *to get information out of us with that yarn about having been locked up because he was a trade unionist.'*

*'Sure, that's why they pulled two fingers off him and goodness knows what else, to make it all sound more convincing.'*

*'I bet he's dining in the Amaya with his pals as we speak, stuffing himself with hake Basque-style and laughing at us all.'*

*'What I think is that he's confessed whatever it was they wanted him to confess and they've chucked him ten kilometres out at sea with a stone tied round his neck.'*

*'He did look like a spook. Thank God I didn't open my mouth. The lot of you will be in a stew.'*

'*You never know, we might even be sent off to jail.*'

For lack of other amusements, the discussions rumbled on until, two days later, the same men who had taken him away brought him back. The first thing all the inmates noticed was that Salgado couldn't stand up and was being dragged along like a bundle. The second thing was that he was as pale as a corpse and drenched in cold sweat. The prisoner had returned half naked and covered in a brownish scab that looked like a mixture of dried blood and excrement. They dropped him on the cell floor as if he were a sack of manure and left without saying a word.

Fermín took him in his arms and laid him down on the bunk. He started to wash him slowly with a few shreds of cloth he tore off his own shirt and a bit of water Bebo brought him on the quiet. Salgado was conscious and breathed with difficulty, but his eyes shone with an inner fire. Where, two days earlier, he'd had a left hand, he now had a throbbing stump of purplish flesh cauterised with tar. While Fermín cleaned his face, Salgado smiled at him with his few remaining teeth.

'Why don't you tell those butchers once and for all what they want to know, Salgado? It's only money. I don't know how much you've hidden, but it's not worth this.'

'Like hell!' he muttered with what little breath he had left. 'That money is mine.'

'It belongs to all those you murdered and robbed, if you don't mind the observation.'

'I didn't rob anyone. They'd robbed the people before that. And if I executed them it was to deliver the justice the people were demanding.'

'Sure. Thank God you came along, the Mediterranean Robin Hood, to right all wrongs and avenge the plight of the common folk.'

'That money is my future,' spat Salgado.

With the damp cloth, Fermín wiped Salgado's cold forehead, lined with scratches.

'One mustn't dream of one's future; one must earn it. And you have no future, Salgado. Neither you, nor a country that keeps producing beasts like you and the governor, and then looks the other way. Between us all we've destroyed the future, and all that awaits us is shit like the shit you're dripping with now and that I'm sick of cleaning off you.'

Salgado emitted a sort of rasping whimper, which Fermín took to be laughter.

'Keep your sermons to yourself, Fermín. Don't pretend you're a hero now.'

'No, there are enough heroes. What I am is a coward. Exactly that,' said Fermín. 'But at least I know it and admit it.'

Fermín went on cleaning him as best he could, silently, and then covered him with the piece of blanket they shared – teeming with nits and stinking of urine. He sat next to the thief until Salgado closed his eyes and fell into a sleep from which Fermín didn't think he was ever going to wake.

'Tell me he's already dead,' came Number 15's voice.

'Bets accepted,' Number 17 added. 'A cigarette that he'll kick the bucket.'

'Go to sleep, or to hell, all of you,' said Fermín.

He curled up at the other end of the cell and tried to nod off, but soon realised he wasn't going to sleep that night. After a while he stuck his head between the bars and let his arms hang over the metal shaft fixed across them. On the other side of the corridor, from the shadows of the cell opposite his, two eyes, gleaming in the light of a cigarette, were watching him.

'You haven't told me what Valls wanted you for the other day,' said Martín.

'You can imagine.'

'Any request out of the ordinary?'

'He wants me to worm out of you something about a cemetery of books, or something like that.'

'Interesting,' said Martín.

'Fascinating.'

'Did he tell you why he was interested in the subject?'

'Quite frankly, Señor Martín, our relationship isn't that close. The governor merely threatens me with mutilation of various sorts unless I carry out his orders within four weeks and I merely say, "Yes, sir".'

'Don't worry, Fermín. In four weeks' time you'll be out of here.'

'Oh, sure, on a beach in the Caribbean, with two well-fed mulatto girls massaging my feet, no less.'

'Have faith.'

Fermín let out a despondent sigh. The cards of his future were being dealt out among lunatics, thugs and dying men.

# 12

THAT SUNDAY, AFTER THE SPEECH IN THE YARD, THE governor cast Fermín a questioning look, rounding it off with a smile that turned his stomach. As soon as the guards allowed the prisoners to fall out, Fermín edged over towards Martín.

'BRILLIANT SPEECH,' MARTÍN REMARKED.

'Historic. Every time that man speaks, the history of Western thought undergoes a Copernican revolution.'

'Sarcasm doesn't suit you, Fermín. It goes against your natural tenderness.'

'Go to hell.'

'I'm on my way. Cigarette?'

'I don't smoke.'

'They say it helps you die faster.'

'Bring it on, then.'

HE DIDN'T MANAGE TO get beyond the first puff. Martín took the cigarette from his fingers and gave him a few pats on the back while Fermín seemed to be coughing up even the memories of his first communion.

'I don't know how you can swallow that. It tastes of singed dogs.'

'It's the best you can get here. Apparently they're made from cigarette stubs picked up in the corridors of the Monumental bullring.'

'The bouquet suggests it's more likely from the urinals.'

'Take a deep breath, Fermín. Feeling better?'

Fermín nodded.

'Are you going to tell me something about that cemetery so that I have a bit of offal to throw at the head swine? It doesn't have to be true. Any nonsense you can come up with will do.'

Martín smiled as he exhaled the fetid smoke through his teeth.

'How's your cellmate, Salgado, the defender of the poor?'

'Here's a story for you. I thought I'd reached a certain age and had seen it all in this circus of a world. But, early this morning, when it looked like Salgado had given up the ghost, I hear him get up and walk over to my bunk like a vampire.'

'He does have something of the vampire,' agreed Martín.

'Anyway, he comes over and stands there staring at me. I pretend to be asleep and when Salgado takes the bait, I see him scurry off to a corner and with the only hand he has left he starts to poke around in what medical science refers to as the rectum or final section of the large intestine,' Fermín continued.

'What did you say?'

'You heard it. Good old Salgado, still convalescing from his most recent session of medieval amputation, decides to celebrate being back on his feet by exploring that long-underrated area of human anatomy where Mother Nature has decreed the sun doesn't shine. I can't believe my eyes and don't even dare breathe. A minute goes by and Salgado looks as if he has two or three fingers, all the ones he has left, stuck in there in search of the philosopher's stone or some very deep piles. All of which is accompanied by a low, hushed moaning which I'm not going to bother to reproduce.'

'I'm dumbfounded,' said Martín.

'Then brace yourself for the grand finale. After a minute or two of prospective digging, he lets out a Saint John of the Cross-type sigh and the miracle happens. When he removes his fingers from anal territory he pulls out something shiny that even from the corner where I'm lying I can certify is no standard faecal arrangement, pardon my French.'

'So what was it, then?'

'A key. Not a spanner, just one of those small keys, the sort used for briefcases or a locker in the gym.'

'What then?'

'Then he takes the key, polishes it with a bit of spit – because I imagine it must have smelled of roses – and then goes over to the wall where, after making sure I'm still asleep, a fact that I confirm through finely rendered snores, like those of a Saint Bernard puppy, he proceeds to hide the key by inserting it in a crack between stones which he then covers with filth and, I dare say, some collateral resulting from his explorations in his nether parts.'

For a while Martín and Fermín looked at one another without speaking.

'Are you thinking what I'm thinking?' asked Fermín.

Martín nodded.

'How much do you reckon the old crap shooter must have hidden in his little nest of greed?' asked Fermín.

'Enough to believe that it's worth his while to lose fingers, hands, part of his testicular mass and God knows what else to keep its whereabouts secret,' Martín guessed.

'And what do I do now? Before I let a snake like the governor snatch Salgado's little treasure – to fund hardback editions of his collected works and buy himself a seat in the Royal Academy of Language – I'd rather swallow that key, or, if necessary, even introduce it into the ignoble part of my own digestive tract.'

'Don't do anything for the time being,' Martín advised. 'Make sure the key is still there and await my instructions. I'm putting the finishing touches to your escape.'

'No offence, Señor Martín, since I'm extremely grateful for your counsel and moral support, but you're getting me to put my head and some other esteemed appendages on the block with this idea of yours, and considering the general consensus that you're as mad as a hatter, it troubles me to think I'm placing my life in your hands.'

'None taken, but, if you don't trust a novelist, who are you going to trust?'

Fermín watched Martín walk off down the yard wrapped in his portable cloud of cigarette-stub smoke.

'Holy mother of God,' he murmured to the wind.

# 13

THE MACABRE BETTING SYNDICATE ORGANISED BY NUMBER 17 continued to thrive for a few more days, during which Salgado sometimes looked as if he were about to expire and then, just as suddenly, would get up, drag himself to the bars of the cell and declaim at the top of his voice the stanza: 'You-fucking-bastards-you're-not-getting-a-penny-out-of-me-you-fucking-sons-of-bitches' and variations on the theme, until he screamed himself hoarse and collapsed exhausted on the floor, from where Fermín had to lift him and take him back to the bed.

'Is old Cockroach succumbing, Fermín?' asked Number 17 every time he heard him slump to the floor.

Fermín no longer bothered giving medical updates on his cellmate. If it happened, they'd soon see the canvas sack passing by.

'Look here, Salgado, if you're going to die, do so once and for all, and if you plan to live, I beg you to do it silently because I'm fed up to the back teeth with your foaming-at-the-mouth recitals,' Fermín told him, tucking him up with a piece of dirty canvas. In Bebo's absence, he'd managed to obtain it from one of the jailers after winning him over with a foolproof strategy for seducing young girls – by overcoming their resistance with carefully measured doses of whipped cream and sponge fingers.

'Don't give me that charitable crap. I know what you're up to. You're no better than this pack of vultures willing to bet their underpants that I'm going to croak,' Salgado replied. He seemed ready to keep up his foul mood to the very end.

'I'm not one to argue with a man in his death throes but I'm letting you know that I haven't bet a single *real* in this gambling den, and if I ever wanted to give myself over to vice it wouldn't be betting on the life of a human being. Although you're as much a human being as I'm a glow-worm,' Fermín pronounced.

'Don't think for a minute that all that talk of yours is going to distract me,' Salgado snapped back maliciously. 'I know perfectly well what you and your bosom friend Martín are plotting with all that *Count of Monte Cristo* business.'

'I don't know what you're babbling about, Salgado. Sleep for a bit, or for a year, since nobody's going to miss you anyhow.'

'If you think you're getting out of this place you're as mad as he is.'

Fermín felt a cold sweat on his back. Salgado bared his smashed teeth in a smile.

'I knew it,' he said.

Swearing under his breath, Fermín curled up in his corner, as far away as he could get from Salgado. The peace only lasted a minute.

'My silence has a price,' Salgado announced.

'I should have let you die when they brought you back,' murmured Fermín.

'As proof of my gratitude I'm prepared to give you a discount,' said Salgado. 'All I ask of you is to do me one last favour and I'll keep your secret.'

'How do I know it's the last?'

'Because you're going to get caught, just like everyone else who's tried to leg it out of here, and after they've riled you for a few days you'll be garrotted in the yard, as an edifying sight for the rest of us. And then I won't be able to ask you for anything else. What do you say? A small favour and my complete co-operation. I give you my word of honour.'

'Your word of honour? Man, why didn't you say so before? That changes everything.'

'Come closer . . .'

Fermín hesitated for a moment, but told himself he had nothing to lose.

'I know that son-of-a-bitch Valls has put you up to it, to find out where I've hidden the money,' he said. 'Don't bother to deny it.'

Fermín shrugged his shoulders.

'I want you to tell him,' Salgado instructed Fermín.

'Whatever you say, Salgado. Where is the money?'

'Tell the governor that he must go alone, in person. If anyone goes with him he won't get a *duro* out of it. Tell him he must go to the old Vilardell factory in Pueblo Nuevo, behind the grave-yard. At midnight. Not before, and not after.'

'Sounds like an episode from *The Phantom*, Salgado, one of the bad ones ...'

'Listen carefully. Tell him he must go into the factory and find the old guards' lodge, next to the textile mill. When he gets there he must knock on the door, and when they ask him who's there, he must say: "Durruti lives".'

Fermín chuckled.

'It's the most idiotic thing I've heard since the governor's last speech.'

'You just tell him what I've told you.'

'And how do you know I won't go there myself? If I follow your cheap melodrama and passwords, I could take the money.'

Avarice shone in Salgado's eyes.

'Don't tell me: because I'll be dead,' Fermín completed.

Salgado's reptilian smile spilled over his lips. Fermín studied those eyes, eaten away by his thirst for revenge. He realised then what Salgado was after.

'It's a trap, isn't it?'

Salgado didn't reply.

'What if Valls survives? Haven't you stopped to think what they'll do to you?'

'Nothing they haven't done to me already.'

'I'd say you've got balls, if it wasn't for the fact that you only have a bit of one left. And if this move of yours doesn't pan out, you won't even have that much,' Fermín suggested.

'That's my problem,' retorted Salgado. 'So what's it to be, Monte Cristo? Is it a deal?'

Salgado offered him his one remaining hand. Fermín stared at it for a few moments before shaking it reluctantly.

# 14

Fermín had to wait for the traditional Sunday lecture after mass and the brief period in the yard to go over to Martín and confide in him what Salgado had asked him to do.

'It won't interfere with the plan,' Martín assured him. 'Do what he's asking you to do. We can't risk a tip-off at this point.'

Fermín, who for days had been hovering between feelings of nausea and a racing heart, dried the cold sweat dripping down his forehead.

'Martín, it's not that I don't trust you, but if this plan you're preparing is so good, why don't you use it to get out of here yourself?'

Martín nodded, as if he'd been expecting that question for days.

'Because I deserve to be here, and even if I didn't, there's nowhere left for me outside these walls. I have nowhere to go.'

'You have Isabella . . .'

'Isabella is married to a man who is ten times better than me. All I would achieve by getting out of here would be to make her miserable.'

'But she's doing everything possible to get you out . . .'

Martín shook his head.

'You must promise me one thing, Fermín. It's all I'm going to ask you to do in exchange for helping you escape.'

This is the month for requests, thought Fermín, nodding readily.

'Whatever you say.'

'If you manage to leave this place I want you, if you can, to take care of her. From a distance, without her knowing, without her even knowing you exist. I want you to take care of her and of her son, Daniel. Will you do that for me, Fermín?'

'Of course.'

Martín smiled sadly.

'You're a good man, Fermín.'

'That's the second time you've told me, and every time it sounds worse to me.'

Martín pulled out one of his stinking cigarettes and lit it.

'We don't have much time. Brians, the lawyer Isabella hired to act on my case, was here yesterday. I made the mistake of telling him what Valls wants me to do.'

'The business about rewriting that garbage of his . . .'

'Exactly. I asked him not to say anything to Isabella, but I know him, and sooner or later he will, and Isabella, whom I know even better, will fly into a rage and come here to threaten Valls with broadcasting his secret from the rooftops.'

'Can't you stop her?'

'Trying to stop Isabella is like trying to stop a cargo train: a fool's errand.'

'The more you talk about her the more I'd like to meet her. I like women with spirit . . .'

'Fermín, let me remind you of your promise.'

Fermín put his hand on his heart and nodded solemnly. Martín continued.

'As I was saying, when this happens, Valls might do something stupid. He's driven by vanity, envy and greed. When he feels he's been cornered he'll make a false move. I don't know what, but I'm sure he'll try to do something. It's important that by then you're already out of here.'

'As you know, I'm not too keen on this place . . .'

'You don't understand. We've got to speed up the plan.'

'When to?'

Martín watched him at length through the curtain of smoke rising from his lips.

'To tonight.'

Fermín tried to swallow, but his mouth felt as if it were full of dust.

'But I don't even know what the plan is yet . . .'

'Listen carefully.'

# 15

That afternoon, before returning to his cell, Fermín approached one of the two guards who had escorted him to Valls's office.

'Tell the governor I need to talk to him.'

'What about?'

'Tell him I have the results he was waiting for. He'll know what I mean.'

Before an hour had passed, the guard and his colleague were at the door of cell number 13 to fetch Fermín. Salgado watched the whole thing eagerly from the bunk as he massaged his stump. Fermín winked at him and set off, escorted by the guards.

The governor received him with an effusive smile and a plateful of delicious pastries from Casa Escribá.

'Fermín, dear friend, what a pleasure to see you here again, ready for an intelligent and productive conversation. Do sit down, please. And enjoy this fine selection of sweets brought to me by the wife of one of the prisoners.'

Fermín, who for days hadn't been able to swallow so much as a birdseed, picked up a ring-shaped pastry so as not to disobey Valls, and held it in his hand as if he were holding an amulet. Valls poured himself a glass of brandy and dropped into his ample general's armchair.

'So? I understand you have good news for me,' the governor said, inviting Fermín to talk.

Fermín nodded.

'In the belles-lettres department, I can assure Your Honour that Martín is more than persuaded and motivated to carry out the polishing and ironing task he was requested to do. Moreover, he remarked that the material you supplied him with, sir, is of such a high quality and so fine, that he thinks it will pose no difficulties. All he needs to do is dot a few i's and cross a few t's in your work of genius to produce a masterpiece worthy of the great Paracelsus.'

Valls paused to absorb Fermín's barrage of words, but nodded politely without removing his frozen smile.

'There's no need for you to sweeten it for me, Fermín. It's enough for me to know that Martín will do what he has to do. We're both aware that he doesn't like the task he's been assigned, but I'm glad he's seeing reason at last and understands that making things possible benefits us all. And now, about the other two points . . .'

'I was coming to that, sir. Concerning the burial ground of the lost volumes . . .'

'The Cemetery of Forgotten Books,' Valls corrected him. 'Have you been able to extract its location from Martín?'

Fermín nodded with utter conviction.

'From what I've been able to gather, the aforementioned ossuary is hidden behind a labyrinth of tunnels and chambers, beneath the Borne market.'

Valls weighed up that revelation, visibly surprised.

'And the entrance?'

'I wasn't able to get that far, sir. I imagine that it must be through some trapdoor camouflaged behind the uninviting paraphernalia and stench of some of the wholesale vegetable stalls. Martín didn't want to talk about it, and I thought that if I pressed him too much he might dig his heels in.'

Valls nodded slowly.

'You did the right thing. Go on.'

'And finally, in reference to Your Excellency's last request, taking advantage of the death throes and moral agonies of that despicable Salgado, I was able to persuade him, in his delirium, to confess where he'd hidden the copious booty from his criminal activities in the service of Freemasonry and Marxism.'

'So, you think he's going to die?'

'Any moment now. I think he's already commended himself to Saint Leon Trotsky and is awaiting his last breath to rise into the politburo of posterity.'

'I told those animals they wouldn't extract anything out of him by force,' Valls muttered under his breath.

'Technically, I believe they extracted a gonad or a limb, but I agree with you, sir, that with vermin like Salgado the only possible method is applied psychology.'

'So then? Where did he hide the money?'

Fermín leaned forward and adopted a confidential tone.

'It's complicated to explain.'

'Don't beat about the bush or I'll send you down to the basement to have your vocal cords refreshed.'

Fermín then proceeded to sell Valls that outlandish plot he'd obtained from Salgado's lips. The governor listened incredulously.

'Fermín, let me warn you that if you're lying you'll be deeply sorry. What they've done to Salgado won't even be a foretaste of what they'll do to you.'

'I can assure Your Lordship that I'm repeating, word for word, what Salgado told me. If you like I'll swear on the irrefutable portrait of Franco that lies on your desk.'

Valls looked him straight in the eye. Fermín held his gaze without blinking, just as Martín had taught him to do. Finally, having procured the information he was looking for, the governor removed his smile as well as the plate of pastries. Without any pretence at cordiality, he snapped his fingers and the two guards came in to lead Fermín back to his cell.

This time Valls didn't even bother to threaten Fermín. As they dragged him down the corridor, Fermín saw the governor's secretary walking past them and stopping outside Valls's office.

'Governor, Sanahuja, the doctor in Martín's cell . . .'

'Yes. What?'

'He says Martín has fainted and thinks it might be something serious. He asks for permission to go to the medicine cabinet and get a few things . . .'

Valls stood up in a fury.

'So what are you waiting for? Go on. Take him there and let him have whatever he needs.'

# 16

FOLLOWING THE GOVERNOR'S ORDERS, A JAILER WAS LEFT posted in front of Martín's cell while Dr Sanahuja treated him. The jailer was a young man of about twenty who was new to the shift. The night shift was supposed to be covered by Bebo, but instead that novice had inexplicably turned up, looking incapable even of sorting out his bunch of keys and more nervous than any of the prisoners. At about nine o'clock the doctor, noticeably tired, walked over to the bars of his cell and spoke to him.

'I need more clean gauze and some antiseptic.'

'I can't abandon my post.'

'And I can't abandon a patient. Please. Gauze and antiseptic.'

The jailer stirred nervously.

'The governor doesn't like it when his instructions are not followed word for word.'

'He'll like it even less if anything happens to Martín because you've ignored me.'

The young jailer assessed the situation.

'Listen, boss,' argued the doctor. 'We're unlikely to walk through the walls or swallow the iron bars . . .'

The jailer swore and rushed off to the medicine cabinet, while Sanahuja stood by the bars of his cell and waited. Salgado had been asleep for a couple of hours, breathing with difficulty. Fermín tiptoed up to the front of his cell and exchanged glances with the doctor. Sanahuja then threw him a parcel, the size of a pack of cards, wrapped in a shred of material and tied with a piece of string. Fermín caught it in the air and quickly retreated to the shadows at the far end of his cell. When the jailer returned with what Sanahuja had asked him for, he peered through the bars, inspecting Salgado's silhouette on the bunk.

'He's on his last legs,' said Fermín. 'I don't think he'll last till tomorrow.'

'You keep him alive until six. I don't want him to screw things up for me. Let him die during someone else's shift.'

'I'll do what is humanly possible, boss,' replied Fermín.

# 17

That night, while Fermín unwrapped the parcel Dr Sanahuja had tossed him from the other side of the corridor, a black Studebaker was driving the governor down the road from Montjuïc towards the dark streets bordering the port. Jaime, the chauffeur, was taking great care to avoid potholes and any jolts that might inconvenience his passenger or interrupt the flow of his thoughts. The new governor was not like the previous one. The previous governor would strike up conversations with him in the car and once in a while he had sat in the front, next to him. Governor Valls never addressed Jaime except to give him an order and rarely caught his eye, unless he'd made a mistake, or driven over a stone, or taken a bend too fast. Then his eyes would smoulder in the rear-view mirror and his face would adopt a sour expression. Governor Valls did not let him turn on the radio because, he said, all the programmes were an insult to his intelligence. Nor did he let Jaime display photographs of his wife and daughter on the dashboard.

Luckily, at that time of night there was no traffic and the route didn't throw up any unwelcome surprises. In just a few minutes the car had passed the old Royal Shipyards, skirted the monument to Columbus and started up the Ramblas. Two minutes later they had reached the Café de la Ópera and stopped. The Liceo audience, on the other side of the street, had already gone in for the evening performance and the Ramblas were almost deserted. The chauffeur got out and, after making sure there was nobody in the way, opened the door for Mauricio Valls. The governor stepped out, looking at the boulevard with indifference, then straightened his tie and brushed off his shoulder pads.

'Wait here,' he said to the driver.

When the governor entered the café, it was almost empty. The clock behind the bar said five minutes to ten. The governor responded to the waiter's greeting with a nod and sat down at a table at the far end. He calmly slipped off his gloves and pulled out his silver cigarette case, the one his father-in-law had given him on his first wedding anniversary. He lit a cigarette and gazed at the old café. The waiter came over with a tray and wiped the table with a damp cloth that smelled of bleach. The governor threw him a look of disdain which the waiter ignored.

'What will the gentleman have?'

'Two camomile teas.'

'In the same cup?'

'No. In separate cups.'

'Is the gentleman expecting someone?'

'Obviously.'

'Very good. Can I get you anything else?'

'Honey.'

'Yes, sir.'

The waiter left unhurriedly, while the governor made some contemptuous remark under his breath. A radio on the counter was murmuring a phone-in programme for lonely hearts, interspersed with publicity from Bella Aurora cosmetics, whose daily use guaranteed perpetual youth and sparkling beauty. Four tables away an elderly man seemed to have fallen asleep with a newspaper in his hands. The rest of the tables were empty. The two steaming cups arrived five minutes later. At a snail's pace, the waiter placed them on the table, followed by a jar of honey.

'Will that be all, sir?'

Valls nodded. He didn't move until the waiter had returned to the bar. Then he proceeded to pull a small bottle out of his pocket. He unscrewed the top, while casting a quick glance at the other customer who still seemed knocked out by his newspaper. The waiter stood behind the bar, with his back to the room, methodically drying glasses with a white cloth.

Valls took the bottle and emptied its contents into the cup on the other side of the table. Then he added a generous dollop of honey and began to stir the camomile with the teaspoon until the honey had dissolved completely. On the radio someone was reading an anguished letter from a faithful listener from Betanzos whose husband, apparently annoyed because she'd burned his All Soul's Day stew, had taken to going to the bar to listen to the football with his friends, was hardly ever home and hadn't gone to mass since that day. She was recommended prayer, patience and to make use of her feminine wiles, but only within the strict limits of the Christian family. Valls checked the clock again. It was a quarter past ten.

# 18

At twenty past ten, Isabella Sempere walked in through the door. She wore a simple coat, no make-up and her hair was tied up. Valls saw her and raised a hand. Isabella paused for a moment to look at him blankly, then slowly walked over to the table. Valls stood up and held out his hand with a friendly smile. Isabella ignored the gesture and sat down.

'I've taken the liberty of ordering two camomile teas. It's the best thing to have on such a chilly evening.'

Isabella nodded absently, avoiding Valls's eyes. The governor studied her closely. As every time she had come to see him, Señora Sempere had made herself look as plain as possible in an attempt to hide her beauty. Valls examined the shape of her lips, her throbbing neck and the swell of her breasts under her coat.

'I'm listening,' said Isabella.

'Above all, let me thank you for agreeing to meet me at such short notice. I received your note this afternoon and thought it would be a good idea to discuss the matter away from the office and the prison.'

Isabella responded with another nod. Valls had a sip of his camomile and licked his lips.

'Excellent. The best in all Barcelona. Taste it.'

Isabella ignored his invitation.

'As you will understand, we can't be discreet enough. May I ask you whether you've told anyone you were coming here tonight?'

Isabella shook her head.

'Your husband, perchance?'

'My husband is stocktaking in the bookshop. He won't get home until the early hours of the morning. Nobody knows I'm here.'

'Shall I get you something else? If you don't feel like a camomile tea . . .'

Isabella shook her head and held the cup in her hands.

'It's fine.'

Valls smiled serenely.

'As I was saying, I got your letter. I quite understand your indignation and wanted to tell you that it's all due to a misunderstanding.'

'You're blackmailing a poor, mentally ill person, your prisoner, by getting him to write a book with which to promote yourself. I don't think I misunderstood anything up to that point.'

Valls slid a hand towards Isabella.

'Isabella . . . May I call you that?'

'Don't touch me, please.'

Valls pulled his hand away, putting on a conciliatory smile.

'All right, but let's talk calmly.'

'There's nothing to talk about. If you don't leave David in peace, I'll take your story and your fraud to Madrid or wherever is required. Everyone will know what sort of a person and what sort of a literary figure you are. Nothing and nobody is going to stop me.'

Isabella's eyes brimmed with tears and the cup of camomile shook in her hands.

'Please, Isabella. Drink a little. It will do you good.'

Isabella drank a couple of sips.

'Like this, with a bit of honey, is how it tastes best,' Valls added.

Isabella took two or three more sips.

'I must say, I do admire you, Isabella,' said Valls. 'Few people would have the courage and the composure to defend a poor wretch like Martín . . . someone whom everyone has abandoned and betrayed. Everyone but you.'

Isabella glanced nervously at the clock above the bar. It was ten thirty-five. She took a couple more sips of camomile and then finished it off.

'You must be very fond of him,' Valls ventured. 'Sometimes I wonder whether, given a bit of time, when you get to know me a bit better and see what I'm really like, you'll become just as fond of me as you are of him.'

She looked at him coldly for a long while, the empty cup in her hands.

'You make me feel sick, Valls. You and all the filth like you.'

Valls smiled warmly.

'I know, Isabella. But it's the filth like me that always rules in this country and the people like you who are always left in the shadow. It makes no difference which side is holding the reins.'

'Not this time. This time your superiors will know what you're doing.'

'What makes you think they'll care, or that they don't do the same or much worse? After all, I'm only an amateur.'

Valls smiled and pulled a folded sheet of paper out of his jacket pocket.

'Isabella, I want you to know I'm not the sort of person you think I am. And to prove it, here is the order for freeing David Martín, effective tomorrow.'

Valls showed her the document. Isabella examined it in disbelief. Valls pulled out his pen and, without further ado, signed it.

'There you are. David Martín is, technically, a free man. Thanks to you, Isabella. Thanks to you . . .'

When Isabella looked at him again her eyes had glazed over. Valls noticed how her pupils were slowly dilating and a film of perspiration appeared over her upper lip.

'Are you all right? You look pale . . .'

Isabella staggered to her feet and held on to the chair.

'Are you feeling dizzy, Isabella? Can I take you somewhere?'

Isabella retreated a few steps and bumped into the waiter as she made her way to the door. Valls remained seated, sipping his camomile tea until the clock said ten forty-five. Then he left a few coins on the table and slowly walked towards the exit. The car was waiting for him on the pavement. The chauffeur stood next to it, holding the door open for him.

'Would the governor like to go home or back to the castle?'

'Home. But first we're going to make a stop in Pueblo Nuevo, in the old Vilardell factory,' he ordered.

On his way to pick up the promised bounty, Mauricio Valls, the illustrious future of Spanish letters, gazed at the procession of black, deserted streets in that accursed Barcelona he so detested, and shed a few tears for Isabella, and for what might have been.

# 19

WHEN SALGADO AWOKE FROM HIS STUPOR AND OPENED his eyes, the first thing he noticed was that there was someone standing motionless at the foot of his bunk, watching him. He felt a slight panic and for a moment thought he was still in the basement room. A flickering light from the oil lamps in the corridor outlined familiar contours.

'Fermín, is that you?' he asked.

The figure in the shadows nodded and Salgado breathed deeply.

'My mouth is dry. Is there any water left?'

Slowly, Fermín drew closer. He had something in his hand: a cloth and a small glass bottle.

Salgado saw Fermín pour the liquid from the bottle on to the cloth.

'What's that, Fermín?'

Fermín didn't reply. His face showed no expression. He leaned over Salgado and looked him in the eye.

'Fermín, no . . .'

Before Salgado was able to utter another syllable, Fermín placed the cloth over his mouth and nose and pressed hard, holding Salgado's head down on the bed. Salgado tossed about with what little strength he had left, while Fermín kept the cloth over his face. Salgado looked at him, terror-stricken. Seconds later, he lost consciousness. Fermín didn't lift the cloth. He counted five more seconds and only then did he remove it. Sitting on the bunk with his back to Salgado, he waited a few minutes. Then, just as Martín had told him to do, he walked over to the door of the cell.

'Jailer!' he called.

He heard the new boy's footsteps approaching down the corridor. In Martín's plan it was supposed to be Bebo doing the night shift, not that moron.

'What's the matter now?' asked the jailer.

'It's Salgado. He's had it.'

The jailer shook his head with exasperation.

'Fucking hell. Now what?'

'Bring the sack.'

The jailer cursed his bad luck.

'If you like, I'll put him in, boss,' Fermín offered.

The jailer nodded with just a hint of gratitude.

'If you bring the sack now, you can go and notify them while I put him in. That way they'll come and collect him before midnight,' Fermín added.

The jailer nodded again and went off in search of the canvas sack. Fermín stood by the door of his cell. On the other side of the corridor, Martín and Sanahuja watched him in silence.

TEN MINUTES LATER, THE jailer returned holding the sack by one end, unable to hide the nausea caused by the stench of rotten flesh it gave off. Fermín moved away to the far end of the cell without waiting to be told. The jailer opened the cell door and threw the sack inside.

'Let them know now, boss. That way they'll take the bacon away before midnight – or we'll have to keep him here until tomorrow night.'

'Are you sure you can manage to put him in on your own?'

'Don't worry, boss, I've had plenty of practice.'

The jailer nodded again, not entirely convinced.

'Let's hope we're in luck and it works out, because his stump is starting to ooze and I can't begin to tell you what that's going to smell like . . .'

'Shit,' said the jailer, scuttling off.

As soon as he heard him reach the end of the corridor, Fermín began to undress Salgado. Then he removed his own clothes and got into the thief's stinking rags. Finally, Fermín put his own clothes on Salgado and placed him on the bed, lying on his side with his face to the wall, and pulled the blanket over him, so that it half covered his face. Then he grabbed the canvas sack and got inside it. He was about to close it when he remembered something.

Hurriedly, he got out again and went over to the wall. With his nails, he scratched the space between two stones where he'd seen Salgado hide the key, until the tip began to show. He tried to pull it out with his fingers, but the key kept slipping and remained stuck between the stones.

'Hurry up,' Martín hissed from the other side of the corridor.

Fermín gripped the key with his nails and pulled hard. The nail of his ring finger was ripped off and for a few seconds he was blinded with pain. Fermín muffled a scream and sucked his finger. The taste of his own blood, salty and metallic, filled his mouth. When he opened his eyes again he noticed that about a centimetre of the key was protruding from the wall. This time he was able to pull it out easily.

He slipped into the sack again and tied the knot from the inside, as best he could, leaving an opening of about a hand's breadth. Holding back the retching he felt rising up his throat, he lay on the floor and tightened the strings until only a small gap was left, the size of a fist. He held his nose shut with his fingers. It was preferable to breathe in his own filth than to smell that rotting stench. Now, all that remained for him to do was wait, he told himself.

# 20

THE STREETS OF PUEBLO NUEVO WERE BURIED IN A THICK, humid fog that slithered up from the citadel of shacks on the Somorrostro beach. The governor's Studebaker advanced slowly through veils of mist, past shadowy canyons formed by factories, warehouses and dark, crumbling outbuildings. In front of them, the car's headlights carved out two tunnels of light. Soon the silhouette of the old Vilardell textile mill peered through the fog. Chimneys and crests of abandoned pavilions and workshops were outlined at the far end of the street. The large entrance was guarded by a spiked gate; behind it, just visible, was a spread of tangled undergrowth out of which rose the skeletons of burned lorries and wrecked wagons. The chauffeur stopped in front of the entrance to the old factory.

'Leave the engine running,' ordered the governor.

The beams from the headlights pierced the blackness beyond the gate, revealing the ruinous state of the plant, bombed during the war and abandoned like so many other buildings all over the city.

On one side, a few huts were boarded up with wooden planks. Next to these, facing a garage that looked as if it had gone up in flames, stood what Valls supposed must be the former home of the security guards. The reddish glow of a candle, or an oil lamp, licked the edges of one of the closed windows. The governor took in the scene unhurriedly from the back seat of the car. After a few minutes' wait, he leaned forward and spoke to the chauffeur.

'Jaime, do you see that house on the left-hand side, opposite the garage?'

It was the first time the governor had addressed him by his first name. Something in that sudden warm and polite tone made the driver prefer his usual cold treatment.

'The lodge, you mean?'

'Exactly. I want you to walk over there and knock on the door.'

'You want me to go in there? Into the factory?'

The governor sighed with impatience.

'Not into the factory. Listen carefully. You see the house, don't you?'

'Yes, sir.'

'Very good. Well, you walk to the gate, you slip in through the gap between the bars, and you go over to the lodge and knock on the door. Everything clear so far?'

The chauffeur nodded with little enthusiasm.

'Right. Once you've knocked, someone will open the door, and then you say to him: "Durruti lives".'

'Durruti?'

'Don't interrupt. You just repeat what I've told you. They'll give you something. Probably a case or a bundle. You bring it back here and that's it. Simple, no?'

The chauffeur had gone pale and kept looking into the rear-view mirror, as if he expected someone or something to spring out from the shadows at any moment.

'Calm down, Jaime. Nothing's going to happen. I'm asking you to do this as a personal favour. Tell me, are you married?'

'I got married three years ago, sir.'

'Ah, that's good. And do you have any children?'

'We have a beautiful two-year-old girl, and my wife is expecting, sir.'

'Congratulations. Family is what matters most, Jaime. You're a good Spaniard. If you'll accept, as an advance christening present, and as proof of my gratitude for your excellent work,

I'll give you a hundred pesetas. And if you do this small favour for me I'll recommend you for a promotion. How would you like an office job in the Council? I have good friends there, and they tell me they're looking for men with character to pull the country out of the black hole the reds have left it in.'

The chauffeur smiled weakly at the mention of money and good prospects.

'Won't it be dangerous, or . . .?'

'Jaime, it's me, the governor. Would I ask you to do something dangerous or illegal?'

The chauffeur looked at him but didn't say anything. Valls smiled at him.

'Repeat what it is you have to do, come on.'

'I go up to the door of the house and knock. When they open the door, I say: "Long live Durruti".'

'Durruti lives.'

'That's it. Durruti lives. They give me a case and I bring it back.'

'And we go home. That simple.'

The chauffeur nodded and, after a moment's hesitation, got out of the car and walked up to the gate. Valls watched his silhouette pass through the beams from the headlights and reach the entrance. There the chauffeur turned for a second to look at the car.

'Go on, you idiot, go in,' murmured Valls.

The chauffeur slipped in between the bars and, picking his way through rubble and weeds, slowly approached the door of the lodge. The governor pulled out the revolver he kept in the inside pocket of his coat and cocked the hammer. The chauffeur reached the door and stopped there. Valls saw him knock twice then wait. Almost a minute went by and nothing happened.

'One more time,' muttered Valls to himself.

The chauffeur was now looking towards the car, as if he didn't know what to do next. Suddenly, a pale yellowish light filled the space where, just a second before, there had been a closed door.

Valls saw the chauffeur uttering the password. He turned one more time to look at the car, smiling. The shot, fired at point-blank range, shattered his temple and went clean through his skull. A mist of blood emerged from the other side and the body, already dead, stood for a moment wrapped in a halo of gunpowder before collapsing to the ground like a broken doll.

Valls stepped hurriedly out of the back seat of the Studebaker and took the wheel. Holding his revolver against the dashboard and pointing it towards the factory entrance with his left hand, he put the car into reverse and pressed down on the accelerator. The car reversed into the darkness, bumping over potholes and puddles that peppered the road. As he drove backwards he was able to see the glare of a few shots hitting the gate, but none of them reached the car. Only when he'd reversed some two hundred metres did he turn the Studebaker around. Then, accelerating fully, he drove away from that place, biting his lips with rage.

# 21

Tied up inside the sack, Fermín could only hear their voices approaching the cell.

'Hey, we've been lucky,' cried the novice jailer.

'Fermín has fallen asleep,' said Dr Sanahuja from his cell.

'Some have it easy,' said the jailer. 'There it is, you can take it away.'

Fermín heard footsteps around him and felt a sudden jerk when one of the two gravediggers firmly retied the knot. Then they picked up the sack between them and, without any care, dragged him along the stone corridor like a dead weight. Fermín didn't dare move a single muscle.

The knocks he received from steps, corners and doors stabbed him without mercy. He put a fist in his mouth and bit it to stop himself from screaming. After what seemed like a long round-about route Fermín noticed a sudden drop in the temperature and the absence of the claustrophobic echo that resounded throughout the castle. They were outdoors. He was hauled for a few metres over a paved surface spattered with puddles that soaked the canvas. The cold air soon pierced the sack.

Finally, he felt he was being lifted and thrown into space. He landed on what seemed to be a hard wooden surface, then heard footsteps moving away. Fermín took a deep breath. The inside of the sack was damp and reeked of excrement, putrid flesh and diesel. Fermín heard a lorry engine start and after a jolt, the vehicle began to move. Soon the downward pull of a slope made the sack roll forward and Fermín deduced that the lorry was trundling down the same road that had brought him to the prison months before. He remembered how the climb up the mountain had been long and full of bends. After a short while, however, he noticed that the vehicle was turning and heading in a new direction, along flat, rough, unpaved ground. They had left the main road and Fermín was sure they were advancing further into the mountain instead of driving down towards the city. Something had gone wrong.

Only then did it occur to him that perhaps Martín had not worked everything out, that he'd missed a key detail. After all, nobody knew for certain what they did with the prisoners' dead bodies. Martín may not have stopped to consider that perhaps they got rid of them by throwing them into a furnace. He imagined Salgado, waking up from his heavy chloroform-induced sleep, laughing and saying that Fermín Romero de Torres, or whatever the hell he was called, before burning in Hell, had burned in Life.

The journey continued for a few minutes. Then, as the vehicle began to slow down, Fermín noticed it for the first time. Never in his life had he smelled anything so revolting. His heart shrank and as an indescribable stench brought on waves of nausea, he wished he'd never listened to that madman, Martín, and had remained in his cell.

# 22

WHEN THE GOVERNOR ARRIVED AT MONTJUÏC CASTLE, HE
stepped out of the car and rushed into his office. His secretary
was ensconced behind his small desk near the door, typing the
day's correspondence with two fingers.

'Leave that and get that son-of-a-bitch Salgado brought here
at once,' he ordered.

The secretary looked at him, disconcerted, wondering
whether he should open his mouth.

'Don't just sit there like a halfwit. Get moving.'

The secretary stood up, looking flustered, avoiding the governor's furious eyes.

'Salgado has died, Governor. Just tonight . . .'

Valls closed his eyes and took a deep breath.

'Governor . . . sir . . .'

Without bothering to explain, Valls ran off and didn't stop
until he reached cell number 13. When he saw him, the young
jailer snapped out of his drowsiness and gave him a military
salute.

'Your Excellency, what . . .'

'Open up. Quick.'

The jailer opened the cell and Valls charged in. He walked
over to the bunk and, grabbing the shoulder of the body lying
on it, pulled hard. Salgado was left face up. Valls leaned over
him and smelled his breath. He then turned towards the jailer,
who was looking at him terror-stricken.

'Where's the body?'

'The men from the undertaker's took it . . .'

Valls slapped him so hard he knocked him over. Two guards had turned up in the corridor, waiting for instructions from the governor.

'I want him alive,' he told them.

The two guards nodded and left at a brisk pace. Valls stayed there, leaning against the bars of the cell shared by Martín and Dr Sanahuja. The jailer, who had got to his feet and hardly dared breathe, thought he saw the governor laughing.

'Your idea, Martín, I suppose?' Valls asked at last.

The governor bowed lightly and, as he walked away down the corridor, slowly clapped his hands.

# 23

FERMÍN COULD FEEL THE LORRY SLOWING DOWN AND negotiating the last obstacles along the dirt track. After a couple of minutes of potholes and groans from the lorry, the engine stopped. The stench wafting in through the canvas was indescribable. The two gravediggers walked round to the rear of the lorry and Fermín heard the click of the metal bar that locked the back panel. Suddenly, a strong pull on the sack flung him into the void.

He hit the ground on his side, a dull pain spreading through his shoulder. Before he could react, the two gravediggers lifted the sack from the stony ground and, holding one end each, carried it uphill until they stopped a few metres further on. They dropped the sack again and then Fermín heard one of them kneel down and start to untie the knot. He could hear the other man's footsteps as he moved away and picked up a metal object. Fermín tried to take in some air but that miasma burned his throat. He shut his eyes and felt the cold breeze on his face. The gravedigger grabbed the sack by the closed end and tugged hard. Fermín's body rolled over stones and puddles.

'Come on, let's count to three,' said one of them.

Four hands gripped him by his ankles and wrists. Fermín struggled to hold his breath.

'Hey, listen, isn't he sweating?'

'How the fuck can a stiff be sweating, you jerk? It must be the puddles. Come on, one two and . . .'

*Three.* Fermín felt himself swing in the air. A moment later he was flying and had abandoned himself to his fate. He opened his eyes in mid-flight and all he managed to see before the impact was that he was plunging into a ditch dug into the mountainside. In the moonlight he could only glimpse something pale covering the ground. Fermín was convinced that what he was seeing were stones and, calmly, in the half-second he took to fall, decided he didn't mind dying.

But the landing was gentle. Fermín's body had fallen on something soft and damp. Five metres further up, one of the gravediggers was holding a spade which he emptied into the air. A whitish powder spread like a shiny mist that caressed his skin and, a second later, began to devour it like acid. The two gravediggers walked away and Fermín stood up to discover he was in an open grave packed with rotting bodies and covered in quicklime. He tried to shake off the fiery dust and scrambled over the bodies until he reached the wall of earth. He climbed up the wall, digging his hands into the earth and ignoring the pain. When he reached the top, he managed to drag himself to a puddle of dirty water and wash off the lime. He stood up and saw the lights of the lorry disappearing into the night. Turning around for a moment to look behind him, Fermín stared at the open grave spreading at his feet like an ocean of tangled corpses. He felt sick and he fell on his knees, vomiting bile and blood over his hands. Panic and the stench of death almost stopped his breathing. Then he heard a rumbling sound in the distance. He looked up and saw the headlights of two cars approaching. He ran to the side of the hill and reached a small esplanade from where he had a view of the sea at the foot of the mountain and the lighthouse of the port at the end of the breakwater.

High above him, Montjuïc Castle rose among black clouds that swept across the sky and masked the moon. The sound of cars was getting closer. Without thinking twice, Fermín threw himself down the slope, falling and rolling through tree trunks, stones and brambles that hit him and tore his skin off in shreds.

He no longer felt pain, or fear, or tiredness when he reached the road, from where he set off running towards the warehouses in the port. He ran without stopping or breathing, losing all sense of time, unaware of the injuries that covered his body.

# 24

DAWN WAS SPILLING OVER THE HORIZON WHEN HE REACHED the boundless labyrinth of shacks blanketing the beach of the Somorrostro. An early mist crept up from the sea, snaking between the rooftops. Fermín wandered through the alleyways and tunnels of the city of the poor until he collapsed between two piles of rubble. He was found by two ragged children, dragging wooden boxes, who stopped to stare at the skeletal figure that seemed to be bleeding from every pore.

Fermín smiled at them and made the victory sign with two fingers. The children looked at one another. One of them said something Fermín couldn't hear. He then abandoned himself to exhaustion and with his eyes half open was aware of being lifted from the ground by four people and then being laid down on a camp bed near a fire. He felt the warmth on his skin and slowly recovered the feeling in his feet, hands and arms. The pain came later, like a slow but unstoppable tide. Around him, hushed voices of women murmured blurred words. They removed the few rags that still clung to him. Cloths soaked in warm water and camphor caressed his naked, broken body with infinite gentleness.

He opened his eyes a fraction when he felt the hand of an old woman on his forehead, her weary, wise gaze fixed on him.

'Where have you come from?' asked that woman whom Fermín, in his delirium, mistook for his mother.

'From among the dead, Mother,' he whispered. 'I've come back from among the dead.'

# Part Three

*Reborn*

# 1

*Barcelona, 1940*

THE INCIDENT AT THE OLD VILARDELL FACTORY NEVER
made the papers. It didn't suit anyone to let the story come
out. What took place there would only be remembered by
those present. That very night, when Mauricio Valls returned
to the castle to discover that prisoner number 13 had escaped,
he informed Inspector Fumero of the political police division
about a tip-off from one of the prisoners. Before sunrise, Fumero and his men were already posted in their positions.

The inspector left two of his men guarding the perimeter and
concentrated the rest at the main entrance, from which, as Valls
had already explained, one could see the guards' lodge. The
body of Jaime Montoya, the prison governor's heroic chauffeur
who had volunteered to enter the premises alone and investi-
gate a prisoner's claim regarding the existence of subversive elements, was still lying there among the rubble. Shortly before
daybreak, Fumero ordered his men to enter the old factory.
They surrounded the lodge and when its occupants, two men
and a young woman, became aware of their presence, only a
minor incident occurred: the woman, who carried a firearm,
shot one of the policemen in the arm. It was just a scratch.
Apart from that slip, Fumero and his men had overpowered the
rebels within thirty seconds.

The inspector then ordered his men to round them all up

into the lodge and drag the body of the dead driver inside too. Fumero didn't ask for names or documents. He had the rebels disrobed and bound hand and foot with wire to some rusty metal chairs lying in a corner. Once the rebels had been tied down, Fumero told his men to leave him alone with them and post themselves by the door of the lodge and by the factory gates to await his instructions. On his own with the prisoners, he closed the door and sat down facing them.

'I haven't slept all night and I'm tired. I want to go home. You tell me where the money and the jewels you're hiding for Salgado are and nothing will happen here, all right?'

The prisoners stared at him with a mixture of bewilderment and terror.

'We don't know anything about jewels or about anyone called Salgado,' said the older man.

Fumero nodded somewhat wearily. His eyes moved unhurriedly over the three prisoners, as if he were able to read their thoughts and was bored by them. After a few moments' uncertainty, he chose the woman and drew his chair closer until he was barely half a metre away from her. The woman was trembling.

'Leave her alone, you son-of-a-bitch,' spat the other, younger man. 'If you touch her I swear I'll kill you.'

Fumero smiled wistfully.

'Your girlfriend is very pretty.'

NAVAS, THE OFFICER POSTED by the door of the lodge, could feel the cold sweat soaking his clothes. He ignored the shrieks coming from inside. When his colleagues threw him a furtive glance from the factory gates, he shook his head.

Nobody exchanged a single word. Fumero had been in the lodge for about half an hour when finally the door opened behind Navas. He stepped aside and avoided looking directly at the damp marks on the inspector's black clothes. Fumero walked slowly towards the gates while Navas, after a brief look inside the lodge, closed the door, trying not to vomit. At a signal from Fumero, two of the men came over carrying cans of petrol and doused the walls of the lodge and the surrounding area. They didn't stay behind to watch it go up in flames.

Fumero was waiting for them, sitting in the passenger seat, when they returned to the car. They drove off in silence as a column of smoke and flames rose above the ruins of the old factory, leaving a trail of ashes spreading in the wind. Fumero lowered the car window and stretched out his hand into the cold, humid air. He had blood on his fingers. Navas drove with his eyes fixed ahead, but all he could see was the pleading look of that young woman, still alive, before he closed the door. Aware that Fumero was watching him, he gripped the wheel tight to hide his trembling.

From the pavement, a group of ragged children watched the car drive by. One of them, making the shape of a gun with his fingers, pretended to be firing at them. Fumero smiled and replied with the same gesture. Seconds later, the car disappeared into the narrow streets surrounding the jungle of chimneys and warehouses, as if it had never been there.

# 2

FERMÍN SPENT SEVEN DAYS IN THE HUT, DELIRIOUS. NO damp cloth managed to calm his fever; no ointment was able to ease the pain which, they said, was consuming him. The old women of the place, who took it in turns to look after him and give him tonics in the hope of keeping him alive, said that the stranger had a demon inside him, the demon of remorse, and that his soul wanted to flee to the end of the tunnel and rest in a dark void.

ON THE SEVENTH DAY, the man whom everyone addressed as Armando and whose authority in the shanty town was second only to God's went over to the hut and sat down next to the sick man. He examined his wounds, lifted his eyelids with his fingers and read the secrets written in his dilated pupils. The old women who nursed him had gathered in a circle behind Armando, waiting in respectful silence. After a while Armando nodded to himself and left the hut. A couple of young men who were waiting by the door followed him as far as the line of surf where the waves broke on the water's edge, and listened carefully to his instructions. Armando watched them leave and stayed on, sitting on the wreck of a trawler that had been washed up by the storm and lay there, halfway between the beach and purgatory.

He lit a small cigar, enjoying it in the dawn breeze. While he smoked and considered what he should do, Armando pulled out a page from *La Vanguardia* he'd been keeping in his pocket for days. There, buried among advertisements for girdles and publicity for the latest shows in the Paralelo district, was a brief news story about the escape of a prisoner from Montjuïc Castle. The item had the stale taste of an official communiqué. The only licence the journalist had allowed himself was a closing remark declaring that never before had anyone succeeded in escaping from that unassailable fortress.

Armando looked up and gazed at the mountain of Montjuïc, rising to the south. The castle, with its crenellated towers outlined in the mist, presided over Barcelona. Armando smiled bitterly. He set fire to the article with the embers from his cigar and watched it turn to ashes in the breeze. As always, newspapers avoided the truth as if their life depended on it, and perhaps with good reason. Everything about that story smelled of half-truths and unspoken details. Among them the claim that nobody had ever been able to escape from Montjuïc Prison. Although in this case, he thought, the news item was probably right, because he, the man they called Armando, only existed in the invisible world of the poor and the untouchables. There are times and places where not to be anyone is more honourable than to be someone.

# 3

THE DAYS DRAGGED. ONCE A DAY, ARMANDO STOPPED by the hut to ask after the dying man. The man's fever made timid attempts at receding and the tangle of bruises, cuts and wounds covering his body seemed to be slowly healing beneath the ointments. He spent most of the day asleep or murmuring incomprehensible words between sleeplessness and slumber.

'Will he live?' Armando sometimes asked.

'He hasn't made up his mind yet,' replied the old woman whom that poor soul had mistaken for his mother.

Days crystallised into weeks, and it soon became evident that nobody was going to come and ask after the stranger: nobody asks for what they'd rather ignore. Normally the police and the Civil Guard didn't enter the Somorrostro. A law of silence made it plain that the city and the world ended at the gates of the shanty town, and both sides were keen to maintain the invisible frontier. Armando knew that many on the other side secretly or openly prayed for a storm that would obliterate the city of the poor, but until that day came, they all preferred to look elsewhere, with their backs to the sea and to the people who barely survived between the water's edge and the jungle of factories of Pueblo Nuevo. Even so, Armando had his doubts. The story he divined behind the outsider they had taken in could well lead to a breach of that law of silence.

\*

A FEW WEEKS LATER, a couple of young policemen turned up asking whether anyone had seen a man who looked like the stranger. Armando remained vigilant for days, but when nobody else came by to look for the man, he concluded that no one wanted to find him. Perhaps he had died and didn't even know it.

A MONTH AND A HALF after his arrival, the wounds on his body began to heal. When the man opened his eyes and asked where he was, they helped him sit up to sip a bowl of broth, but they didn't tell him anything.

'You must rest.'

'Am I alive?' he asked.

Nobody confirmed whether he was or wasn't. He spent much of the day asleep, or overcome by a weariness that never left him. Every time he closed his eyes and gave himself up to exhaustion, he travelled to the same place. In his dream, which recurred night after night, he scaled the walls of a bottomless mass grave strewn with corpses. When he reached the top and turned to look behind him, he saw the flood of ghostly bodies stirring like an eddy of eels. The dead bodies opened their eyes and climbed the walls, following him. They trailed him over the mountain and returned to the streets of Barcelona, looking for their old dwelling places, knocking on the doors of those they had once loved. Some went in search of their murderers and combed the city, thirsty for revenge, but most of them only wanted to return to their homes, to their beds, and embrace the children, wives and lovers they had left behind. Yet nobody would open the door to them. Nobody would hold their hands or wanted to kiss their lips. The dying man, bathed in sweat, woke up in the dark every night with the deafening cries of the dead in his soul.

\*

A STRANGER OFTEN VISITED him. He smelled of tobacco and eau de cologne, two substances that were hard to come by in those days. He sat on a chair by his side, looking at him with impenetrable eyes. His hair was black as tar and his features sharp. When he noticed that the patient was awake, he smiled at him.

'Are you God or the devil?' the dying man once asked him.

The stranger shrugged and thought about it.

'A bit of both,' he answered at last.

'In principle, I'm an atheist,' the patient informed him. 'Although in fact I have a lot of faith.'

'Like so many. Rest now, my friend. Heaven can wait. And hell is too small for you.'

# 4

BETWEEN VISITS FROM THE STRANGE GENTLEMAN WITH the jet-black hair, the convalescent would let himself be fed, washed and dressed in clean clothes that proved too big for him. When he was finally able to stand up and take a few steps on his own, they led him down to the edge of the sea where he bathed his feet and felt the Mediterranean light caressing his skin. One day he spent the entire morning watching a group of ragged children with dirty faces playing in the sand, and he thought perhaps he would like to live, at least a little longer. As time went by, memories and anger began rising to the surface, and with them both the wish to return to the city and the fear of doing so.

Legs, arms and other parts began to function more or less as he remembered. He recovered the rare pleasure of peeing into the wind with no burning sensations or shameful mishaps and told himself that a man who could urinate standing up and without help was a man in a fit state to face his responsibilities. That same night, in the early hours, he rose quietly and walked through the citadel's narrow alleyways as far as the boundary marked by the railway tracks. On the other side stood the forest of chimneys and the cemetery's skyline of angels and mausoleums. Further in the distance, in a tableau of lights that spread up the hillsides, lay Barcelona. He heard footsteps behind him and when he turned round he was met by the serene gaze of the man with the jet-black hair.

'You've been reborn,' he said.

'Well, let's hope this time around things turn out better. I've had a pretty bad time so far . . .'

The man with the jet-black hair smiled.

'Allow me to introduce myself. I'm Armando, the Gypsy.'

Fermín shook his hand.

'Fermín Romero de Torres, not a Gypsy, but still of relatively good coinage.'

'Fermín, my friend: I get the impression that you're considering going back to those people.'

'You can't make a leopard change its spots,' Fermín proclaimed. 'I've left a few things unfinished.'

Armando nodded.

'I understand. But not yet, dear friend,' he said. 'Have patience. Stay with us for a time.'

THE FEAR OF WHAT awaited him on his return and the generosity of those people kept him there until one Sunday morning, when he borrowed a newspaper some children had found in the bin of a refreshment stall on La Barceloneta beach. It was hard to tell how long the newspaper had been lying among the rubbish, but it was dated three months after the night of his escape. He combed the pages searching for a hint, a sign or some mention, but there was nothing. That afternoon, when he'd already made up his mind to return to Barcelona at nightfall, Armando approached Fermín and told him that one of his men had gone over to the *pensión* where he used to live.

'Fermín, you'd better not go round there to fetch your things.'

'How did you know my address?'

Armando smiled, avoiding the question.

'The police told them you'd died. A notice of your death appeared in the papers weeks ago. I didn't say anything because I realise that to read about one's own passing when one is convalescing doesn't help.'

'What did I die of?'

'Natural causes. You fell down a ravine when you were trying to flee from the law.'

'So, I'm dead?'

'As dead as the polka.'

Fermín weighed up the implications of his new status.

'And what do I do now? Where do I go? I can't stay here for ever, taking advantage of your kindness and putting you all in danger.'

Armando sat down next to him and lit one of the cigarettes he himself rolled. It smelled of eucalyptus.

'Fermín, you can do what you want, because you don't exist. I'd almost suggest that you stay here, because you're now one of us, people who have no name and are not documented anywhere. We're ghosts. Invisible. But I know you must return and resolve whatever you've left behind out there. Unfortunately, once you leave this place I can't offer you my protection.'

'You've already done enough for me.'

Armando patted Fermín's shoulder and handed him a folded sheet of paper he carried in his pocket.

'Leave the city for a while. Let a year go by and, when you return, begin here,' he said, moving away.

Fermín unfolded the sheet of paper and read:

FERNANDO BRIANS
LAWYER

*Calle de Caspe, 12*
*Attic Floor, room 1*
*Barcelona. Telephone 564375*

'How can I repay you for everything you've done for me?'

'One day, when you've sorted out your business, come by and ask for me. We'll go and see Carmen Amaya dance and you can tell me how you managed to escape from up there. I'm curious,' said Armando.

Fermín looked into those black eyes and nodded slowly.

'What cell were you in, Armando?'

'Cell thirteen.'

'Were those crosses on the wall yours?'

'Unlike you, Fermín, I *am* a believer, but I've lost my faith.'

That afternoon nobody said goodbye to Fermín or tried to stop him leaving. He set off, one more invisible person, towards the streets of a Barcelona that smelled of electricity. In the distance the towers of the Sagrada Familia seemed stranded in a blanket of red clouds that threatened a storm of biblical proportions, and he went on walking. His feet took him to the bus depot on Calle Trafalgar. There was some money in the pockets of the coat Armando had given him, and he bought a ticket for the longest trip available. He spent the night on the bus, driving through deserted roads under the rain. The following day he did the same, until, after three days on trains, on foot and on midnight buses, he reached a place where the streets had no name and the houses had no numbers and where nothing or no one could remember him.

HE HAD A HUNDRED jobs and no friends. He made money, which he spent. He read books that spoke of a world in which he no longer believed. He started to write a letter that he never knew how to end, battling with reminiscences and remorse. More than once he walked up to a bridge or a precipice and gazed calmly at the chasm below. At the last moment the memory of that promise would always return, and the look in the eyes of the Prisoner of Heaven. After a year, Fermín left the room he had rented above a café and, with no baggage other than a copy of *City of the Damned* he'd found in a flea market – possibly the only book of Martín's that hadn't been burned and which Fermín had read a dozen times – he walked two kilometres to the train station and bought the ticket that had been waiting for him all those months.

'One way to Barcelona, please.'

The ticket-office clerk issued the ticket and gave it to him with a disdainful look.

'Rather you than me,' he said. 'With all those goddam Catalan dogs.'

# 5

*Barcelona, 1941*

IT WAS STARTING TO GET DARK WHEN FERMÍN STEPPED OFF
the train in the Estación de Francia. A cloud of steam and soot
belched out by the engine stole along the platform, masking
the passengers' feet as they descended after the long journey.
Fermín joined the silent procession towards the exit, among
people in threadbare clothes, dragging suitcases held together
with straps, people aged well before their time carrying all their
belongings in a bundle, children with empty eyes and emptier
pockets.

A pair of Civil Guards patrolled the entrance. Fermín saw
how they followed the passengers with their eyes and stopped
some of them at random to ask for documentation. He kept
walking in a straight line towards one of them. When he was
only about a dozen metres away, he noticed that the Civil Guard
was watching him. In Martín's novel, the book that had kept
Fermín company all those months, one of the characters swore
that the best way of disarming the authorities was to speak to
them first before they addressed you. So before the officer was
able to point him out, Fermín walked straight up to the man
and said in a calm voice:

'Good evening, chief. Would you be so kind as to tell me
where I can find the Hotel Porvenir? I believe it's in Plaza Palacio,
but I hardly know the city.'

The Civil Guard examined him silently, somewhat disconcerted. His colleague had moved closer, covering his right side.

'You'll have to ask someone when you get out,' he said in a rather unfriendly tone.

Fermín nodded politely.

'That's what I'll do. I'm sorry to have bothered you.'

He was about to continue walking towards the entrance hall when the other officer took hold of his arm.

'Plaza Palacio is on the left as you go out. Opposite the Military Headquarters.'

'Most obliged. Have a good evening.'

The Civil Guard let go of him and Fermín walked away slowly, pacing himself, until he reached the entrance hall and then the street.

A SCARLET SKY CURVED over Barcelona. The city looked dark, entwined with sharp, black silhouettes. A half-empty tram hauled itself along, shedding a flickering light on the cobblestones. Fermín waited for it to go by before crossing to the other side. As he stepped over the shining rails he gazed into the distance, where the sides of Paseo Colón seemed to converge and the hill and castle of Montjuïc loomed above the city. He looked down again and set off up Calle Comercio towards the Borne market. The streets were deserted and a cold breeze blew through the alleyways. He had nowhere to go.

He remembered Martín telling him that years ago he'd lived in that area, in a large old house buried in the shadowy canyon of Calle Flassaders, next to the old Mauri chocolate factory. Fermín headed off in that direction but when he arrived he realised that the building in question had been shelled during the war. The authorities hadn't bothered to remove the rubble, so the neighbours had piled it up out of the way, presumably to make room for them to walk along the street, which was narrower than the corridors of some homes in the smarter parts of town.

Fermín looked around him. A dim glow of bulbs and candles

drifted down from the balconies. He moved further into the ruins, jumping over debris, broken gargoyles and beams twisted into improbable knots, looking for a space among the wreckage. At last he lay down under a stone that still had number 30 engraved on it, David Martín's former address. Covering himself with his coat and the old newspapers he wore under his clothes, he curled up into a ball, closed his eyes and tried to get to sleep.

Half an hour went by and the chill was starting to seep into his bones. A humid wind licked the ruins, searching for holes and cracks. Fermín opened his eyes and stood up. He was trying to find a more sheltered place when he noticed a figure watching him from the street. Fermín froze. The figure took a few steps towards him.

'Who goes there?' asked the figure.

The figure advanced a little further and the far-off light of a street lamp revealed the profile of a tall, well-built man dressed in black. Fermín noticed the collar: a priest. He raised both hands in a gesture of peace.

'I was leaving, Father. Please, don't call the police.'

The priest looked him up and down. His eyes seemed harsh, and he had the air of someone who had spent half his life lifting sacks in the port instead of chalices.

'Are you hungry?' he asked.

Fermín, who would have eaten any of those rough stones if someone had sprinkled a few drops of olive oil over them, shook his head.

'I've just had dinner at the Siete Puertas and I've stuffed myself silly with lobster stew,' he said.

The priest gave him a hint of a smile. He turned round and started walking.

'Come on,' he ordered.

# 6

FATHER VALERA LIVED ON THE TOP FLOOR OF A BUILDING
at the end of Paseo del Borne, overlooking the market rooftops.
Fermín quickly polished off three bowlfuls of thin soup and a
few bits of stale bread, together with a glass of watered-down
wine the priest placed in front of him, while he eyed him with
curiosity.

'Aren't you having dinner, Father?'

'I don't usually eat dinner. You enjoy it. I see your hunger
goes all the way back to 1936.'

While Fermín slurped his soup with its garnish of bread, he
let his eyes roam around the dining room. Next to him, a glass
cabinet displayed a collection of plates and glasses, various figures of saints and what looked like a modest set of silver cutlery.

'I've also read *Les Misérables*, so don't even think of it,' warned
the priest.

Fermín nodded, ashamed.

'What's your name?'

'Fermín Romero de Torres, at your service, *Monsignore*.'

'Are they after you, Fermín?'

'Depends how you look at it. It's a complicated matter.'

'It's none of my business if you don't want to tell me. But with
clothes like those you can't wander around out there. You'll end
up in jail before you even reach Vía Layetana. They're stopping
a lot of people who have been lying low for a while. You must
be very careful.'

'As soon as I gain access to some monetary funds that I've had in deep storage, I thought I'd drop by El Dique Flotante and come out looking my usual dapper self.'

'No doubt. But for the time being, humour me. Stand up a moment, will you?'

Fermín put down the spoon and stood up. The priest examined him carefully.

'Ramón was twice your size, but I think some of the clothes from when he was young would fit you.'

'Ramón?'

'My brother. He was killed down there, in the street, by the front door, in May 1938. They were looking for me, but he confronted them. He was a fine musician. He played in the municipal band. Principal trumpet.'

'I'm so sorry, Father.'

The priest shrugged his shoulders.

'More or less everyone has lost someone, whatever side they belong to.'

'I don't belong to any side,' Fermín replied. 'What's more, I think flags are nothing but painted rags that represent rancid emotions. Just seeing someone wrapped up in one of them, spewing out hymns, badges and speeches, gives me the runs. I've always thought that anyone who needs to join a herd so badly must be a bit of a sheep himself.'

'You must have a very hard time in this country.'

'You have no idea. But I always tell myself that having direct access to *serrano* ham makes up for everything. And anyhow, it's the same the world over.'

'That's true. Tell me, Fermín. How long since you last tasted real *serrano* ham?'

'March sixth 1934. Los Caracoles on Calle Escudellers. Another life.'

The priest smiled.

'You can stay here for tonight, Fermín, but tomorrow you'll have to find some other place. People talk. I can give you a bit of money for a *pensión*, but don't forget they all ask for identity cards and register their lodgers' names with the police.'

'That goes without saying, Father. Tomorrow, before sunrise, I'll vanish faster than goodwill. And I won't accept a single *céntimo* from you. I've already taken enough advantage of your . . .'

The priest put a hand up and shook his head.

'Let's see how some of Ramón's things look on you,' he said, rising from the table.

FATHER VALERA INSISTED ON providing Fermín with a pair of slightly worn shoes, a modest but clean wool suit, a couple of changes of underwear and a few personal toiletries which he put in a suitcase. A shining trumpet was displayed on one of the shelves, next to a number of photographs of two smiling, good-looking young men, in what looked like the annual *fiestas* of the Gracia district. One had to look closely to realise that one of them was Father Valera, who now looked thirty years older.

'I have no hot water. And they don't fill the tank till the morning, so either you wait, or you use the water jug.'

While Fermín washed himself as best he could, Father Valera prepared a pot of coffee with some sort of chicory mixed with other substances that looked vaguely suspicious. There was no sugar but that cup of dirty water was warm and the company was pleasant.

'Anyone would say we're in Colombia, enjoying the finest selection of coffee beans,' said Fermín.

'You're a peculiar fellow, Fermín. Can I ask you something personal?'

'Will the secrecy of the confessional cover it?'

'Let's say it will.'

'Fire away.'

'Have you killed anyone? During the war, I mean.'

'No,' replied Fermín.

'I have.'

Fermín went rigid, his cup half empty. The priest lowered his eyes.

'I've never told anyone.'

'It remains bound by the secrecy of the confessional,' Fermín assured him.

The priest rubbed his eyes and sighed. Fermín wondered how long this man had lived there alone, harbouring that secret and the memory of his dead brother.

'You must have had your reasons, Father.'

The priest shook his head.

'God has abandoned this country,' he said.

'Don't worry then. As soon as he sees what's brewing north of the Pyrenees, he'll come back with his tail between his legs.'

The priest kept quiet for a long time. They finished off the ersatz coffee and Fermín, to cheer up the poor priest, who seemed to look gloomier with every passing minute, poured himself a second cup.

'Do you really like it?'

Fermín nodded.

'Would you like me to hear your confession?' the priest suddenly asked him. 'I'm not joking now.'

'Don't be offended, Father, but I don't really believe in that sort of thing . . .'

'But perhaps God believes in you.'

'I doubt it.'

'You don't have to believe in God to confess. It's something between you and your conscience. What is there to lose?'

DURING THE NEXT COUPLE of hours Fermín told Father Valera everything he'd kept to himself since he fled from the castle over a year ago. The priest listened to him attentively, nodding every now and then. At last, when Fermín felt he had said it all and the stone slab that had been suffocating him for months without him realising had been lifted, Father Valera pulled out a flask of liqueur from a drawer and, without asking, poured what was left of it into a glass and handed it to Fermín.

'I was hoping for absolution, Father, not a reward of a swig of cognac.'

'It comes to the same thing. Besides, I'm no longer in a position to forgive or to judge anyone, Fermín. But I think you needed to get all that off your chest. What are you going to do now?'

Fermín shrugged.

'If I've returned, and I'm risking my neck by doing so, it's because of the promise I made to Martín. I must find the lawyer and then Señora Isabella and that boy, Daniel, and protect them.'

'How?'

'I don't know. I'll think of something. Any suggestions?'

'But you don't even know them. They're just strangers that a man you met in prison told you about . . .'

'I know. When you put it that way it sounds crazy, doesn't it?'

The priest was looking at him as if he could see through his words.

'Might it not be that you've seen so much misery and so much evil among men that you want to do something good, even if it's madness?'

'And why not?'

Valera smiled. The priest took the glass with the untouched drink from Fermín's hands and knocked it back.

'I knew God believed in you.'

# 7

THE FOLLOWING DAY, FERMÍN TIPTOED OUT OF THE FLAT so as not to disturb Father Valera, who had fallen asleep on the sofa with a book of poems by Machado in his hand and was snoring like a fighting bull. Before leaving he kissed him on the forehead and left the silverware – which the priest had wrapped in a napkin and slipped into his suitcase – on the dining-room table. Then he set off down the stairs with clean clothes and a clean conscience, determined to stay alive, at least for a few more days.

That day the sun was strong and a fresh breeze swept over the city. The sky looked bright and steely, casting long shadows as people walked by. Fermín spent the morning strolling through streets he remembered, stopping in front of shop windows and sitting on benches to watch pretty girls go by – and they all looked pretty to him. Around noon he walked over to a café at the entrance to Calle Escudellers, near the Los Caracoles restaurant of such happy memories. The café itself was notorious among those with fearless and undemanding palates for offering the cheapest sandwiches in town. The trick, said experts, was not to ask about the ingredients.

Sporting his smart new clothes and an armour of newspapers packed beneath them to lend him some bulk, a hint of muscles and low-cost warmth, Fermín sat at the bar, checked the list of delicacies within reach of modest pockets and began negotiating with the waiter.

'I have a question, young man. In today's special, peasant's bread with *mortadella* and cold cuts from Cornellá, does the bread come with fresh tomato?'

'Just arrived from our market garden in El Prat, behind the sulphuric acid plants.'

'A premium bouquet. And tell me, my good man, does this establishment extend credit to suitable individuals?'

The waiter lost his cheerful expression and withdrew behind the bar, hanging his rag over his shoulder with a hostile gesture.

'Not even to God almighty.'

'I see. And would you consider making an exception in the case of a decorated disabled war hero?'

'Scram, or we'll call the police.'

In light of the stringent policies being enforced, Fermín beat a hasty retreat, searching for a quiet corner where he could reconsider his plans. He'd just settled on the steps of the building next door when a young girl, who couldn't have been a day older than seventeen but already possessed the curves of a budding starlet, walked past him and fell flat on her face.

Fermín stood up to help her and had only just taken hold of her arm when he heard a voice that made the words from the hostile waiter who had sent him on his way sound like heavenly music.

'Look here, you goddam slut, don't give me this crap or I'll slice your face up and dump you in the street, which is already filled with unemployed cut-up whores.'

The author of such a notable speech turned out to be a sallow-skinned pimp with a questionable eye for fashion. Despite the fact that the man was twice Fermín's size, and was holding what appeared to be a sharp object, or at least a fairly pointy one, Fermín, who was beginning to be fed up to his back teeth with bullies, stood between the girl and her aggressor.

'And who the fuck are you, you loser? Go on, beat it before I cut your face up.'

Fermín felt the girl grip his arms in fear. She smelled of a particular mixture of sweet cinnamon and refried calamari. A quick glance was enough for Fermín to realise that the situation was unlikely to be resolved through diplomacy, so he decided to move into action. After a lightning assessment of his opponent he concluded that the grand total of his body mass was mainly flab, and that when it came to actual muscle, or grey matter, he was not packing a lethal punch.

'Don't talk to me in that way, even less to the young lady.'

The pimp looked at him in astonishment, as if he hadn't taken in the words. A second later, the individual, who was expecting anything from this wimp except a fight, got the surprise of his life when a suitcase slammed into his soft parts and sent him to the ground clutching his privates. This was followed by four or five knocks in strategic places inflicted with the leather corners of the case that left him, at least for a short while, notably lacking in any mood to fight back.

A group of passers-by who had witnessed the incident began to applaud and, when Fermín turned to check whether the girl was all right, he was welcomed by her adoring look, laced with undying gratitude and tenderness.

'Fermín Romero de Torres, at your service, miss.'

The girl stood on her toes and kissed his cheek.

'I'm Rociíto.'

The specimen at his feet was gasping and struggling to get up. Before the balance of the contest stopped favouring him, Fermín decided to distance himself from the scene of the confrontation.

'We'd better make haste and shove off,' he announced. 'Now we've lost the initiative, the battle will go against us . . .'

Rociíto took his arm and guided him through the twisted web of narrow streets that led to Plaza Real. Once they were in the sunlight and in the open, Fermín stopped for a second to recover his breath. Rociíto noticed that Fermín was becoming increasingly pale. He looked unwell. She guessed that the emotions induced by the skirmish, or perhaps plain old hunger, had caused a drop in her brave champion's blood pressure. She walked him to the terrace of the Hostal Dos Mundos, where Fermín collapsed into one of the chairs.

Rociíto, who might have been seventeen but had a clinical eye that many an experienced doctor would have coveted, proceeded to ask for a selection of tapas with which to revive him. When Fermín saw the feast arriving, he was alarmed.

'Rociíto, I don't have a *céntimo* on me . . .'

'It's on me,' she cut in proudly. 'Gotta take care of my man and keep 'im well nourished.'

Rociíto kept stuffing him with small *chorizos*, bread and spicy potatoes, all washed down with a monumental pitcher of beer. Fermín slowly revived and recovered his lively colouring to the girl's visible satisfaction.

'For dessert, if you like, I can serve you up a house special that will knock you sideways,' offered the young woman, licking her lips.

'Listen, kid, shouldn't you be at school right now, with the nuns?'

Rociíto laughed at his joke.

'You rogue, you've sure got a mouth!'

As the feast went on, Fermín realised that, if it depended on the girl, he had before him a promising career as a procurer. But matters of greater importance claimed his attention.

'How old are you, Rociíto?'

'Eighteen and a half, Señorito Fermín.'

'You look older.'

'It's me tits. Got them when I was thirteen. A joy to look at, aren't they, even though I shouldn't say so.'

Fermín, who hadn't laid eyes on such a conspiracy of curves since his longed-for days in Havana, tried to recover his common sense.

'Rociíto,' he began, 'I can't take care of you . . .'

'I know, Señorito Fermín. Don't think me stupid. I know you're not the sort of man to live off a woman. I might be young, but I know how to see 'em coming . . .'

169

'You must tell me where I can send you a proper refund for this handsome banquet. Right now you catch me at a rather delicate financial moment . . .'

Rociíto shook her head.

'I've a room here, in the *hostal*. I share it with Lali, but she's out all day because she works the merchant ships . . . Why don't you come up, señorito, and I'll give you a massage?'

'Rociíto . . .'

'It's on the house . . .'

Fermín gazed at her with a touch of melancholy.

'You have sad eyes, Señorito Fermín. Let little Rociíto cheer you up, even if it's just for a while. What harm can there be in that?'

Fermín looked down in embarrassment.

'How long is it since you've been with a real woman?'

'I can't even remember.'

Rociíto offered him a hand and, pulling him behind her, took him up to a tiny room with just enough space for a ramshackle bed and a sink. A small balcony looked out on the square. The girl drew the curtain and in a flash removed the floral-print dress she was wearing next to her bare skin. Fermín gazed at that miracle of nature and let himself be embraced by a heart almost as old as his own.

'We don't need to do anything, if you don't want, all right?'

Rociíto laid him down on the bed and stretched out next to him. She held him tight and stroked his head.

'Shhh, shhh,' she whispered.

With his face buried in that eighteen-year-old bosom, Fermín burst into tears.

WHEN EVENING FELL AND Rociíto had to begin her shift, Fermín pulled out the piece of paper Armando had given him a year ago, with the address of Brians, the lawyer, and decided to pay him a visit. Rociíto insisted on lending him some loose change, enough to take a tram or two and have a coffee. She made him swear, time and time again, that he would come back to see her, even if it was just to take her to the cinema or to mass: she had a particular devotion for Our Lady of Carmen and she loved ceremonies, especially if there was singing involved. Rociíto went down the stairs with him, and when they said goodbye she gave him a kiss on the lips and a nip on the bum.

'Gorgeous,' she said as she watched him leave under the arches of the square.

As Fermín crossed Plaza de Cataluña, a ribbon of cloud was beginning to swirl in the sky. The flocks of pigeons that usually flew over the square had taken shelter in the trees and waited impatiently. People could smell the electricity in the air as they hurried towards the entrances of the metro. An unpleasant wind had started to blow, dragging a tide of dry leaves along the ground. Fermín quickened his pace and by the time he reached Calle Caspe, the rain was bucketing down.

# 8

Brians was a young man with the air of a Bohemian student who looked as if he survived on salty crackers and coffee, which is what his office smelled of. That, and dusty paper. The lawyer's workplace was a small, cramped room at the end of a dark corridor, perched on the attic floor of the same building that housed the great Tivoli Theatre. Fermín found him still there at eight-thirty in the evening. He opened the door in his shirtsleeves and acknowledged his visitor with a nod and a sigh.

'Fermín, I suppose. Martín spoke to me about you. I was beginning to wonder when you'd be coming by.'

'I've been away for a while.'

'Of course. Come in, please.'

Fermín followed him into the cubicle.

'What a night, eh?' said the lawyer. He sounded nervous.

'It's only water.'

Fermín looked around him and noticed only one chair. Brians offered it to him and sat on a pile of volumes on criminal and civil law.

'I'm still waiting for the furniture.'

Fermín could see there wasn't even room for a pencil sharpener in that place, but thought it best not to open his mouth. On the table was a plate with a grilled-meat sandwich and a beer. A paper napkin informed him that the sumptuous dinner came from the café on the ground floor.

'I was about to eat. I'll be happy to share it with you.'

'No, no, go ahead, you young ones need to grow and besides, I've had my dinner.'

'Can't I offer you anything? Coffee?'

'If you have a Sugus . . .'

Brians rummaged in a drawer that held just about everything except Sugus sweets.

'A liquorice lozenge?'

'I'm fine, thanks.'

'Then, if you don't mind . . .'

Brians gave the sandwich a hearty bite, munching with gusto. Fermín wondered which of them looked more famished. Next to the desk, the door to an adjoining room stood ajar. Fermín caught a glimpse of an unmade folding bed, a coat stand with crumpled shirts and a pile of books.

'Do you live here?' asked Fermín.

Clearly the lawyer Isabella had been able to afford for Martín was not a high-flyer. Brians followed Fermín's eyes and gave him a modest smile.

'This is, temporarily, my office and my home, yes,' Brians replied, leaning over to close his bedroom door.

'You must think I don't look much like a lawyer. You're not the only one. So does my father.'

'Pay no attention. My father was always fond of telling us we were nothing but a useless lot of imbeciles who would end up lifting rocks at a quarry, if we were lucky. And look at me now, as cool as they come. Succeeding in life when your family believes in you and supports you, what's the merit in that?'

Brians nodded reluctantly.

'If you look at it that way . . . Truth be told, I only established myself on my own a short time ago. Before that I used to work for a well-known lawyer's practice just round the corner, on Paseo de Gracia. But we fell out over a number of things. It hasn't been easy since then.'

'Don't tell me. Valls?'

Brians nodded, finishing off his beer in three gulps.

'From the moment I accepted Señor Martín's case, Valls didn't stop until he'd got almost all my clients to leave me and I was laid off. The few who followed me are the ones who don't have a *céntimo* and can't pay my fees.'

'And Señora Isabella?'

A shadow fell over the lawyer's face. He left the beer glass on the desk and looked hesitantly at Fermín.

'Don't you know?'

'Know what?'

'Isabella Sempere is dead.'

# 9

THE STORM POUNDED OVER THE CITY. FERMÍN HELD A CUP of coffee in his hands while Brians, standing by the open window, watched the rain lash the roofs of the Ensanche district and recounted Isabella's last days.

'She fell ill suddenly, without any explanation. If you'd known her . . . Isabella was young, full of life. She had an iron constitution and had survived the hardships of war. It all happened overnight. The night you managed to escape from the castle, Isabella came home late. When her husband found her, she was kneeling down in the bathroom, sweating and with palpitations. She said she wasn't feeling well. They called the doctor, but before he arrived she started having convulsions and throwing up blood. The doctor said it was food poisoning and told her to follow a strict diet for a few days, but by the morning she was worse. Señor Sempere wrapped her up in blankets and a neighbour who was a taxi driver drove them to the Hospital del Mar. She'd broken out in dark blotches, like ulcers, and her hair was coming out in handfuls. In the hospital they waited a couple of hours but in the end the doctors refused to see her because someone in the waiting room, a patient who hadn't been seen yet, said he knew Sempere and accused him of being a communist or some such nonsense. I suppose he did it to jump the queue. A nurse gave them a syrup which, she said, would help Isabella clean out her stomach, but Isabella couldn't swallow anything. Sempere didn't know what to do. He took her home and started to call one doctor after another. Nobody knew what was wrong with her. A medical assistant who was a regular customer at the bookshop knew someone who worked at the Hospital Clínico. Sempere took Isabella there.'

'IN THE CLÍNICO SEMPERE was told it might be cholera and he must take her home, because there was an outbreak and the hospital was overflowing. A number of people in the area had already died. Every day Isabella was worse. She was delirious. Her husband did everything he could. He moved heaven and earth, but after a few days she was so weak he couldn't even take her to the hospital. She died a week after falling ill, in the flat on Calle Santa Ana, above the bookshop . . .'

A long silence reigned between them, punctuated only by the splattering rain and the echo of thunder moving away as the wind abated.

'It wasn't until a month later that I heard she'd been seen one night in the Café de la Ópera, opposite the Liceo. She was sitting with Mauricio Valls. Ignoring my advice, Isabella had threatened him with exposing his plan to use Martín to rewrite some crap of his with which he expected to become famous and be showered with medals. I went there to find out more. The waiter remembered that Valls had arrived before her in a car and that he'd asked for two camomile teas and honey.'

Fermín weighed up the young lawyer's words.

'And you believe Valls poisoned her?'

'I can't prove it, but the more I think about it, the more obvious it seems to me. It had to be Valls.'

Fermín stared at the floor.

'Does Señor Martín know?'

Brians shook his head.

'No. After your escape, Valls ordered Martín to be held in a solitary confinement cell in one of the towers.'

'What about Doctor Sanahuja? Didn't they put them together?'

Brians gave a dejected sigh.

'Sanahuja was court-martialled for treason shortly after your escape. He was shot a week later.'

Another long silence flooded the room. Fermín stood up and began to walk around in circles, looking agitated.

'And why has nobody looked for me? After all, I'm the cause of all this . . .'

'You don't exist. To avoid loss of face before his superiors and the end of a promising career working for the regime, Valls summoned the patrol he'd sent out to search for you and made them swear that they'd gunned you down while you were trying to escape along the slopes of Montjuïc, and they'd flung your body into the common grave.'

Fermín tasted the anger on his lips.

'Well, look here, I've half a mind to go up to the offices of the Military Government right now and invite them to kiss my resurrected arse. I'd like to see how Valls explains my return from the grave.'

'Don't talk nonsense. You wouldn't solve anything by doing that. You'd simply be taken up to Carretera de las Aguas and shot in the back of the head. That worm isn't worth it.'

Fermín nodded in assent, but the feelings of shame and guilt were gnawing at his insides.

'What about Martín? What will happen to him?'

Brians shrugged.

'What I know is confidential. It can't go beyond these four walls. There's a jailer in the castle, a guy called Bebo, who owes me more than a couple of favours. They were going to kill a brother of his but I managed to get his sentence commuted to ten years in a Valencia prison. Bebo is a decent guy and tells me everything he sees and hears in the castle. Valls won't allow me to see Martín, but through Bebo I've found out that he's alive and that Valls keeps him locked up in the tower and watched round the clock. He's given him pen and paper. Bebo says Martín is writing.'

'Writing what?'

'Goodness knows. Valls believes, or so Bebo tells me, that Martín is working on the book he asked him to write, based on his notes. But Martín, who, as you and I know, is not quite in his right mind, seems to be writing something else. Sometimes he reads out loud what he's written, or he stands up and starts walking round the cell, reciting bits of dialogue or whole sentences. Bebo does the night shift by his cell, and whenever he can he slips him cigarettes and sugar lumps, which is all he eats. Did Martín ever talk to you about something called *The Angel's Game*?'

Fermín shook his head.

'Is that the title of the book he's working on?'

'That's what Bebo believes. From what he's been able to piece together from what Martín tells him and what he overhears him saying to himself, it sounds like some sort of autobiography or confession . . . If you want my opinion, Martín has realised he's losing his mind, so he's trying to write down what he remembers before it's too late. It's as if he were writing himself a letter to find out who he is . . .'

'And what will happen when Valls discovers that he hasn't followed his orders?'

Brians gave him a mournful look.

# 10

Round about midnight it stopped raining. From the lawyer's attic Barcelona looked lugubrious beneath a sky of low clouds that swept over the rooftops.

'Do you have anywhere to go, Fermín?' asked Brians.

'I have a tempting offer to start a career as a gigolo and body-guard and move in with a wench who is a bit flighty but has a good heart, and spectacular bodywork. But I don't see myself playing the role of a kept man even at the feet of the Venus of Jerez.'

'I don't like the thought of you living on the streets, Fermín. It's dangerous. You can stay here as long as you like.'

Fermín looked around him.

'I know this isn't the Hotel Colón, but I have a camp bed in the back there, I don't snore and, quite frankly, I could use the company.'

'Don't you have a girlfriend?'

'My fiancée was the daughter of the founding partner in the firm from which Valls and company managed to get me fired.'

'You're paying dearly for this Martín business. A vow of poverty and chastity.'

Brians smiled.

'Give me a lost cause and you'll make me happy.'

'That makes two of us. All right then, I'll take you up on your generous offer. But only if you allow me to help and contribute. I can clean, tidy up, type, cook and offer you advice as well as investigative and security services. And if, in a moment of weakness, you find yourself in a tight spot and need to unwind a bit, I'm sure that through my friend Rociíto I can provide you with professional services that will leave you as good as new: when you're young and tender you have to watch out for a build-up of seminal fluids going to your head, or you could make matters worse.'

Brians shook his hand.

'That's a deal. I hereby hire you as assistant articled clerk for Brians & Brians, defenders of the insolvent.'

'As my name is Fermín, I swear that before the week is over I will have found you a customer of the sort who pays up front and in cash.'

THAT IS HOW Fermín Romero de Torres moved temporarily into Brians's minuscule office, where he began by rearranging, cleaning and updating all his files, folders and open cases. Within a couple of days the practice looked as if it had trebled in size thanks to Fermín, who had left the place as clean as a pin. Fermín spent most of the day closeted in the office, but he devoted a couple of hours to sundry expeditions from which he returned with handfuls of flowers he'd nicked from the lobby of the Tivoli Theatre, a bit of coffee – which he obtained by buttering up a waitress from the bar on the ground floor – and fine foods from the Quílez grocers, which he charged to the account of the legal firm that had fired Brians, having first introduced himself as their new errand boy.

'Fermín, this ham is fabulous, where did you get it?'

'Try the Manchego, it's out of this world.'

He spent the mornings going through all Brians's cases and copying his notes out neatly. In the afternoons he would pick up the telephone and, working his way through the directory, plunge into a search for solvent clients. When he sniffed a possibility, he would then round off the phone call with a visit to the prospect's address. Out of a total of fifty cold calls to businesses, professionals and private citizens in the district, ten turned into visits and three into new clients for Brians.

The first of these was a widow who had entered into a dispute with an insurance company because they'd refused to make the payment due on the death of her husband, arguing that the cardiac arrest he had suffered after a huge dish of red-hot spicy prawns at the Siete Puertas restaurant was in fact a case of suicide, not covered by the policy. The second was a taxidermist to whom a retired bullfighter had taken the five-hundred-kilo Miura bull with which he'd ended his career in the rings. Once the bull was stuffed, the bullfighter had refused to pay for it and take it home. He said that the glass eyes the taxidermist had given it made it look as if it were possessed by malevolent forces from the other side, and he'd rushed out of the shop claiming Gypsy sorcery had brought on an irritable colon emergency. And the third client was a tailor from Ronda San Pedro who had had five perfectly healthy molars extracted by a dentist with no qualifications but plenty of gall. They were small cases, but all the clients had paid a deposit and signed a contract.

'Fermín, I'm going to put you on the payroll.'

'I won't hear of it. Consider my services strictly pro bono.'

Fermín refused to accept any emolument for his good offices, except occasional small loans with which on Sunday afternoons he took Rociíto to the cinema, to dance at La Paloma or to the funfair at the top of the Tibidabo mountain. Romance was in the air, and Fermín was slowly reclaiming his old self. Once, in the funfair's hall of mirrors, Rociíto gave him a love bite on the neck that smarted for a whole week. On another occasion, taking advantage of the fact that they were the only passengers on the full-sized aeroplane replica that gyrated, suspended from a crane, between Barcelona and the blue heavens, Fermín recovered full command of his manhood after a long absence from the scenarios of rushed love.

\*

181

Not long after that, one lazy afternoon when Fermín was savouring Rociíto's splendid attributes on the top of the big wheel, it occurred to him that those times, against all expectations, were turning out to be good times. Then he felt afraid, because he knew they couldn't last long and those stolen drops of happiness and peace would evaporate sooner than the youthful bloom of Rociíto's flesh and eyes.

# 11

THAT SAME NIGHT, FERMÍN SAT IN THE OFFICE WAITING for Brians to return from his rounds of courts, offices, practices, prisons and the thousand and one audiences with the high and mighty he had to endure to obtain information. It was almost eleven when he heard the young lawyer's footsteps approaching down the corridor. He opened the door for him and Brians came in dragging his feet and his soul, looking more crestfallen than ever. He collapsed in a corner and put his hands over his head.

'What's happened, Brians?'

'I've just come from the castle.'

'Bad news?'

'Worse. Valls refused to see me. They made me wait for four hours and then they told me to leave. They've withdrawn my visitor's licence and my permit for entering the premises.'

'Did they let you see Martín?'

Brians shook his head.

'He wasn't there.'

Fermín looked at him without understanding. Brians didn't speak for a few moments, searching for the right words.

'When I was leaving Bebo followed me and told me what he knew. It happened two weeks ago. Martín had been writing like a man possessed, day and night, barely sleeping. Valls suspected something was up and instructed Bebo to confiscate the pages Martín had written so far. Three guards were needed to hold him down and pull the manuscript from him. He'd written over five hundred pages in under two months.

'Bebo handed them to Valls, and when Valls started to read, it seems he flew into a rage.'

'It wasn't what he was expecting, I take it . . .'

Brians shook his head.

'Valls spent all night reading and the following morning went up to the tower, escorted by four of his men. He had Martín shackled hand and foot and then stepped into the cell. Bebo was listening through a chink in the cell door and heard part of the conversation. Valls was furious. He told him he was very disappointed in him. He'd handed him the seeds of a masterpiece and Martín, ungratefully, instead of following his instructions, had embarked on that rubbish that made no sense whatsoever. "This isn't the book I was expecting from you, Martín," Valls kept repeating.'

'And what did Martín say?'

'Nothing. He ignored him. As if he weren't there. Which made Valls all the more furious. Bebo heard Valls slap and punch Martín, but Martín didn't utter a sound. When Valls grew tired of hitting and insulting him and getting no response at all, Bebo says that Valls pulled out a letter he had in his pocket, a letter Señor Sempere had written to Martín months before which had been confiscated. In this letter there was a note Isabella had written to Martín on her deathbed . . .'

'Son-of-a-bitch . . .'

'Valls left him there, locked up with that letter, because he knew that nothing would hurt him more than to know Isabella had died . . . Bebo says that when Valls left and Martín read the letter he started to scream, and he screamed all night, banging on the walls and the iron door with his hands and with his head . . .'

Brians looked up and Fermín knelt down in front of him and put a hand on his shoulder.

'Are you all right, Brians?'

'I'm his lawyer,' he said in a shaky voice. 'I'm supposed to protect him and get him out of there . . .'

'You've done everything you could, Brians. And Martín knows that.'

Brians dissented, murmuring to himself.

'And that's not the end of it,' he said. 'Bebo told me that since Valls didn't allow him any more paper, Martín started writing on the back of the pages the governor had thrown in his face. And as he had no ink, he would cut his hands and arms and use his own blood . . .

'Bebo tried to talk to him, to calm him . . . He no longer accepted the cigarettes or the sugar lumps he liked so much . . . He didn't even acknowledge Bebo's presence. Bebo thinks that when he heard about Isabella's death he lost his sanity altogether and moved into the hell he'd created in his mind . . . At night he shouted so loud everyone could hear him. Rumours began to circulate among visitors, prisoners and the prison staff. Valls was getting nervous. Finally, he ordered two of his gunmen to take Martín away one night . . .'

Fermín gulped.

'Where to?'

'Bebo isn't sure. From what he was able to hear, he thinks he was taken to an old house next to Güell Park . . . it seems that during the war a number of men were killed in that place and then buried in the garden . . . When the gunmen returned they told Valls that everything had been taken care of, but Bebo told me that on that very night he heard them talking among themselves and they seemed rattled. Something had happened in the house. It seems there was someone else there.'

'Someone?'

Brians shrugged his shoulders.

'So then David Martín is alive?'

'I don't know, Fermín. Nobody knows.'

# 12

*Barcelona, 1957*

FERMÍN WAS SPEAKING IN A FEEBLE VOICE AND LOOKED disconsolate. Conjuring up those memories seemed to have left him lifeless. I poured him one last glass of wine and watched him dry his tears with his hands. I handed him a napkin but he ignored it. The rest of the Can Lluís clientele had gone home some time ago, and I imagined that it must be past midnight, but nobody had wanted to disturb us and they'd left us alone in the dining room. Fermín looked at me exhausted, as if having revealed the secrets he'd kept for so many years had robbed him of his will to live.

'Fermín . . .'

'I know what you're going to ask me. The answer is no.'

'Fermín, is David Martín my father?'

Fermín looked at me severely.

'Your father is Señor Sempere, Daniel. You must never be in any doubt about that. Never.'

I nodded. Fermín remained anchored in his chair, looking absent, staring into space.

'What about you, Fermín? What happened to you?'

Fermín took a while to reply, as if that part of the story were completely unimportant.

'I went back to the streets. I couldn't stay there, with Brians. Nor could I stay with Rociíto. Nor with anyone else . . .'

Fermín broke off his account, and I took up the thread of the narrative for him.

'You returned to the streets, a beggar without a name, with nobody and nothing in the world, a man whom everyone thought was mad and who would have wished to die, had it not been for a promise he had made . . .'

'I'd promised Martín I'd take care of Isabella and her son . . . of you. But I was a coward, Daniel. I was in hiding for so long, I was so frightened of returning, that when I did your mother was no longer there . . .'

'And is that why I found you that night in Plaza Real? It wasn't a coincidence? How long had you been following me?'

'Months. Years.'

I imagined him following me as a child, when I went to school, when I played in Ciudadela Park, when I stopped with my father in front of that shop window to gaze at the pen I believed blindly had belonged to Victor Hugo, when I sat in Plaza Real to read to Clara and caress her with my eyes, thinking nobody could see me. A beggar, a shadow, a figure nobody noticed and all eyes avoided. Fermín, my protector and friend.

'And why didn't you tell me the truth years later?'

'At first I wanted to, but then I realised that it would do you more harm than good. Nothing could change the past. I decided to hide the truth because I thought it best for you to be more like your father and less like me.'

We fell into a long silence during which we eyed each other furtively, not knowing what to say.

'Where's Valls?' I asked at last.

'Don't even think of it,' Fermín cut in.

'Where is he now?' I asked again. 'If you don't tell me I'll find out myself.'

'And what will you do? Will you turn up at his house, ready to kill him?'

'Why not?'

Fermín laughed bitterly.

'Because you have a wife and a son, because you have a life ahead of you and people who love you and whom you love. Because you have it all, Daniel.'

'All except my mother.'

'Revenge won't give you back your mother, Daniel.'

'That's easy to say. Nobody murdered yours . . .'

Fermín was about to say something, but he bit his tongue.

'Why do you think your father never told you about the war, Daniel? Do you think he doesn't imagine what happened?'

'If that's so, why did he keep quiet? Why didn't he do anything?'

'Because of you, Daniel. Because of you. Your father, like so many people who had to live through those years, swallowed everything and kept quiet. They just had to lump it. You pass them in the street every day and don't even see them. They've rotted away all these years with that pain inside them so that you, and others like you, could live. Don't you dare judge your father. You have no right to.'

I felt as if my best friend had slapped me.

'Don't be angry with me, Fermín . . .'

Fermín shook his head.

'I'm not angry.'

'I'm just trying to take all this in, Fermín. Let me ask you a question. Just one.'

'About Valls? No.'

'Just one question, Fermín. I swear. If you don't want to, you don't have to reply.'

Fermín nodded reluctantly.

'Is this Mauricio Valls the same Valls I think he is?' I asked.

Fermín nodded.

'The very one. The one who was Minister of Culture until about four or five years ago. The one who appeared in the papers every other day. The great Mauricio Valls. Author, editor, thinker and messiah of the national intellectual class. *That* Valls,' said Fermín.

I realised I'd seen that man's photograph in the papers dozens of times, that I'd heard his name being mentioned and had seen it printed on the spines of some of the books we had in the shop. Until that night, the name Mauricio Valls was just one more in that dim parade of dignitaries one barely notices but which always seems to be there. Until that night, if anyone had asked me who Mauricio Valls was, I would have said he was only vaguely familiar to me, a public figure of those blighted years to whom I'd never paid much attention. Until that night it would never have crossed my mind to imagine that one day that name, that face, would thereafter be the name and the face of the man who murdered my mother.

'But . . .' I protested.

'No buts. You said one more question and I've answered it already.'

'Fermín, you can't leave me like this . . .'

'Listen carefully, Daniel.'

Fermín looked me in the eye and gripped my wrist.

'I swear that, when the moment is right, I myself will help you find that son-of-a-bitch, if it's the last thing I do in my life. Then we'll settle our scores with him. But not now. Not like this.'

I looked at him doubtfully.

'Promise me you won't do anything stupid, Daniel. Promise you'll wait for the right moment.'

I looked down.

'You can't ask me that, Fermín.'

'I can and I must.'

At last I nodded, and Fermín let go of my arm.

# 13

WHEN I FINALLY GOT HOME IT WAS ALMOST TWO IN THE morning. I was about to walk through the front door of the building when I noticed there was light inside the shop, a faint glow coming from behind the back-room curtain. I stepped in through the side door in the hallway and found my father sitting at his desk, enjoying the first cigarette I'd seen him smoke in years. In front of him, on the table, lay an open envelope and the pages of a letter. I pulled a chair over and sat down facing him. My father stared at me, sunk in an impenetrable silence.

'I didn't know you smoked,' I ventured.

He simply shrugged.

'Good news?' I asked, pointing at the letter.

My father handed it to me.

'It's from your Aunt Laura, the one who lives in Naples.'

'I have an aunt in Naples?'

'She's your mother's sister, the one who went to live in Italy with her mother's side of the family the year you were born.'

I nodded absently. I didn't remember her. Her name belonged among the strangers who came to my mother's funeral all those years ago, and whom I'd never seen again.

'She says she has a daughter who is coming to study in Barcelona and wants to know whether she can stay here for a while. Her name is Sofía.'

'It's the first time I've ever heard her mentioned,' I said.

'That makes two of us.'

The thought of my father sharing his flat with a teenager who was a perfect stranger seemed unlikely.

'What are you going to say to her?'

'I don't know. I'll have to say something.'

We continued sitting there quietly for almost a minute, gazing at one another without daring to speak about the matter that really filled our minds – not the visit of an unknown cousin.

'I suppose you were out with Fermín,' my father said at last, putting out his cigarette.

I nodded.

'We had dinner at Can Lluís. Fermín finished everything, down to the napkins. I saw Professor Alburquerque there when we arrived and told him to drop by the bookshop.'

The sound of my own voice reciting banalities had an accusatory echo. My father observed me tensely.

'Did Fermín tell you what's been the matter with him lately?'

'I think it's nerves, because of the wedding and all that stuff that doesn't agree with him.'

'And that's it?'

A good liar knows that the most efficient lie is always a truth that has had a key piece removed from it.

'Well, he told me about the old days, about when he was in prison and all that.'

'Then he must have told you about Brians, the lawyer. What did he say?'

I wasn't sure what my father knew or suspected, so I decided to tread carefully.

'He told me he was imprisoned in Montjuïc Castle and that he managed to escape with the help of a man called David Martín. Apparently you knew him.'

My father was silent for a while.

'Nobody has dared to say this to my face, but I know there are people who at the time believed, and still believe, that your mother was in love with Martín,' he said with such a sad smile that I knew he considered himself one of them.

My father had a tendency to grin the way some people do when they're trying to hold back their tears.

'Your mother was a good woman. A good wife. I wouldn't like you to think strange things about her because of what Fermín may have told you. He didn't know her. I did.'

'Fermín didn't insinuate anything,' I lied. 'Just that Mum and Martín were bound by a strong friendship and that she tried to help him get out of the prison by hiring that lawyer, Brians.'

'I suppose he will also have spoken to you about that man, Valls...'

I hesitated for a second before nodding. My father saw the consternation in my eyes and shook his head.

'Your mother died of cholera, Daniel. Brians – I'll never know why – insists on accusing that man, just a bureaucrat with delusions of grandeur, of a crime for which he has no evidence or proof.'

I didn't say anything.

'You must get that idea out of your head. I want you to promise you're not even going to think about this.'

I sat there with my mouth shut, wondering whether my father was really as naive as he appeared to be or whether the pain of her loss had blinded him and pushed him towards the convenient cowardice of survivors. I recalled Fermín's words and told myself that neither I nor anyone else had any right to judge him.

'Promise you won't do anything stupid, and you won't look for this man,' he insisted.

I nodded without conviction. He grabbed my arm.

'Swear you won't. For the sake of your mother's memory.'

I felt a pain gripping my face and realised I was gnashing my teeth so strongly they were in danger of cracking. I looked away but my father wouldn't let go of me. I stared into his eyes, and until the last second, thought I might be able to lie to him.

'I swear on my mother's memory that I won't do anything while you live.'

'That is not what I asked you.'

'It's all I can give you.'

My father dropped his head between his hands and took a deep breath.

'The night your mother died, upstairs, in the flat . . .'

'I remember it clearly.'

'You were five.'

'I was four.'

'That night, Isabella asked me never to tell you what had happened. She thought it was better that way.'

It was the first time I'd heard him refer to my mother by her name.

'I know, Dad.'

He looked into my eyes.

'Forgive me,' he whispered.

I held my father's gaze. Sometimes he seemed to grow a little older just by looking at me and remembering. I stood up and hugged him quietly. He held me tight, and when he burst into tears the anger and the pain he'd buried in his soul all those years gushed out like blood. I knew then, without being able to explain clearly why, that slowly, inexorably, my father had begun to die.

# Part Four

*Suspicion*

# 1

*Barcelona, 1957*

THE FIRST GLINT OF DAYBREAK FOUND ME IN THE DOOR-way of little Julián's bedroom. For once he was sound asleep, far from everything and everyone, with a smile on his lips. I heard Bea's footsteps approaching and felt her hands on my back.

'How long have you been standing here?' she asked.

'A while.'

'What are you doing?'

'I'm looking at him.'

Bea walked up to Julián's cot and leaned over to kiss his fore-head.

'What time did you come in last night?'

I didn't reply.

'How is Fermín?'

'Not too bad.'

'And you?' I tried to smile. 'Do you want to talk about it?' she insisted.

'Some other day.'

'I thought there were no secrets between us,' said Bea.

'So did I.'

She looked at me in surprise.

'What do you mean, Daniel?'

'Nothing. I don't mean anything. I'm very tired. Shall we go back to bed?'

Bea took my hand and led me to the bedroom.

We lay down on the bed and I embraced her.

'I dreamed about your mother tonight,' said Bea. 'About Isabella.'

The rain began to pelt against the windowpanes.

'I was a little girl, and she was holding my hand. We were in a large and very old house, with huge rooms and a grand piano, and a glass-covered balcony that looked on to a garden with a pond. There was a little boy by the pond. He looked just like Julián, but I knew that it was really you, don't ask me why. Isabella knelt down by my side and asked me whether I could see you. You were playing by the water with a paper boat. I said I could. Then she told me to look after you. To look after you for ever because she had to go far away.'

We lay there without speaking for a long time, listening to the patter of the rain.

'What did Fermín tell you last night?'

'The truth,' I replied. 'He told me the truth.'

As I tried to reconstruct Fermín's story Bea listened in silence. At first I felt anger welling up inside me again, but as I advanced through the story I was overwhelmed by sadness and despair. It was all new to me and I still didn't know how I was going to be able to live with the secrets and implications of what Fermín had revealed to me. Those events had taken place almost twenty years before, and the passage of time had turned me into a mere spectator in a play where the course of my fate had been determined.

When I finished talking, I noticed the anxious look in Bea's eyes. It wasn't hard to guess what she was thinking.

'I've promised my father that during his lifetime I won't look for that man, Valls, or do anything else,' I added, to reassure her.

'During *his* lifetime? And what happens afterwards? Haven't you thought about us? About Julián?'

'Of course I have. And you must not worry,' I lied. 'After talking to my father I've understood that all this happened a long time ago and there's nothing we can do to change it.'

Bea seemed rather unconvinced.

'It's the truth . . .' I lied again.

She held my gaze for a few moments, but those were the words she wanted to hear and she finally surrendered to the temptation of believing them.

# 2

THAT AFTERNOON, WITH THE RAIN STILL LASHING THE flooded, deserted streets, the grim figure of Sebastián Salgado appeared outside the bookshop. He was observing us with his unmistakable predatory air through the shop window, the lights from the nativity scene illuminating his ravaged face. His suit – the same old suit he'd worn on his first visit – was soaking wet. I went over to the door and opened it for him.

'Lovely manger,' he said.

'Aren't you coming in?'

I held the door open and Salgado limped in. After a few steps he stopped, leaning on his walking stick. Fermín eyed him suspiciously from the counter. Salgado smiled.

'It's been a long time,' he intoned.

'I thought you were dead,' replied Fermín.

'I thought you were dead, too, as did everyone else. That's what they told us. That you'd been caught trying to escape and they'd shot you.'

'Fat chance.'

'To be honest, I always hoped you'd managed to slip away. You know: the devil looks after his own, and all that . . .'

'You move me to tears, Salgado. When did you get out?'

'About a month ago.'

'Don't tell me you were let out for good behaviour,' said Fermín.

'I think they got tired of waiting for me to die. Do you know

I was granted a pardon? I've got it on a sheet of paper, signed by General Franco himself.'

'You must have had it framed, I'm sure.'

'I've put it in a place of honour: above the toilet, in case I ever run out of tissue.'

Salgado took a few more steps towards the counter and pointed to a chair in a corner.

'Do you mind if I sit down? I'm still not used to walking more than ten metres in a straight line and I get tired very easily.'

'It's all yours,' I offered.

He fell into the chair and took a deep breath as he rubbed his knee. Fermín looked at him like someone who has spied a rat climbing out of a toilet.

'Funny, isn't it, to think that the one person everyone thought would be the first to kick the bucket turns out to be the last . . . Do you know what has kept me alive all these years, Fermín?'

'If I didn't know you so well I'd say it was the Mediterranean diet and the fresh sea air.'

Salgado gave an attempt at a laugh that sounded like a hoarse cough or his bronchial tubes on the verge of collapse.

'You never change, Fermín. That's why we got along so famously back then. What times those were. But I don't want to bore the young man here with memories of the good old days. This generation isn't interested in our stuff. They're into the charleston, or whatever they call it these days. Shall we talk business?'

'I'm listening.'

'You're the one who must do the talking, Fermín. I've already said all I had to say. Are you going to give me what you owe me? Or are we going to have to kick up a fuss you'd do better to avoid?'

Fermín remained impassive for a few moments, leaving us in an uncomfortable silence. Salgado was staring straight at him with venom in his eyes. Fermín gave me a look I didn't quite understand and sighed dejectedly.

'You win, Salgado.'

He pulled a small object out of his pocket and handed it to him. A key. *The key*. Salgado's eyes lit up like those of a child. He got to his feet and slowly approached Fermín, accepting the key with his remaining hand, trembling with emotion.

'If you're planning to reintroduce it into restricted areas of your anatomy, I beg you to step into the bathroom for the sake of decorum. This is a family venue, open to the general public,' Fermín warned him.

Salgado, who seemed to have recovered the bloom of first youth, broke into a smile of boundless satisfaction.

'Come to think of it, you've actually done me a huge favour keeping it for me all these years,' he declared.

'That's what friends are for,' answered Fermín. 'God bless, and don't hesitate never to come back here again.'

Salgado smiled and winked at us. He walked towards the door, already lost in thought. Before stepping into the street he turned round for a moment and raised a hand in a conciliatory farewell.

'I wish you luck and a long life, Fermín. And rest assured, your secret is safe with me.'

We watched him leave in the rain, an old man anyone might have thought was at death's door but who, I was sure, didn't feel the cold raindrops lashing at him then, or even the years of imprisonment and hardships he carried in his blood. I glanced at Fermín, who seemed nailed to the ground, looking pale and confused at the sight of his old cellmate.

'Are we going to let him go just like that?' I asked.

'Have you a better plan?'

# 3

After the proverbial minute's wait, we hurried down the street armed with dark raincoats and an umbrella the size of a parasol that Fermín had bought in one of the bazaars in the port – intending to use it both winter and summer for his escapades to La Barceloneta beach with Bernarda.

'Fermín, with this thing we stick out like a sore thumb,' I warned him.

'Don't worry. I'm sure the only thing that swine can see are gold doubloons raining down from heaven,' replied Fermín.

Salgado was some hundred metres ahead of us, hobbling briskly under the rain along Calle Condal. We narrowed the gap a little, just in time to see him about to climb on to a tram going up Vía Layetana. We sprinted forward, closing the umbrella as we ran, and by some miracle managed to leap on to the tram's running board. In the best tradition of those days we made the journey hanging from the back. Salgado had found a seat in the front, offered to him by a Good Samaritan, who couldn't have known who he was dealing with.

'That's what happens when people reach old age,' said Fermín. 'Nobody remembers they've been bastards too.'

The tram rumbled along Calle Trafalgar until it reached the Arco de Triunfo. We peered inside and saw that Salgado was still glued to his seat. The ticket collector, a man with a bushy moustache, scowled at us.

'Don't think that because you're hanging out there I'm going to give you a discount. I've had an eye on you ever since you jumped on board.'

'Nobody cares about social realism any more,' murmured Fermín. 'What a country.'

We handed him a few coins and he gave us our tickets. We were beginning to think Salgado must have fallen asleep when, as the tram turned into the road leading to the Estación del Norte, he stood up and pulled the chain to request a stop. The driver was now slowing down, so we jumped off opposite the palatial art nouveau headquarters of the Hydroelectric Company and followed the tram on foot to the stop. We saw Salgado step down, assisted by two passengers, and then head off towards the train station.

'Are you thinking what I'm thinking?' I asked.

Fermín nodded. We followed Salgado to the station's grand entrance hall, camouflaging ourselves – or perhaps making our presence painfully obvious – behind Fermín's oversized umbrella. Once inside, Salgado approached a row of metal lockers lined up along one of the walls like miniature niches in a cemetery. We sat on a bench in the shadows of the hall. Salgado was standing in front of the countless lockers, staring at them, utterly absorbed.

'Do you think he's forgotten where he hid the booty?' I asked.

'Of course he hasn't. He's been waiting twenty years for this moment. He's simply savouring it.'

'If you say so . . . But he's forgotten, if you ask me.'

We remained there, watching and waiting.

'Fermín, you never really told me where you hid the key when you escaped from the castle . . .'

Fermín threw me a hostile glance.

'Forget it,' I conceded.

The wait continued a few minutes longer.

'Perhaps he has an accomplice . . .' I said, 'and he's waiting for him.'

'Salgado isn't the sharing sort.'

'Perhaps there's someone else who . . .'

'Shhh,' Fermín hushed me, pointing at Salgado, who had moved at last.

The old man walked over to one of the lockers and placed his hand on the metal door. He pulled out the key, inserted it in the lock, opened the door and looked inside. At that precise moment a pair of Civil Guards doing their rounds turned into the entrance hall from the station platforms and walked over to where Salgado was standing, trying to pull something out of the locker.

'Oh dear, oh dear . . .' I murmured.

Salgado turned and greeted the two officers. They exchanged a few words and one of them pulled a case out of the locker and left it on the floor by Salgado's feet. The thief thanked them effusively for their help and the Civil Guards touched their three-cornered hats and continued on their beat.

'God bless Spain,' murmured Fermín.

Salgado grabbed the case and dragged it along to another bench, at the opposite end from where we were sitting.

'He's not going to open it here, is he?' I asked.

'He has to make sure it's all there,' replied Fermín. 'That nasty piece of work has put up with years of misery to recover his treasure.'

Salgado looked around him a few times to make sure there was nobody nearby, and finally decided to take action. We saw him open the suitcase just a few centimetres and peer inside.

He remained like that for almost a minute, motionless. Fermín and I looked at one another without understanding. Suddenly Salgado closed the suitcase and got up, then walked off towards the exit, leaving the suitcase behind him in front of the open locker.

'But what's he doing?' I asked.

Fermín stood up and signalled to me.

'You get the suitcase, and I'll follow him . . .'

Without giving me time to reply, Fermín hastened towards

the exit. I hurried over to the place where Salgado had abandoned the case. A smart alec, who was reading a newspaper on a nearby bench, had also set eyes on it and, looking both ways first to check that nobody was watching, got up and was preparing to swoop on it like a bird of prey. I quickened my pace. The stranger was about to grab the case when, by the miracle of a split second, I managed to snatch it from him.

'That suitcase isn't yours,' I said.

The individual fixed me with a hostile look and clutched the handle.

'Shall I call the Civil Guards?' I asked.

Looking flustered, the scamp let go of the case and moved swiftly away in the direction of the platforms. I took it over to the bench and, after making sure no one was looking, opened it.

It was empty. Salgado's treasure was gone.

Only then did I hear shouts and turned my head to discover that some incident had occurred outside the station. I got to my feet and looked through the glass doors. The two Civil Guards were pushing their way through a circle of bystanders that had congregated in the rain. When the crowd parted, I saw Fermín kneeling on the ground, holding Salgado in his arms. The old man's eyes were staring into space.

A woman came into the station, a hand clamped over her mouth.

'What happened?' I asked.

'A poor old man, he just keeled over . . .' she said.

I went outside and walked across to the knot of people observing the scene. I could see Fermín looking up and exchanging a few words with the Civil Guards. One of them was nodding. Fermín then took off his raincoat and spread it over Salgado's corpse, covering his face. By the time I arrived there, a three-fingered hand was peeping out from under the garment. On the palm, shining in the rain, was the key. I protected Fermín with the umbrella and put a hand on his shoulder. We slowly moved away.

'Are you all right, Fermín?'

My good friend shrugged.

'Let's go home,' he managed to say.

# 4

As we left the station behind us, I took off my raincoat and put it over Fermín's shoulders. He'd abandoned his on Salgado's body. I didn't think my friend was in a fit state to take a long walk, so I hailed a taxi. I opened the door for him and, once he was seated, closed it and got in on the other side.

'The suitcase was empty,' I said. 'Someone played a dirty trick on Salgado.'

'It takes a thief to catch a thief . . .'

'Who do you think it was?'

'Perhaps the same person who said I had his key and told him where he could find me,' Fermín murmured.

'Valls?'

Fermín gave a dispirited sigh.

'I don't know, Daniel. I no longer know what to think.'

I noticed the taxi driver looking at us in the mirror, waiting.

'We're going to the entrance to Plaza Real, on Calle Fernando,' I said.

'Aren't we going back to the bookshop?' asked Fermín, who didn't have enough fight left in him even to argue about a taxi ride.

'I am. But you're going to Don Gustavo's, to spend the rest of the day with Bernarda.'

We made the journey in silence, staring out at Barcelona, a blur in the rain. When we reached the arches on Calle Fernando, where years before I'd first met Fermín, I paid the fare and we got out. I walked Fermín as far as Don Gustavo's front door and gave him a hug.

'Take care of yourself, Fermín. And eat something, or Bernarda will get a bone sticking into her on the wedding night.'

'Don't worry. When I set my mind to it, I can put on more weight than an opera singer. As soon as I go up to the flat I'll gorge myself with those almond cakes Don Gustavo buys in Casa Quílez, and by tomorrow I'll look like a stuffed turkey.'

'I hope so. Give my best to the bride.'

'I will, although with things the way they are on the legal front and with all that red tape, I can see myself living in sin.'

'None of that. Remember what you once told me? That destiny doesn't do home visits, that you have to go for it yourself?'

'I must confess I took that sentence from one of Carax's books. I liked the sound of it.'

'Well, I believed it and still do. That's why I'm telling you that your destiny is to marry Bernarda on the arranged date with all your papers in order – with priests, rice and your name and surnames.'

My friend looked at me sceptically.

'As my name is Daniel, you're getting married with all due pomp and ceremony,' I promised Fermín. He looked so dejected I thought nothing would manage to revive his spirits: not a packet of Sugus, not even a good movie at the Fémina Cinema with Kim Novak sporting one of her glorious brassieres that defied gravity.

'If you say so, Daniel . . .'

'You've given me back the truth,' I said. 'I'm going to give you back your name.'

# 5

That afternoon, when i returned to the bookshop, I set in motion my plan for rescuing Fermín's identity. The first step consisted in making a few phone calls from the back room and establishing a course of action. The second required gathering the right team of recognised experts.

The following day turned out to be pleasant and sunny. Around noon I walked over to the library on Calle del Carmen, where I'd arranged to meet Professor Alburquerque, convinced that whatever he didn't know, nobody knew.

I found him under the tall arches of the main reading room, surrounded by piles of books and papers, concentrating, pen in hand. I sat down opposite him, on the other side of the table, and let him get on with his work. It took him almost a minute to become aware of my presence. When he looked up he stared at me in surprise.

'That must be really good stuff,' I ventured.

'I'm working on a series of articles on Barcelona's accursed writers,' he explained. 'Do you remember someone called Julián Carax, an author you recommended a few months ago in the bookshop?'

'Of course,' I replied.

'Well, I've been looking into him and his story is truly extraordinary. Did you know that for years a diabolical character went around the world searching for Carax's books and burning them?'

'You don't say,' I said, feigning surprise.

'It's a very odd case. I'll let you read it when I've finished.'

'You should write a book on the subject,' I proposed. 'A secret history of Barcelona seen through its accursed writers, those forbidden in the official version.'

The professor considered the idea, intrigued.

'It had occurred to me, I must say, but I have so much work, what with my newspaper articles and the university . . .'

'If you don't write it, nobody will . . .'

'Yes, well, maybe I'll take the plunge and get on with it. I don't know where I'll find the time, but . . .'

'Sempere & Sons can offer you its full catalogue and any assistance you may need.'

'I'll bear it in mind. So? Shall we go for lunch?'

PROFESSOR ALBURQUERQUE CALLED IT a day and we set off for Casa Leopoldo, where we sat down with a glass of wine and some sublime *serrano* ham tapas, to wait for two plates of bull's-tail stew, the day's special.

'How's our good friend Fermín? A couple of weeks ago, when I saw him in Can Lluís, he looked very downcast.'

'Oddly enough, he's the person I wanted to talk to you about. It's a rather delicate matter, and I must ask you to keep it between ourselves.'

'But of course. What can I do?'

I PROCEEDED TO OUTLINE the problem as concisely as I could, without touching upon thorny or unnecessary details. The professor sensed that there was plenty more to the story than I was telling him, but he displayed his customary discretion.

'Let's see if I've understood,' he said. 'Fermín cannot make use of his identity because, officially, he was pronounced dead almost twenty years ago and therefore, in the eyes of the state, he doesn't exist.'

'Correct.'

'But, from what you tell me, I gather that this identity that was cancelled was also fictitious, an invention of Fermín himself during the war, to save his skin.'

'Correct.'

'That's where I get lost. Help me, Daniel. If Fermín thought up a false identity once, why can't he make up another one now to get married with?'

'For two reasons, Professor. The first is purely practical and that is, whether he uses his name or another invented one, currently Fermín does not possess any legal identity. Therefore, whatever identity he decides to use must be created from scratch.'

'But he wants to continue being Fermín, I suppose.'

'Exactly. And that is the second reason, which is not practical but spiritual, so to speak, and far more important. Fermín wants to continue being Fermín because that is the person Bernarda has fallen in love with, the man who is our friend, the one we all know and the one *he* wants to be. The person he used to be hasn't existed for years. It's a skin he sloughed off. Not even I, who am probably his best friend, know what name he was given when he was christened. For me, and for all those who love him, and especially for himself, he is Fermín Romero de Torres. And when you think of it, if it's a question of creating a new identity for him, why not create his present one?'

Professor Alburquerque finally nodded in assent.

'Correct,' he pronounced.

'So, do you think this is feasible, Professor?'

'Well, it's a quixotic mission if ever there was one,' considered the professor. 'How to endow the gaunt knight Don Fermín de la Mancha with lineage, greyhound and a sheaf of false documents with which to pair him off with his beautiful Bernarda del Toboso in the eyes of God and the register office?'

'I've been thinking about it and consulting legal books,' I said. 'In this country, a person's identity begins with a birth certificate, which, when you stop to consider, is a very simple document.'

The professor raised his eyebrows.

'What you're suggesting is delicate. Not to say a serious crime.'

'Unprecedented, in fact, at least in the judicial annals. I've verified it.'

'Have you? Please continue, this is getting better.'

'Let's suppose that someone, hypothetically speaking, had access to the offices of the Civil Registry and could, to put it bluntly, *plant* a birth certificate in the archives . . . Wouldn't that provide sufficient grounds to establish a person's identity?'

The professor shook his head.

'Perhaps for a newborn child. But if we're speaking, hypothetically, of an adult, we'd have to create an entire documentary history. And even if you had access, hypothetically, to the archives, where would you get hold of those documents?'

'Let's say I was able to create a series of credible facsimiles. Would you think it possible then?'

The professor considered the matter carefully.

'The main risk would be that someone uncovers the fraud and wants to bring it to light. Bearing in mind that in this case the so-called accuser who could have spilled the beans regarding documental irregularities is deceased, the problem would boil down to a), being able to gain access to the archives and introduce a file into the system with a fictitious but plausible identity and b), generating the whole string of documents required to establish that identity. I'm talking about papers of all shapes and sizes, and all sorts of certificates including certificates of baptism from parish churches, identity cards . . .'

'With regard to point a), I understand that you're writing a series of articles on the marvels of the Spanish legal system, commissioned by the Council for a report on that institution. I've been looking into it a little and discovered that during the war, a number of archives in the Civil Registry were bombed. That means that hundreds, even thousands, of identities must have been reconstructed any old how. I'm no expert, but I imagine that this would open a gap or two which someone well informed, well connected and with a plan could take advantage of . . .'

The professor looked at me out of the corner of his eye.

'I see you've been doing some serious research, Daniel.'

'Forgive me, Professor, but Fermín's happiness is worth that and much more.'

'And it does you credit. But it could also earn whoever attempted to do such a thing a heavy sentence if he was caught red-handed.'

'That's why I thought that if someone, hypothetically, had access to one of those reconstructed archives in the Civil Registry, he could take a helper along with him who would, so to speak, assume the more risky part of the operation.'

'If that were the case, the hypothetical helper would have to be able to guarantee the facilitator a twenty per cent lifelong discount on the price of any book bought at Sempere & Sons. Plus an invitation to the wedding of the newborn.'

'That's a done deal. And I'd even raise that to twenty-five per cent. Although, come to think of it, I know someone who, hypothetically, would be prepared to collaborate pro bono, just for the pleasure of scoring a goal against a rotten, corrupt regime, receiving nothing in exchange.'

'I'm an academic, Daniel. Emotional blackmail doesn't work with me.'

'For Fermín, then.'

'That's another matter. Let's go into the technicalities.'

I pulled out the one-thousand-peseta note Salgado had given me and showed it to him.

'This is my budget for running costs and issuance of documents,' I remarked.

'I see you're sparing no expense. But you'd do better to put that money aside for other endeavours that will be required by this noble deed. My services come free of charge,' replied the professor. 'The bit that worries me most, dear assistant, is the much-needed documentary trail. Forget all the new public works and prayer books: the new centurions of the regime have also doubled the already colossal structure of the state bureaucracy, worthy of the worst nightmares of our friend Franz Kafka. As I say, a case like this will require generating all kinds of letters, applications, petitions and other documents that must look credible and have the consistency, tone and smell that are characteristic of a dusty, dog-eared and unquestionable file . . .'

'We're covered on that front,' I said.

'I'm going to have to be given the list of accomplices in this conspiracy, to make sure you're not bluffing.'

I went on to explain the rest of my plan.

'It could work,' he concluded.

As soon as the main dish arrived, we wrapped up the matter and the conversation took a different direction. Although I'd been holding back during the entire meal, by the time coffee was served, I could no longer restrain myself. Feigning a certain indifference, I asked innocently:

'By the way, Professor, the other day a customer was chatting to me about something in the bookshop and the name Mauricio Valls cropped up – the one who was Minister of Culture and all those things. What do you know about him?'

The professor raised an eyebrow.

'About Valls? What everyone knows, I suppose.'

'I'm sure you know much more than everyone, Professor. Much more.'

'Well, actually, I hadn't heard that name for a while, but until not long ago Mauricio Valls was a real big shot. As you say, he was our famous new Minister of Culture for a few years, head of a number of institutions and organisations, a man well placed in the regime and of great prestige in those circles, patron to many, golden boy of all the cultural pages in the Spanish press . . . As I say, a big shot.'

I smiled weakly, pretending to be pleasantly surprised.

'And he isn't any longer?'

'Quite frankly, I'd say he disappeared off the map a while ago, or at least from the public scene. I'm not sure whether he was given some embassy or some post in an international institution, you know how these things work. But in fact I've lost track of him lately . . . I know he set up a publishing house with a number of partners some years ago. The business does very well – it doesn't stop bringing out new books. In fact, once a month I receive an invite for the launch of one of their titles . . .'

'And does Valls go to these events?'

'He used to, years ago. We always joked about the fact that he spoke more about himself than about the book or the author he was presenting. But that was some time ago. I haven't seen him for years. May I ask why this interest, Daniel? I didn't think of you as someone keen on our literature's small vanity fair.'

'I'm just curious.'

'I see.'

While Professor Alburquerque paid the bill, he looked at me askance.

'Why is it that I always think you're not even telling me a quarter of the story?'

'One day I'll tell you the rest, Professor. I promise.'

'You'd better, because cities have no memory and they need someone like me, a sage with his feet on the ground, to keep it alive.'

'This is the deal: you help me solve Fermín's problem and in exchange, one day I'll tell you things that Barcelona would rather forget. For your secret history.'

The professor held out his hand and I shook it.

'I'll take your word for it. Now, returning to the subject of Fermín and the documents we're going to have to pull out of a hat . . .'

'I think I have the right man for the job.'

# 6

Oswaldo Darío de Mortenssen, prince of Barcelona scribes and an old acquaintance of mine, was enjoying a break after his lunch, in his booth next to La Virreina Palace, sipping a double espresso with a dash of cognac and smoking a cigar. When he saw me approaching he raised a hand in greeting.

'The prodigal son returns. Have you changed your mind? Shall we get going on that love letter that will give you access to the forbidden zips and buttons of the desired young lady?'

I showed him my wedding ring again and he nodded, remembering.

'I'm sorry. Force of habit. You're one of the old guard. What can I do for you?'

'The other day I remembered why your name sounded familiar to me, Don Oswaldo. I work in a bookshop and I found a novel of yours from 1933, *The Riders of Twilight*.'

That sparked a host of memories. Oswaldo smiled nostalgically.

'What times those were . . . Barrido and Escobillas, my publishers, ripped me off to the last *céntimo*, the swines. May they roast for ever in hell. Still, the pleasure of writing it – nobody can take that away from me.'

'If I bring it along one day, will you sign it for me?'

'Of course. It was my swansong. The world wasn't ready for a western set in the Ebro delta, with bandits on canoes instead of horses, and mosquitoes the size of watermelons.'

'You're the Zane Grey of the Spanish coast.'

'I wish. What can I do for you, young man?'

'Lend me your talent and cunning for an equally worthy venture.'

'I'm all ears.'

'I need you to help me invent a documentary past for a friend, so he can marry the woman he loves without legal impediments.'

'A good man?'

'The best I know.'

'If that's the case, it's a deal. My favourite scenes were always weddings and christenings.'

'We'll need official applications, reports, petitions, certificates – the whole shooting match.'

'That won't be a problem. We'll delegate part of the logistics to Luisito, whom you already know. He's completely trustworthy and a master in twelve different calligraphies.'

I pulled out the one-thousand-peseta note the professor had refused and handed it to him. Oswaldo put it away swiftly, his eyes as big as saucers.

'And they say you can't make a living from writing in Spain,' he said.

'Will that cover the working expenses?'

'Amply. When I've got it all organised I'll let you know what the whole operation adds up to, but off the top of my head I'd guess that three or four hundred will get us there.'

'I leave that to your discretion, Oswaldo. My friend Professor Alburquerque . . .'

'Fine writer . . .' Oswaldo cut in.

'And an even better gentleman. As I say, my friend, the professor, will drop by and give you a list of the documents required, and all the details. If there's anything you need, you'll find me at the Sempere & Sons bookshop.'

His face lit up when he heard the name.

'Ah, the sanctuary. As a young man I used to go round every

Saturday and those encounters with Señor Sempere opened my eyes.'

'That would have been my grandfather.'

'I haven't been there for years. My finances are tight, and I've taken to borrowing books from libraries.'

'Well, do pay us the honour of returning to the bookshop, Don Oswaldo. Consider it your home and we can always sort something out with prices.'

'I will.'

He put out a hand and I shook it.

'It's a pleasure to do business with the Semperes.'

'May it be the first of many such occasions.'

'What happened to the lame man whose eyes twinkled at the sight of gold?'

'Turned out that all that glittered wasn't gold,' I said.

'A sign of our times . . .'

# 7

*Barcelona, 1958*

THAT MONTH OF JANUARY CAME WRAPPED IN BRIGHT ICY skies that blew powdery snow over the city's rooftops. The sun shone every day, casting sharp angles of light and shadow on the façades of a crystalline Barcelona. Double-decker buses drove by with the top tier empty, and passing trams left a halo of steam on the tracks.

Christmas lights glowed in garlands of blue fire all over the old town and carols bearing sugary wishes of goodwill and peace trickled out of a thousand and one loudspeakers by shop doors. The Yuletide message was so pervasive that a policeman guarding the nativity scene set up by the town hall in Plaza San Jaime turned a blind eye when someone had the bright idea of placing a Catalan beret on the Infant Jesus – ignoring the demands of a group of pious old women who expected him to haul the man off with a slap to police headquarters. In the end, someone from the archbishop's office reported the incident and three nuns turned up to restore order.

CHRISTMAS SALES HAD PICKED up, and a seasonal star in the shape of black numbers in the accounts of Sempere & Sons guaranteed that we would at least be able to cope with the electricity and heating bills. With a bit of luck, we might even enjoy a proper hot meal once a day. My father seemed to have recovered his spirits and decreed that this year we wouldn't wait so long before decorating the bookshop.

'We're going to have that crib hanging around for a long time,' grumbled Fermín with little or no enthusiasm.

After 6 January, the feast of the Three Kings, my father instructed us to wrap up the nativity scene carefully and take it down to the basement for storage until the following Christmas.

'With care,' warned my father. 'I don't want to be told that the boxes slipped accidentally, Fermín.'

'With the utmost care, Señor Sempere. I'll vouch for the integrity of the crib with my life, and that includes all the farm animals dotted round the swaddled Messiah.'

Once we had made room for the boxes containing all the Christmas decorations, I paused for a moment to have a quick look round the basement and its forgotten corners. The last time we'd been there, the conversation had covered matters that neither Fermín nor I had brought up again, but they still lay heavily on my mind at least. Fermín seemed to read my thoughts, and he shook his head.

'Don't tell me you're still thinking about that idiot's letter.'

'Every now and then.'

'You won't have said anything to Doña Beatriz, I hope.'

'No. I put the letter back in her coat pocket and didn't say a word.'

'What about her? Didn't she mention that she'd received a letter from Don Juan Tenorio?'

I shook my head. Fermín screwed up his nose, as if to say that it wasn't a good sign.

'Have you decided what you're going to do?'

'What about?'

'Don't act innocent, Daniel. Are you or are you not going to follow your wife to her potential tryst with that old boyfriend at the Ritz and cause a little stir?'

'You're presupposing that she'll be going there,' I protested.

'Aren't you?'

I looked down, upset with myself.

'What kind of a husband doesn't trust his wife?' I asked.

'Would you like me to give you a list of names and surnames, or will statistics do?'

'I trust Bea. She wouldn't cheat on me. She isn't like that. If she had anything to say to me, she'd say it to my face, without lying.'

'Then you don't have anything to worry about, do you?'

Something in Fermín's tone made me think that my suspicions and insecurities had disappointed him. Although he was never going to admit it, I was sure it saddened him to think I devoted my time to unworthy thoughts and to doubting the sincerity of a woman I didn't deserve.

'You must think I'm a fool.'

Fermín shook his head.

'No. I think you're a fortunate man, at least when it comes to love. And like most people who are so fortunate, you don't realise it.'

A knock on the door at the top of the stairs interrupted us.

'Unless you've discovered oil down there, will you please come back up right away, there's work to do,' called my father.

Fermín sighed.

'Since he's got out of the red he's become a tyrant,' he said.

THE DAYS CRAWLED BY. Fermín had at last agreed to delegate the preparations for the wedding and the banquet to my father and Don Gustavo, who had taken on the role of parental authorities. As best man, I advised the presiding committee, but mine was a merely honorary title since Bea acted as chief executive and artistic director and coordinated all those involved with an iron fist.

'Fermín, I have orders from Bea to take you along to Casa Pantaleoni to try on your suit.'

'A striped prisoner's suit is all I'm going to wear . . .'

I'd given him my word that when the time came his name

would be in order and his friend the parish priest would be able to intone those words: 'Do you, Fermín, take Bernarda to be your lawful wedded wife?' without us all ending up in the police station. But as the date drew closer Fermín was being eaten up by anxiety. Bernarda survived the suspense by means of prayers and egg-yolk flans, although, once her pregnancy had been confirmed by a trustworthy, discreet doctor, she spent much of her day fighting nausea and dizziness. Everything seemed to indicate that Fermín's firstborn was going to be a handful.

THOSE WERE DAYS OF apparent and deceptive calm, but beneath the surface I'd succumbed to a dark, murky current that was slowly dragging me into the depths of a new and irresistible emotion: hatred.

In my spare time, without telling anyone where I was going, I would slip out and walk over to the nearby Ateneo Library on Calle Canuda, where I tracked every step of Mauricio Valls's life in the newspaper room. What for years I'd regarded as an indistinct and uninteresting figure took on a painful clarity and precision that increased with every passing day. My investigation allowed me to reconstruct Valls's public career during the last fifteen years, piece by piece. A lot of water had flowed under the bridge since his early days with the regime. With time and good contacts, if one were to believe what the papers said (something Fermín compared to believing that orange squash was obtained by squeezing fresh oranges from Valencia), Don Mauricio Valls had seen his wishes come true and become a shining star in Spain's literary and artistic firmament.

His ascent had been nothing short of spectacular. From 1944 onwards he landed posts and official appointments of growing importance in the country's cultural and academic institutions. His articles, talks and publications multiplied. Any self-respecting award ceremony, conference or cultural event required the participation and presence of Don Mauricio. In 1947, with a couple of business partners, he created Ediciones Ariadna, a publishing company with offices in Madrid and Barcelona mostly devoted to his self-promotion, which the press spared no effort in canonising as the 'most prestigious editorial brand' in Spanish literature.

By 1948, the same papers began to refer regularly to Mauricio Valls as 'the most brilliant and well-respected intellectual in the New Spain'. The country's self-appointed intelligentsia and those who aspired to join the club seemed to be conducting a passionate romance with Don Mauricio. Journalists covering the cultural pages went out of their way to extol Valls, seeking his favour and, with luck, the publication by Ediciones Ariadna of some manuscript they'd been keeping in a drawer, so that they could become part of the official scene and taste at least a few sweet crumbs falling from his table.

Valls had learned the rules of the game and controlled the board better than anyone. At the start of the fifties, his fame and influence had already extended beyond official circles and were beginning to seep into so-called civil society and its members. Mauricio's slogans had been fashioned into a canon of revealed truths adopted by the same three or four thousand Spaniards who saw themselves as the chosen few and who made it a matter of pride to parrot the gospel like diligent pupils while looking down at the lowbrow masses.

En route to the top, Valls had gathered around him a clique of like-minded characters who ate out of his hand and were gradually placed at the head of institutions and in positions of power. If anyone dared question Valls's words or his worth, such an individual would be mercilessly crucified by the press. After being ridiculed in malicious terms, the poor wretch would end up as a pariah, a beggar to whom all doors were slammed shut and whose only alternatives were obscurity or exile.

I SPENT ENDLESS HOURS reading every word as well as between the lines, comparing different versions of the story, cataloguing dates and making lists of successes and potential skeletons in cupboards. In other circumstances, if the purpose of my study had been purely anthropological, I would have taken my hat off to Don Mauricio and his masterly moves. Nobody could deny that he'd learned to read the heart and soul of his fellow citizens and pull the strings that moved their desires, hopes and dreams. He knew the game inside out, and nobody played it better.

If I was left with anything after endless days submerged in the official version of Valls's life, it was the belief that the building blocks of a new Spain were being set in place and that Don Mauricio's meteoric ascent to the altars of power exemplified a rising trend that, in all probability, would outlast the dictatorship and put down deep and immovable roots throughout the entire country for decades to come.

In 1952 Valls reached the summit of his career when he was named Minister of Culture for a three-year period, a position on which he capitalised to consolidate his authority and place his lackeys in the last few posts he had not yet managed to control. His public projection took on a golden monotony: his words were quoted as the source of all wisdom. His presence on jury panels, tribunals and all sorts of formal audiences was constant, while his arsenal of diplomas, laurels and medals continued to grow.

And then, suddenly, something strange happened.

I wasn't aware of it at first. The litany of praise and news flashes continued relentlessly, but after 1956, I spotted a detail buried among all those reports which was in stark contrast to everything published prior to that date. The tone and content of the articles were unchanged, but by reading each one of them and comparing them, I noticed something.

Don Mauricio Valls had never again appeared in public.

His name, his prestige, his reputation and his power were still going from strength to strength. There was just one piece missing: his person. After 1956 there were no photographs, no mention of his attendance nor any direct references to his participation in official functions.

The last cutting confirming Mauricio Valls's presence was

dated 2 November 1956, when he received an award for the year's most distinguished achievements in publishing. The solemn ceremony, held in Madrid's Círculo de Bellas Artes, was attended by the highest authorities and the cream of society. The text of the news report followed the usual, predictable lines of the genre, in other words a short item couched in flattering tones. The most interesting thing about it was the accompanying photograph, the last published picture of Valls, taken shortly before his sixtieth birthday. Elegantly dressed in a well-cut suit, he was smiling modestly as he received a standing ovation from the audience. Some of the usual crowd at that type of event appeared next to Valls and, behind him, slightly off-camera, their expression serious and impenetrable, stood two individuals ensconced behind dark glasses, dressed in black, who didn't seem to be part of the ceremony. They looked severe and disconnected from the whole farce. Vigilant.

NOBODY HAD PHOTOGRAPHED Don Mauricio or seen him in public after that night in the Círculo de Bellas Artes. However hard I tried, I didn't find a single appearance. Tired of pursuing avenues that seemed to lead nowhere, I went back to the beginning and pieced his story together, until I got to know it as if it were my own. I sniffed his trail in the hope of finding a clue, some sign that might tell me where he was. Where was that man who smiled in photographs and paraded his vanity through endless pages with an entourage of flatterers, hungry for favours?

MY HATRED GREW DURING those solitary afternoons in the old Ateneo library, where not so long ago I'd devoted my cares to nobler causes, like the smooth skin of my first impossible love, the blind Clara, or the mysteries of Julián Carax and his novel *The Shadow of the Wind*. The harder it became to follow Valls's trail, the more I refused to admit that he had the right to disappear and erase his name from history. From my history. I needed to know what had happened to him. I needed to look him in the eye, even if it was just to remind him that someone, a single person in the entire universe, knew who he really was and what he had done.

# 8

ONE AFTERNOON, TIRED OF CHASING GHOSTS, I CANCELLED my session at the newspaper library and went out for a stroll with Bea and Julián through a clean, sunny Barcelona I had almost forgotten. We walked from home to Ciudadela Park. I sat on a bench and watched Julián play with his mother on the lawn. As I gazed at them I reminded myself of Fermín's words. A fortunate man, that was me, Daniel Sempere. A fortunate man who had allowed blind resentment to grow inside him until he felt sick at the very thought of himself.

I watched Julián devote himself to one of his grand passions: crawling about on all fours until he was filthy. Bea kept a close eye on him. Every now and then he would pause and turn towards me. Suddenly, a gust of air lifted Bea's skirt and Julián burst out laughing. I clapped and Bea gave me a disapproving look. I searched my son's eyes: soon, I thought, they'll begin to look at me as if I were the wisest man in the world, the bearer of all answers. I decided never to mention the name of Mauricio Valls again or pursue his shadow.

Bea came over and sat down beside me. Julián crawled after her as far as the bench. When he reached my feet I picked him up and he set about cleaning his hands on the lapels of my jacket.

'Just back from the dry cleaner's,' said Bea.

I shrugged, resigned. Bea leaned over and took my hand.

'Nice legs,' I said.

'I don't see what's so amusing. Your son will pick that up from you. Thank goodness there was nobody around.'

'There was a little old grandad hiding behind a newspaper over there. I think he's collapsed with tachycardia.'

Julián decided that the word 'tachycardia' was the funniest thing he'd heard in his life, and we spent a good part of the journey home singing 'ta-chy-car-dia' while Bea walked a few steps in front of us, fuming.

THAT NIGHT, 20 JANUARY, Bea put Julián to bed and then fell asleep on the sofa next to me, while I reread, for the third time, one of David Martín's old novels. It was the copy Fermín had found during his months of exile, after his escape from the prison, and had kept all those years. I liked savouring every turn of phrase and dissecting the architecture of every sentence. I thought that if I could decode the music of his prose I might discover something about that man whom I'd never known and whom everyone assured me was not my father. But that night I couldn't do it. Before reaching the end of a single paragraph, my thoughts would fly from the page and all I could see in front of me was that letter from Pablo Cascos Buendía, arranging to meet my wife the following day at the Ritz, at two o'clock in the afternoon.

At last I closed the book and gazed at Bea, sleeping by my side, sensing that she held a thousand times more secrets than David Martín's stories about the sinister city of the damned. It was after midnight when Bea opened her eyes and caught me scrutinising her. She smiled at me, but a flicker of anxiety crossed her face.

'What's on your mind?' she asked.

'I was thinking about how lucky I am,' I said.

Bea stared at me, unconvinced.

'You say that as if you didn't believe it.'

I stood up and put out a hand to her.

'Let's go to bed,' I invited.

She took my hand and followed me down the corridor to the bedroom. I lay down on the bed and looked at her in silence.

'You've been acting strangely, Daniel. What's wrong? Have I said something?'

I shook my head and gave her a smile as innocent as a white lie. Bea slowly began to undress. When she removed her clothes she never turned round, or hid in the bathroom or behind a door, as the official marriage-guidance booklets advised. I watched her calmly, reading the lines of her body. Bea's eyes were fixed on mine. She slipped on that nightdress I detested and got into bed, turning her back on me.

'Goodnight,' she said, her voice tense and, to someone who knew her well, annoyed.

'Goodnight,' I whispered.

Listening to her breathing I knew that it took her over half an hour to fall asleep, but in the end she was too exhausted to dwell on my peculiar behaviour. As I lay by her side, I wondered whether I should wake her to beg her forgiveness or simply kiss her. I did nothing. I remained there, motionless, gazing at the curve of her back and feeling that dark force inside me whispering that in a few hours Bea would go to meet her ex-fiancé and those lips and that skin would belong to another, as his corny letter seemed to insinuate.

WHEN I AWOKE, BEA had left. I hadn't managed to get to sleep until daybreak, and when the church bells struck nine o'clock I woke up with a start and got dressed in the first clothes I found. Outside, a cold Monday awaited me, sprinkled with snow-flakes that drifted in the air and settled on passers-by like glass spiders hanging from invisible threads. When I walked into the bookshop, my father was standing on the stool he climbed on to every morning to change the date on the calendar. 21 January.

'Oversleeping is not acceptable when you're over twelve,' he said. 'It was your turn to open up today.'

'Sorry. Bad night. It won't happen again.'

I spent a couple of hours trying to occupy my mind and my hands with menial tasks in the bookshop, but all I could do was think of that damned letter that I kept reciting to myself. Halfway through the morning Fermín came over to me surreptitiously and offered me a Sugus sweet.

'Today's the day, isn't it?'

'Shut up, Fermín,' I shot back at him, so brusquely that my father raised his eyebrows.

I took refuge in the back room and heard them murmuring. I sat at my father's desk and stared at the clock. It was one-twenty in the afternoon. I tried to let the minutes go by but the hands of the clock seemed unwilling to move. When I returned to the shop Fermín and my father gave me a worried look.

'Daniel, you might like to take the rest of the day off,' said my father, 'Fermín and I will manage on our own.'

'Thanks. I think I will. I've hardly slept, and I'm not feeling very well.'

I didn't have the courage to look at Fermín as I slipped out through the back room. I walked up the five flights of stairs with leaden feet. When I opened the front door of the apartment I heard water running in the bathroom. I dragged myself to the bedroom and stopped in the doorway. Bea was sitting on the edge of the bed. She hadn't seen me or heard me come in. I watched her as she slipped on her silk stockings and got dressed with her eyes fixed on the mirror. She didn't notice my presence for a couple of minutes.

'I didn't know you were there,' she said halfway between surprise and irritation.

'Are you going out?'

She nodded as she put on scarlet lipstick.

'Where are you going?'

'I have a couple of errands to do.'

'You're looking very pretty.'

'I don't like going out looking a mess,' she replied.

I regarded her as she applied her eyeshadow. 'A *fortunate man*,' said the sarcastic voice.

'What errands?' I asked.

Bea turned to look at me.

'What?'

'I was asking you what errands you have to do.'

'A few things. This and that.'

'And Julián?'

'My mother came to fetch him. She's taken him out for a walk.'

'I see.'

Bea came closer and, putting aside her irritation, gave me a worried look.

'Daniel, what's the matter with you?'

'I didn't sleep a wink last night.'

'Why don't you take a nap? It will do you good.'

'Good idea,' I agreed.

Smiling wanly, Bea took me round to my side of the bed. She helped me lie down, covered me with the bedspread and gave me a kiss on the forehead.

'I'll be late,' she said.

I watched her leave.

'Bea . . .'

She stopped halfway down the corridor and turned round.

'Do you love me?' I asked.

'Of course I love you. Don't be silly.'

I heard the door close and then Bea's feline footsteps in her stiletto heels going down the stairs. I picked up the phone and waited for the operator to speak.

'The Ritz Hotel, please.'

The line took a few seconds to connect.

*'Ritz Hotel, good afternoon, how can I help you?'*

'Could you check whether you have someone staying at the hotel, please?'

*'May I have the name of the guest?'*

'Cascos. Pablo Cascos Buendía. I think he must have arrived yesterday . . .'

*'Just a minute please . . .'*

A long minute's wait, hushed voices, echoes down the line.

'Sir . . .'

'Yes?'

*'I can't see any reservation in that name, sir . . .'*

I felt enormously relieved.

'Could the reservation have been made under a company name?'

*'I'll just check.'*

This time the wait was shorter.

*'Yes, you were right. Señor Cascos Buendía. Here it is, Continental Suite. The reservation was made by the Ariadna publishing company.'*

'What did you say?'

*'I was saying, sir, that Señor Cascos Buendía's booking is in the name of Ediciones Ariadna. Would you like me to put you through to his room?'*

The phone slipped out of my hands. Ariadna was the publishing firm Mauricio Valls had started up years ago.

Cascos worked for Valls.

I slammed down the phone and went out into the street following my wife, my heart poisoned with suspicion.

# 9

THERE WAS NO TRACE OF BEA AMONG THE CROWD FILING past Puerta del Ángel towards Plaza de Cataluña. I assumed that was the way my wife would have chosen to go to the Ritz, but with Bea you never knew. She liked trying out different routes between destinations. After a while I gave up and guessed she must have taken a taxi – a bit more in keeping with the stylish clothes she'd chosen for the occasion.

It took me fifteen minutes to get to the hotel. Although it can't have been more than ten degrees Centigrade I was perspiring and short of breath. The doorman eyed me suspiciously, but he opened the door and allowed me in with the merest hint of a bow. The layout of the lobby puzzled me: it looked like the setting for a spy story or a decadent romantic saga. My limited experience of luxury hotels had not prepared me to work out what was what. I noticed a counter, behind which stood a conscientious receptionist observing me with a mixture of curiosity and alarm. I walked over to him with a smile that failed to impress him.

'The restaurant, please?'

The receptionist examined me with polite scepticism.

'Do you have a reservation, sir?'

'I have a meeting with a hotel guest.'

The receptionist smiled coldly and nodded.

'You'll find the restaurant at the end of that corridor, sir.'

'Much obliged.'

I made my way there with my heart in my mouth. I had no idea what I was going to say or do when I came face to face with Bea and that man. I was met by the head waiter who stopped me in my tracks. His expression, behind a stiff smile, betrayed scant approval of my attire.

'Do you have a reservation, sir?' he asked.

I shoved him aside and walked into the dining hall. Most tables were empty. An elderly couple with a mummified air and nineteenth-century manners interrupted their solemn soup-sipping to stare at me in disgust. A few more tables were occupied by what seemed to be dull businessmen accompanied by one or two incongruously attractive ladies, most likely to be billed as corporate expenses. There was no sign of Cascos or Bea.

The head waiter was approaching, flanked by two assistants. I turned round to face him and smiled politely.

'Didn't Señor Cascos Buendía have a reservation for two o'clock?' I asked.

'Señor Cascos asked to have his meal taken up to his suite,' the head waiter informed me.

I checked my watch. It was twenty past two. I made my way to the corridor with the lifts. One of the doormen had his eye on me but before he could reach me I'd already slipped into one of the lifts. I pressed the button for one of the upper floors, forgetting that I had no idea where the Continental Suite was.

'*Start at the top*,' I told myself.

I got out of the lift on the seventh floor and began to wander down grand corridors, all of them deserted. After a while I came across a door leading to the fire-escape stairs and walked down to the floor below. I went from door to door, looking unsuccessfully for the Continental Suite. It was two-thirty by my watch. On the fifth floor I came across a maid dragging a trolley filled with feather dusters, bars of soap and towels and asked her where the suite was. She gave me a worried look, but I must have frightened her enough for her to point upwards.

235

'Eighth floor.'

I preferred to avoid the lifts in case the hotel staff were looking for me. Three flights of stairs and a long corridor later I
reached the doors of the Continental Suite dripping with sweat.
I stood there for a second to catch my breath, trying to imagine
what was going on behind the thick wooden door and wondering whether I still had enough common sense to walk away. I
thought I could see someone observing me from the other end
of the corridor and feared it might be one of the doormen, but
when I looked closer the figure disappeared round the corner. It
must have been another hotel guest, I imagined. Finally I rang
the doorbell.

# 10

I heard footsteps. The image of Bea doing up her blouse flashed through my mind. A turn of the doorknob. I clenched my fists. A guy with slicked-back hair, wearing a white bathrobe and five-star hotel slippers, opened the door. Some years had passed, but one never forgets faces one wholeheartedly detests.

'Sempere?' he asked incredulously.

The punch landed between his upper lip and his nose. I felt his flesh and cartilage tearing under my fist. Cascos put his hands to his face and staggered, blood spouting through his fingers. I pushed him hard against the wall and stepped into the room. I heard Cascos tumble to the floor behind me. The bed was made and a steaming plate of food lay on a table facing the terrace with a privileged view of the Gran Vía. Only one place had been set. I turned and confronted Cascos, who was trying to get up by holding on to a chair.

'Where is she?'

Cascos's face was deformed with pain, blood dripping down on to his chest. I could see I'd cut his lip open and almost certainly broken his nose. I noticed a sharp burning sensation on my knuckles, and when I looked at my hand I saw I'd grazed my skin when I smashed his face in. I felt no remorse whatsoever.

'She didn't come. Happy?' spat Cascos.

'Since when do you devote your time to writing to my wife?'

I thought he was laughing, and before he could utter another word I hurled myself against him again and dealt him a second punch with all my pent-up anger. The blow loosened his teeth and left my hand feeling numb. Cascos groaned in agony and collapsed into the chair he had been leaning on. When he saw me bending over him he covered his face with his arms. I sank my hands into his neck and pressed my fingers into his flesh as if I were trying to rip out his throat.

'What have you got to do with Valls?'

Cascos stared at me with a terrified expression, convinced that I was going to kill him then and there. He mumbled something unintelligible. Saliva and blood dripped from his mouth on to my hands.

'Mauricio Valls. What have you got to do with him?'

My face was so close to his I could see my reflection in his pupils. The capillaries in his eyes were starting to burst and a web of black lines opened up towards the iris. Realising I was choking him, I let go of him abruptly. Cascos made a rasping sound as he took in air and felt his neck. I sat down on the bed opposite him. My hands were trembling and covered in blood. I went into the bathroom and washed them. I splashed my face and hair with cold water, and when I saw my reflection in the mirror I barely recognised myself. I'd been on the point of killing a man.

# 11

WHEN I RETURNED TO THE ROOM, CASCOS WAS STILL
slumped on the chair, panting. I filled a glass with water and
handed it to him. Seeing me approach again he moved to one
side, expecting another blow.

'Here,' I said.

He opened his eyes and when he saw the glass he seemed
uncertain for a moment or two.

'Here,' I repeated. 'It's only water.'

He accepted the glass with a trembling hand and took it
to his lips. I noticed that I'd broken some of his teeth. Cascos
groaned and his eyes filled with tears from the pain when the
cold water touched the dental pulp exposed beneath the enamel.
We remained silent for over a minute.

'Shall I call a doctor?' I asked at last.

He looked up and shook his head.

'Go away before I call the police.'

'Tell me what you have to do with Mauricio Valls and I'll go,'
I looked at him coldly.

'He's . . . he's one of the partners of the publishing house
where I work.'

'Did he ask you to write that letter?'

Cascos hesitated. I stood up and took a step towards him. I
grabbed his hair and pulled hard.

'Don't hit me again,' he pleaded.

'Did Valls ask you to write that letter?'

Cascos was avoiding my eyes.

'It wasn't him,' he managed to say.

'Who, then?'

'One of his secretaries, Armero.'

'Who?'

'Paco Armero. He's an employee at the firm. He told me to renew contact with Beatriz. He said that if I did there would be something for me. A reward.'

'Why did you have to renew contact with Bea?'

'I don't know.'

I made as if to hit him again.

'I don't know,' whimpered Cascos. 'It's the truth.'

'And that's why you asked her to meet you here?'

'I still love Beatriz.'

'Pretty way of showing it. Where is Valls?'

'I don't know.'

'How can you not know where your boss is?'

'Because I don't know him. OK? I've never seen him. I've never spoken to him.'

'Explain.'

'I started working for Ariadna a year and a half ago, in the Madrid office. In all this time I've never seen him. Nobody has.'

He stood up slowly and walked over to the telephone. I didn't stop him. He picked up the receiver, his eyes poisoned with hatred.

'I'm going to call the police . . .'

'That won't be necessary,' came a voice from the hallway.

I turned to discover Fermín, in what I imagined must be one of my father's suits, holding up a card vaguely resembling some kind of police badge.

'Inspector Fermín Romero de Torres. Police. Someone has reported a disturbance. Which of you two can sum up what has taken place here?'

I don't know who was more disconcerted, Cascos or me. Fermín took advantage of the situation to pull the receiver gently away from Cascos's hand.

240

'Allow me,' he said, brushing him to one side. 'I'll call headquarters.'

He pretended to dial a number and smiled at us.

'Give me headquarters, please. Yes, thank you.'

He waited a few seconds.

'Yes, Mari Pili, it's me, Romero de Torres. Put me through to Palacios. Yes, I'll wait.'

While Fermín pretended to wait and covered the receiver with his hand, he gestured to Cascos.

'Have you banged your head on the bathroom door, or is there anything you wish to declare?'

'This savage attacked me and tried to kill me. I want to press charges immediately. I want to see him behind bars before the end of the day.'

Fermín gave me an officious look and nodded.

'Indeed. We have a dungeon that's just the ticket, rats and all.'

He pretended to hear something on the telephone and signalled to Cascos to be quiet.

'Yes, Palacios. At the Ritz. Yes. It's a 424. One person wounded. Mostly facial. It depends. I'd say a real mess. Fine. I'll proceed immediately to the suspect's summary arrest.'

He put down the phone.

'All sorted.'

Fermín came over to me and, grabbing my arm with authority, motioned for me to keep quiet.

'Don't say a word. Anything you say now will be used against you and all your criminal associates till justice is served.'

Doubled up with pain and confused by Fermín's peculiar display of procedural methods, Cascos stared at the scene in disbelief.

'Aren't you going to handcuff him?'

'This being a posh establishment, we'll put the shackles on him in the police car. Standard procedure, sir.'

Cascos, who was still bleeding and was probably seeing double, barred our way with little conviction.

'Are you sure you're a policeman?'

'Elite corps. I'll get room service to bring you up a tartar steak right away so you can treat your injuries with a soothing mask. Works wonders for bags under the eyes and close-up bruising, take it from a pro. My esteemed colleagues will swing by later to take your statement and prepare the official charges to make sure this rascal receives an airtight conviction for hard labour in a high-security Moroccan prison,' he recited, moving Cascos's arm out of the way and pushing me as fast as he could towards the exit.

# 12

We hailed a taxi outside the hotel door and travelled along Gran Vía in silence for a while.

'Jesus, Mary and Joseph!' Fermín finally burst out. 'Are you mad? I look at you and I don't know who you are . . . What were you trying to do? Kill that imbecile?'

'He works for Mauricio Valls,' was my only answer.

Fermín rolled his eyes.

'Daniel, this obsession of yours is beginning to get out of hand. I wish I hadn't told you all that . . . Are you all right? Let's have a look at your hand . . .'

I showed him my fist.

'For God's sake.'

'How did you know . . . ?'

'Because I know you as if I'd given birth to you, even if there are days when I almost regret I do,' he said furiously.

'I don't know what came over me . . .'

'Well, I know exactly what came over you. And I don't like it. I don't like it one bit. That's not the Daniel I know. And it's not the Daniel I want for a friend.'

My hand was hurting, but to know I'd disappointed Fermín hurt far more.

'Fermín, please don't get angry with me.'

'Oh, excuse me! Maybe you just want me to hand you a medal . . .'

For a while we didn't speak, each looking out on his side of the street.

'Thank God you came,' I said at last.

'Did you think I was going to leave you on your own?'

'You won't tell Bea, will you?'

'Sure, and then I'll write a letter to the editor of *La Vanguardia* setting out your exploits so everybody can rejoice in your bravery.'

'I don't know what I was thinking . . .'

He looked at me severely but finally relaxed his expression and patted my hand. I swallowed my pain.

'Let's not go on about it. I suppose I would have done the same.'

I gazed at Barcelona marching past the windows.

'What was the card?'

'What?'

'The police ID card you showed . . . What was it?'

'The parish priest's Barcelona Football Club card. Expired.'

'You were right, Fermín. I've been a fool to suspect Bea.'

'I'm always right. I was born like that.'

I had to bow to the evidence and keep my mouth shut. I'd already said enough stupid things for one day. Fermín had gone very quiet and seemed preoccupied. It troubled me to think I'd caused him such disappointment that he didn't know what to say to me.

'What's on your mind, Fermín?'

He turned, looking concerned.

'I was thinking about that man.'

'Cascos?'

'No. Valls. About what that idiot said earlier. About its significance.'

'What do you mean?'

Fermín's face was grim.

'I mean that what worried me before was that you wanted to find Valls.'

'And now it doesn't?'

'There's something that worries me more, Daniel.'

244

'What?'

'That he may be the one looking for you.'

We stared at each other.

'Have you any idea why?' I asked.

Fermín, who always had a reply for everything, slowly shook his head and looked away.

We spent the rest of the journey in silence. When I got home I went straight up to the flat, took a long hot shower and swallowed four aspirins. Then I lowered the blinds and, hugging a pillow that smelled of Bea, fell asleep like the idiot I was, wondering where she was – that woman for whom I didn't mind having made such a huge fool of myself.

# 13

'I LOOK LIKE A HEDGEHOG,' DECLARED BERNARDA, STARING at her hundredfold image reflected in the mirrored room of Modas Santa Eulalia.

Kneeling down at her feet, two seamstresses went on marking the bridal dress with dozens of pins, watched closely by Bea, who walked in circles round Bernarda inspecting every pleat and every seam as if her life depended on it. Bernarda, standing with arms outstretched in the hexagonal fitting room, hardly dared breathe, but her eyes were riveted on the different angles of her figure as she searched for signs of swelling around her belly.

'Are you sure it's not noticeable, Señora Bea?'

'Not a bit. Flat as a pancake. Where you should be, of course.'

'Oh, I don't know, I don't know . . .'

Bernarda's ordeal and the seamstresses' efforts to adjust and tailor continued for another half-hour. When there didn't seem to be any pins left in the world with which to skewer poor Bernarda, the firm's star couturier and creator of the dress drew the curtain aside and made an appearance. After a quick survey and a few corrections on the lining of the skirt, he gave his approval and snapped his fingers at his assistants, ordering them to make themselves scarce.

'Not even Balenciaga could have made you look so beautiful,' he concluded happily.

Bea smiled and nodded.

The couturier, a slender gentleman with affected manners and theatrical gestures who went simply by the name of Evaristo, kissed Bernarda on the cheek.

'You're the best model in the world. The most patient and long-suffering. It has been hard work, but well worth it.'

'And do you think, sir, that I'll be able to breathe in this dress?'

'My darling, you're marrying an Iberian macho buck in the Holy Mother Church. Your breathing days are over, believe me. Anyhow, a wedding dress is like a diving bell: it's not ideal for breathing. The fun begins when they take it off you.'

Bernarda crossed herself at the couturier's insinuations.

'What I'm going to ask you to do now is remove the dress with the greatest care. The seams are loose and with all those pins I wouldn't like to see you walking up to the altar looking like a colander,' said Evaristo.

'I'll help her,' said Bea.

Casting a meaningful look at Bea, Evaristo inspected her from head to toe.

'And when am I going to be able to dress and undress *you*, my love?' he asked, flouncing off through the curtain.

'What a look the rascal gave you!' said Bernarda. 'I didn't think he was into female company, if you get my meaning.'

'I think Evaristo keeps all sorts of company, Bernarda.'

'Is that possible?' she asked.

'Come on, let's try to get you out of this without dropping a single pin.'

While Bea freed Bernarda from her captivity, the maid swore under her breath.

Ever since she'd found out the price of that dress, which her employer, Don Gustavo, had insisted on paying out of his own pocket, Bernarda had been in a terrible state.

'Don Gustavo should never have spent such a bundle. He insisted that it had to be here, the most expensive shop in Barcelona I'm sure, and on hiring this guy Evaristo, who is a halfnephew of his or something like that. Apparently Evaristo says that any fabric that isn't from Casa Gratacós gives one a rash. And they're so pricey!'

'Don't look a gift horse in the mouth . . . Besides, Don Gustavo is thrilled that you'll be getting married in style. He's like that. You're the daughter he never had.'

'I'm his maid, and I would have been quite happy wearing my mother's wedding dress, with a couple of alterations, and Fermín doesn't care. Every time I show him a new dress all he wants to do is take it off me . . . And look what that's led to, may God forgive me,' said Bernarda, patting her belly.

'Bernarda, I was also pregnant when I got married and I'm sure God has far more pressing things to worry about.'

'That's what my Fermín says, but I don't know . . .'

'You listen to Fermín and don't worry about anything.'

In her slip, and exhausted after standing for two hours in high heels with her arms stretched out, Bernarda fell into an armchair and sighed.

'Poor thing, he's lost so much weight, he's as thin as a rake. I'm really worried about him.'

'You'll see how he gets better from now on. Men are like that. They're like geraniums. When they look as if they're ready to be tossed into the bin, they revive.'

'I don't know, Señora Bea. Fermín seems very depressed to me. He tells me he wants to get married, but I have my doubts.'

'Come on, he's crazy about you, Bernarda.'

Bernarda shrugged.

'Look, I'm not as stupid as I seem. Since I was thirteen all I've done is clean houses and I may not understand a lot of things, but I know that my Fermín has seen the world and he's had his share of adventures. He never tells me anything about his life before we met, but I know he's had other women and he's been round the block a few times.'

'And he's ended up choosing you out of them all. So there.'

'I know. But you know what I'm afraid of, Señora Bea? That

248

I'm not good enough for him. When I see him looking at me spellbound and he tells me he wants us to grow old together and all that sweet-talk he comes up with, I always think that one morning he'll wake up and look at me and he'll say: "Where on earth did I find this dimwit?"'

'I think you're wrong, Bernarda. Fermín will never think that. He has you on a pedestal.'

'Well, that's not a good thing either. I've seen a lot of gentlemen, the sort who put their wives on pedestals as if they were the Virgin Mary, who then run after the first pretty young thing they see passing by, like dogs after a bitch on heat. You wouldn't believe the times I've seen that with these little eyes God gave me.'

'But Fermín isn't like that, Bernarda. Fermín is one of the good ones. One of the few. Men are like chestnuts they sell in the street: they're all hot and they all smell good when you buy them, but when you take them out of the paper cone you realise that most of them are rotten inside.'

'You're not saying that because of Señor Daniel, are you?'

Bea took a while to reply.

'No. Of course not.'

Bernarda glanced at her.

'Everything all right at home, Señora Bea?'

Bea fiddled with a pleat on the shoulder strap of Bernarda's slip.

'Yes, Bernarda. The trouble is that I think we've both gone and got ourselves husbands who have a secret or two.'

Bernarda nodded.

'Sometimes they're like children.'

'Men. What do you expect?'

'But the thing is, I like them,' said Bernarda. 'And I know that's a sin.'

Bea laughed.

'And how do you like them? Like Evaristo?'

'No, good heavens, no. If he keeps looking at himself in the mirror he'll wear it out! A man who takes longer than me to get smartened up gives me the creeps. I like them a bit rougher, I'm afraid. I know my Fermín isn't exactly what you'd call handsome. But he is to me – handsome and good. And very manly. In the end, I think that's what matters, that he's truly a good person and that he's real. That he's someone you can hold on to on a cold winter's night and who knows how to make you feel warm inside.'

Bea smiled in assent.

'Amen. Although a birdie told me the one you liked was Cary Grant.'

Bernarda blushed.

'Don't you? Not to marry, of course. I'd say he fell in love the first time he looked at himself in the mirror. But between you and me, and may God forgive me, I wouldn't say no to a good squeeze from him . . .'

'What would Fermín say if he heard you, Bernarda?'

'What he always says. "After all, we're all going to get eaten up by worms in the end . . ."'

Part Five

*The Name of the Hero*

# 1

*Barcelona, 1958*

MANY YEARS LATER, THE TWENTY-THREE GUESTS GATHERED there to celebrate the occasion would look back and remember the historic eve of the day when Fermín Romero de Torres abandoned his bachelorhood.

'It's the end of an era,' proclaimed Professor Alburquerque, raising his glass of champagne in a toast, voicing better than anyone what we were all feeling.

Fermín's stag night, an event whose effects on the global female population Gustavo Barceló compared to the death of Rudolf Valentino, took place on a clear February night of 1958. The venue was the magnificent dance hall of La Paloma, where the groom had in the past performed some heart-rending tangos, attaining moments that would now enter the secret dossier of a distinguished career at the service of the eternal female. My father, who for once in his life had been persuaded to leave home, had secured the services of a semi-professional dance band, La Habana del Baix Llobregat, who agreed to play for a knockdown price a selection of Fermín's favourite fare: mambos, *guarachas* and *sones montunos* that transported the groom to his faraway days of intrigue and international glamour in the great gaming salons of a forgotten Cuba. Everyone, to a greater or lesser degree, let their hair down, throwing themselves on to the dance floor to shake a leg in Fermín's honour.

Barceló had convinced my father that the glasses of vodka he kept handing him were mineral water with a few drops of anisette, and soon we were all able to witness an unprecedented sight: Señor Sempere dancing cheek-to-cheek with one of the easy ladies brought along by Rociíto – the true life and soul of the party – to brighten up the event.

'Dear God,' I murmured as I watched my father with that veteran madam of the night, swaying his hips and bumping his backside against hers in time to the beat.

Barceló circulated among the guests, handing out cigars and the little cards he'd had printed to commemorate the occasion, at a firm specialising in mementoes for first communions, christenings and funerals. The fine paper card depicted a caricature of Fermín dressed up as an angel, his hands together as in prayer, with the following message:

FERMÍN ROMERO DE TORRES

*19??–1958*

*The great lover retires*

*1958–19??*

*The paterfamilias arises*

For the first time in ages, Fermín was happy and calm. Half an hour before the start of the bash I'd taken him along to Can Lluís, where Professor Alburquerque certified that he'd been at the Civil Registry that very morning, armed with the entire dossier of documents and papers masterfully produced by Oswaldo Darío de Mortenssen and his assistant, Luisito.

'Dear Fermín,' the professor announced. 'Allow me to welcome you officially to the world of the living. With our friends from Can Lluís as witnesses, Don Daniel Sempere and I hereby present you with a brand-new you, which comes with this fresh and legitimate identity card.'

An emotional Fermín examined his new documentation.

'How did you manage such a miracle?'

'We'll spare you the technicalities,' said the professor. 'What really matters is that when you have a true friend who is ready to take the risk and move heaven and earth so that you can get married with everything in order and start bringing offspring into the world to continue the Romero de Torres line, almost anything is possible, Fermín.'

Fermín looked at me with tears in his eyes and hugged me so tight I thought I was going to suffocate. I'm not ashamed to admit that it was one of the happiest moments in my life.

# 2

HALF AN HOUR OF MUSIC, DRINKS AND NAUGHTY DANCING
had gone by when I took a breather and walked over to the
bar to ask for something non-alcoholic. I didn't think I could
swallow another drop of rum and lemon, the evening's official beverage. The waiter served me a glass of cold sparkling
water and I leaned my back against the bar to take in the fun. I
hadn't noticed that Rociíto was standing at the other end. She
was holding a glass of champagne, watching the party she had
organised with a melancholy expression. From what Fermín
had told me, I worked out that Rociíto must be close to her
thirty-fifth birthday, but almost twenty years in the profession
had taken their toll and even in the multicoloured half-light the
crowned queen of Calle Escudellers appeared older.

I went up to her and smiled.

'Rociíto, you're looking more beautiful than ever,' I lied.

She was wearing her smartest clothes and her hair showed
the stunning handiwork of the best hairdresser in the Raval, but
what really struck me was how sad she looked that night.

'Are you all right, Rociíto?'

'Look at 'im, poor thing. All skin and bone, and he's still in
the mood for dancing. He always was a great dancer.'

Her eyes were glued to Fermín and I knew that she would
always see in him the champion who had saved her from that
small-time pimp. After her twenty years of working the streets,
he was probably one of the few worthwhile men she'd met.

'Don Daniel, I didn't want to say anything to Fermín, but I won't be going to the wedding tomorrow.'

'What are you saying, Rociíto? Fermín had saved you a place of honour . . .'

Rociíto lowered her eyes.

'I know, but I can't be there.'

'Why?' I asked, although I could guess what the reply would be.

'Because it would make me really sad, and I want Señorito Fermín to be happy with his missus.'

Rociíto had started to cry. I didn't know what to say, so I hugged her.

'I've always loved him, you know? Ever since we met. I know I'm not the right woman for him. I know he sees me as . . . well, he sees me as Rociíto.'

'Fermín loves you very much, you must never forget that.'

The woman moved away and dried her tears in embarrassment. She smiled and shrugged her shoulders.

'Forgive me. You see, I'm so stupid: soon as I drink a couple of drops I don't even know what I'm saying.'

'That's all right.'

I offered her my glass of water and she accepted it.

'One day you realise your youth has passed you by and the train's left, if you see what I mean.'

'There's always another train. Always.'

Rociíto nodded.

'That's why I'm not going to the wedding, Don Daniel. Some months ago I met this gentleman from Reus. He's a good man. A widower. A good father. Owns a scrapyard, and whenever he's in Barcelona he comes to see me. He's asked me to marry him. We're not kidding ourselves, not him or me, you know? Growing old on your own is very hard, and I know I don't have the figure to be on the street any more. Jaumet, the man from Reus, he's asked me to go on a journey with him. His children have already left home and he's been working all his life. He says he wants to see a bit of the world before it's too late, and he's asked me to go with him. As his wife, not a tart you use and then chuck out. The boat leaves tomorrow morning early. Jaumet says a captain can marry a couple on the high seas and if not, we'll look for a priest in any old port.'

'Does Fermín know?'

As if he'd heard us from afar, Fermín stopped bopping about on the dance floor and looked at us. He stretched his arms out towards Rociíto and gave her that silly look of someone in urgent need of a kiss and a cuddle that had always served him so well. Rociíto laughed, muttering under her breath, and before joining the love of her life on the dance floor for a last bolero, she turned to me and said:

'Take good care of him, Daniel. There's only one Fermín.'

The band had stopped playing and the dance floor opened up to receive Rociíto. Fermín took her hands. The lamps in La Paloma were slowly dimmed and from among the shadows the beam from a spotlight cast a hazy circle of light at the couple's feet. The others drew aside and the orchestra gently struck up the slow rhythms of the saddest bolero ever written. Fermín put his arm round Rociíto's waist. Looking into each other's eyes, far from the world, the lovers of that Barcelona that would never return danced close together for the last time. When the music died away Fermín kissed her on the lips and Rociíto, bathed in tears, stroked his cheek, then walked slowly towards the exit without saying goodbye.

# 3

THE ORCHESTRA CAME TO THE RESCUE WITH A *GUARACHA* and Oswaldo Darío de Mortenssen, who from writing so many love letters had become an encyclopedia of sad tales, encouraged everyone to return to the dance floor and pretend they hadn't noticed anything. Looking somewhat crestfallen, Fermín walked over to the bar and sat on a stool next to me.

'Everything all right, Fermín?'

He nodded weakly.

'I think a bit of fresh air would do me good, Daniel.'

'Wait here for me, I'll get our coats.'

We were walking down Calle Tallers towards the Ramblas when, about fifty metres ahead of us, we glimpsed a familiar-looking figure, moving along slowly.

'Hey, Daniel. Isn't that your father?'

'The very one. And he's soused.'

'The last thing I ever expected to see in this world,' said Fermín.

'If you didn't expect it, imagine me!'

We quickened our pace until we caught up with him and when he saw us, my father smiled, glassy-eyed.

'What's the time?' he asked.

'Very late.'

'That's just what I thought. Hey Fermín, what a great party. And what girls. There were some bums in there worth going to war for.'

I rolled my eyes. Fermín took my father's arm and guided his steps.

'Señor Sempere, I never thought I'd have to say this, but you're suffering from alcohol poisoning and you'd better not say anything that you might later regret.'

My father nodded, suddenly embarrassed.

'It's that devil, Barceló. I don't know what he's given me, and as I'm not used to drinking . . .'

'Never mind. Just take a glass of bicarbonate of soda and sleep it off. Tomorrow morning you'll be as fresh as a daisy and no damage done.'

'I think I'm going to be sick.'

Between us, we held him upright while the poor man threw up everything he'd drunk. I held his sweat-drenched forehead with my hand and when we were sure there was nothing left inside him, not even his first plate of baby food, we settled him for a moment on the steps of someone's front door.

'Take a deep, slow breath, Señor Sempere.'

My father nodded with his eyes shut. Fermín and I exchanged glances.

'Listen, weren't you going to get married soon?'

'Tomorrow afternoon.'

'Hey, congratulations!'

'Thank you, Señor Sempere. So, what do you say? Do you think we can make it home bit by bit?'

My father nodded.

'There's a brave man, we're almost there.'

A cool, dry wind helped clear my father's head. By the time we walked up Calle Santa Ana ten minutes later, he'd sized up the situation and the poor man was mortified with embarrassment. He'd probably never been drunk before in his life.

'Please, not a word about this to anyone,' he pleaded.

WE WERE ABOUT TWENTY metres away from the bookshop when I noticed someone sitting in the main doorway of the

260

building. The large street lamp from Casa Jorba, on the corner with Puerta del Ángel, outlined the silhouette of a young girl clutching a suitcase on her knees. When she saw us she stood up.

'We have company,' murmured Fermín.

My father saw her first. I noticed something strange in his expression, a tense calm that gripped him as if he'd suddenly recovered his sobriety. He advanced towards the girl but suddenly stood petrified.

'Isabella?' I heard him say.

Fearing the drink was still clouding his judgement and that he might collapse then and there, in the middle of the street, I took a few steps forward. Then I saw her.

# 4

SHE CAN'T HAVE BEEN MORE THAN SEVENTEEN. AS SHE emerged into the light cast by the street lamp, she smiled timidly at us, lifting a hand as if in greeting.

'I'm Sofía,' she said, with a light accent.

My father stared at her in astonishment, as if he'd seen a ghost. I gulped, feeling a shiver run through my body. That girl was the spitting image of my mother: she had the same face that appeared in the set of photographs my father kept in his desk.

'I'm Sofía,' the girl repeated, looking uncomfortable. 'Your niece. From Naples . . .'

'Sofía,' stammered my father. 'Ah, Sofía.'

Thank God Fermín was there to take hold of the situation. After bringing me to my senses with a slap on the wrist, he explained that Señor Sempere was feeling a little under the weather.

'You see, we're just back from a wine-tasting event, and it only takes a glass of Vichy water to put the poor man in a trance. Pay no attention to him, *signorina,* he doesn't usually look so plastered.'

We found the urgent telegram sent by Aunt Laura, the girl's mother, announcing her arrival. It had been slipped under the door while we were out.

Up in the flat, Fermín settled my father on the sofa and ordered me to prepare a pot of strong coffee. In the meantime, he engaged in conversation with the girl, asking her about her trip and bringing up all manner of banalities while my father slowly came back to life.

With her delightful accent and her vivacious air, Sofía told us she'd arrived at the Estación de Francia that night at half past ten. From the station she had taken a taxi to Plaza de Cataluña. When she discovered there was no one at home, she'd sheltered in a nearby bar until they closed. Then she'd sat down to wait in the doorway, trusting that someone would turn up sooner or later. My father remembered the letter from her mother telling him that Sofía was coming to Barcelona, but he hadn't imagined it was going to be so soon.

'I'm very sorry you had to wait in the street,' he said. 'Normally, I never go out, but tonight was Fermín's bachelor party and . . .'

Delighted with the piece of news, Sofía jumped up and congratulated Fermín with a peck on the cheek. And although he had now retired from active duty, Fermín couldn't restrain himself and invited her to the wedding on the spot.

We'd been chatting away for about half an hour when Bea, who was returning from Bernarda's own hen party, heard voices on her way up the stairs and rang the doorbell. When she stepped into the dining room and saw Sofía, she went pale and glanced at me.

'This is my cousin Sofía, from Naples,' I announced. 'She's come to Barcelona to study and she's going to stay here for a while . . .'

Bea tried to conceal her alarm and greeted her with absolute normality.

'This is my wife, Beatriz.'

'Bea, please. Nobody calls me Beatriz.'

Time and coffee slowly softened the impact of Sofía's arrival and after a bit, Bea suggested that the poor soul must be exhausted and had better get some sleep. Tomorrow would be another day, she said, even if it was a wedding day. It was decided that Sofía would move into the room that had been my bedroom when I was a child and, after making sure my father wasn't going to fall into a coma again, Fermín packed him off to bed too. Bea told Sofía she would lend her one of her dresses for the ceremony and when Fermín, whose breath smelled of champagne from two metres off, was on the point of making some inappropriate remark on the similarities and differences between their shapes and sizes, I gave him a jab in the ribs with my elbow to shut him up.

A PHOTOGRAPH OF MY parents on their wedding day observed us from a shelf.

The three of us sat there, in the dining room, gaping at it in disbelief.

'Like two peas in a pod,' murmured Fermín.

Bea looked at me out of the corner of her eye, trying to read my thoughts. She took my hand with a cheerful expression, ready to change the subject.

'So tell me, how was the celebration?'

'Dignified and restrained. How was the ladies' party?'

'Ours was anything but that.'

Fermín threw me a serious look.

'I told you that when it comes to such matters women are far more loutish than us.'

Bea gave us a quizzical smile.

'Who are you calling loutish, Fermín?'

'Forgive this unpardonable slip, Doña Beatriz. It's the bubbly in my bloodstream that's making me talk nonsense. I swear to God that you're a model of virtue and decorum and this humble servant of yours would rather be struck dumb and spend the rest of his days in a Carthusian cell in silent penitence than insinuate that you possess the remotest hint of loutishness.'

'No such luck,' I remarked.

'We'd better not discuss this any further,' Bea cut in, looking at us as if we were both eleven years old. 'And now I suppose you're going to take your customary pre-wedding walk down to the breakwater,' she said.

Fermín and I looked at one another.

'Go on. Off you go. And you'd better make it to the church on time tomorrow . . .'

# 5

THE ONLY PLACE WE FOUND OPEN AT THAT TIME OF NIGHT was El Xampanyet, on Calle Montcada. They must have felt sorry for us because they let us stay for a bit while they cleaned up, and when they closed, hearing that Fermín was hours away from becoming a married man, the owner expressed his condolences and presented us with a bottle of house medicine.

'Be brave, and may God be with you,' he pronounced.

We wandered through the narrow streets of the Ribera quarter, putting the world to rights, as we usually did, until the sky took on a purple hue and we knew the time had come for the groom and his best man – in other words, me – to head for the breakwater. There we would sit once again to greet the dawn facing the greatest mirage in the universe: the reflection of Barcelona awakening in the harbour waters.

WE SAT THERE WITH our legs dangling over the jetty to share the bottle we'd been given at El Xampanyet. Between one gulp and the next, we gazed silently at the city, tracing the flight of a flock of seagulls over the dome of La Mercé Church and watching them draw an arc between the towers of the Post Office building. In the distance, crowning the mountain of Montjuïc, the castle loomed darkly, a ghostly bird of prey scrutinising the city at its feet, expectant.

The silence was broken by a ship's horn. On the other side of the National Dock a large cruiser was weighing anchor. Pulling away from the pier, it set sail with a surge of the propellers, leaving a wide wake behind it on the waters of the port. Dozens of passengers came out to wave from the stern. I wondered whether Rociíto was among them, next to her mature, handsome scrap merchant from Reus. Fermín watched the ship, deep in thought.

'Do you think Rociíto will be happy, Daniel?'

'What about you, Fermín? Will you be happy?'

We saw the cruiser move into the distance and the figures grow smaller until they became invisible.

'Fermín, there's one thing that intrigues me. Why didn't you want anyone to give you wedding presents?'

'I don't like to put people in a tight spot. And besides, what were we going to do with sets of glasses, teaspoons with the Spanish shield and all that kind of stuff people give at weddings?'

'Well, I was looking forward to giving you a present.'

'You've already given me the biggest present anyone could give me, Daniel.'

'That doesn't count. I'm talking about a present for personal use and enjoyment.'

Fermín looked intrigued.

'Don't tell me it's a porcelain Madonna or a figurine of Saint Teresa. Bernarda has such an ample collection already that I don't know where we're going to find room to sit down.'

'Don't worry. It's not an object.'

'Don't tell me it's money . . .'

'As you know, I don't have a *céntimo*, unfortunately. The one with the funds is my father-in-law, and he doesn't splash it about.'

'These new Francoists are as tight as two coats of paint.'

'My father-in-law is a good man, Fermín. Don't have a go at him.'

'Let's draw a line under the matter, but don't change the subject now you've put the sweet in my mouth. What present?'

'Guess.'

'A batch of Sugus sweets.'

'Cold, cold . . .'

Fermín arched his eyebrows, dying with curiosity. Suddenly, his eyes lit up.

'No . . . It was about time.'

I nodded.

'There's a time for everything. Now, listen carefully. You mustn't tell anyone what you're about to see today, Fermín. No one . . .'

'Not even Bernarda?'

# 6

THE FIRST LIGHT OF THE DAY SPILLED LIKE LIQUID COPPER over the cornices of Rambla de Santa Mónica. It was a Sunday morning and the streets were quiet and deserted. When we entered the narrow alleyway of Calle Arco del Teatro, the ghostly beam of light penetrating from the Ramblas dimmed and by the time we reached the large wooden door we had become submerged in a city of shadows.

I climbed the steps and rapped with the knocker a few times. The echo trailed off inside, like ripples on a pond. Fermín, who had assumed a respectful silence and looked like a boy on his first day of school, turned to me anxiously.

'Isn't it rather early to call?' he asked. 'I hope the chief doesn't get annoyed . . .'

'This isn't a department store. There are no opening times,' I reassured him. 'And here the chief is called Isaac. Don't speak unless he asks you something first.'

Fermín nodded compliantly.

'Not a peep.'

A couple of minutes later I heard the dance of cogs, pulleys and levers operating the lock and I stepped down again. The door opened just a fraction and the vulturine face of Isaac Montfort, the keeper, peered round with its usual steely look. The keeper's eyes alighted first on me and, after a quick glance at Fermín, proceeded to X-ray, catalogue and examine him from head to toe.

'This must be the illustrious Fermín Romero de Torres,' he murmured.

'At your service, and God's and . . .'

I silenced Fermín with a nudge and smiled at the severe keeper.

'Good morning, Isaac.'

'A good morning, Sempere, will be one when you don't call at dawn, or while I'm in the toilet, or on a religious holiday,' replied Isaac. 'Come on, in with you.'

The keeper opened the door a bit further and we slid through. When the door closed behind us, Isaac retrieved his oil lamp from the floor and Fermín was able to observe the elaborate movements of the lock as it folded back upon itself like the insides of the biggest clock in the world.

'A burglar could age like a good Camembert trying to prise this one open,' he let slip.

I threw him a warning glance and he quickly put a finger to his lips.

'Collection or delivery?' asked Isaac.

'Well, you see, I've been meaning to bring Fermín here for ages so he could get to know the place first-hand. I've often talked to him about it. He's my best friend, and he's getting married today, at noon,' I explained.

'Gracious,' said Isaac. 'Poor thing. Are you sure you wouldn't like me to offer you nuptial asylum here?'

'Fermín is quite convinced about getting married, Isaac.'

The keeper looked Fermín up and down. Fermín smiled apologetically.

'What courage.'

Isaac guided us along the wide corridor to the entrance of the gallery leading into the large hall. I let Fermín walk ahead of me so that he could discover with his own eyes a vision that no words could describe.

*

His TINY FIGURE WAS engulfed by the great beam of light pouring down from the glass dome in the ceiling. Brightness fell in a vaporous cascade over the sprawling labyrinth of corridors, tunnels, staircases, arches and vaults that seemed to spring from the floor like the trunk of an endless tree of books and branched heavenwards displaying an impossible geometry. Fermín stepped on to a gangway extending like a bridge into the base of the structure. He gazed at the sight, open-mouthed. I drew up to him and put a hand on his shoulder.

'Welcome to the Cemetery of Forgotten Books, Fermín.'

# 7

IN MY EXPERIENCE, WHENEVER SOMEONE DISCOVERED that place, their reaction was always one of bewitchment and amazement. The beauty and the mystery of the premises reduced the visitor to a silent, dream-like contemplation. Naturally, Fermín had to be different. He spent the first half-hour hypnotised, wandering like a man possessed through every nook and cranny of the large jigsaw formed by the winding labyrinth. He stopped to rap his knuckles against flying buttresses and columns, as if he doubted their solidity. He stood at different angles and perspectives, forming a spyglass with his hands and trying to decipher the logic of the construction. He walked through the spiral of libraries with his large nose almost touching the infinite rows of spines running along endless pathways, making a mental note of titles and cataloguing whatever he discovered on his way. I followed a few steps behind him, with a mixture of alarm and anxiety.

I was beginning to suspect that Isaac was going to kick us out of there when I bumped into the keeper on one of the bridges suspended between book-lined vaults. To my surprise, not only did he show no sign of irritation but he was smiling good-humouredly as he watched Fermín's progress during his first exploration of the Cemetery of Forgotten Books.

'Your friend is a rather peculiar specimen,' Isaac reckoned.

'You haven't scratched the surface yet.'

'Don't worry about him, leave him alone. He'll come down from his cloud eventually.'

'What if he gets lost?'

'He seems to be on the ball. He'll work it out.'

I wasn't so sure, but I didn't want to contradict Isaac. I walked with him to the room that doubled as his office and accepted the cup of coffee he was offering me.

'Have you explained the rules to your friend?'

'Fermín and rules are incompatible notions. But I have summed up the basics and he replied with a convincing: "But of course, who do you take me for?"'

While Isaac filled my cup again he caught me gazing at a photograph of his daughter Nuria hanging above his desk.

'It will soon be two years since she left us,' he said with a sadness that cut through the air.

I looked down, distressed. A hundred years could go by and the death of Nuria Montfort would still be on my mind, as would the certainty that if I'd never met her she might still be alive. Isaac caressed the photograph with his eyes.

'I'm getting old, Sempere. It's about time someone took my post.'

I was about to protest at such a suggestion when Fermín walked in with his face all flushed, and panting as if he'd just run a marathon.

'So?' asked Isaac. 'What do you think?'

'Glorious. Although it doesn't appear to have a toilet. At least not that I noticed.'

'I hope you didn't pee in some corner.'

'I made a superhuman effort to hold it in and make it back here.'

'It's that door on the left. You'll have to pull the chain twice, the first time it never works.'

While Fermín relieved himself, Isaac poured out a cup of coffee which awaited him steaming hot when he returned.

'I have a few questions I'd like to ask you, Don Isaac.'

'Fermín, I don't think . . .' I pleaded.

'It's fine. Go ahead, ask.'

'The first lot is related to the history of the premises. The second one concerns technical and architectural works. And the third is basically bibliographic . . .'

Isaac laughed. It was the first time I'd ever heard him laugh, and I didn't know whether to take it as a sign from heaven or the presage of some imminent disaster.

'First you'll have to choose the book you want to save,' Isaac proposed.

'I've had my eye on a few, but even if it's just for sentimental reasons, I've selected this one, if that's all right.'

He pulled a book out of his pocket. It was bound in red leather, with the title embossed in gold letters and an engraving of a skull on the title page.

'Well I never: *City of the Damned, episode thirteen: Daphne and the impossible staircase*, by David Martín,' Isaac read.

'An old friend,' Fermín explained.

'You don't say. Strangely enough, there was a time when I'd often see him around here,' said Isaac.

'That must have been before the war,' I remarked.

'No, no . . . I saw him some time later.'

Fermín and I looked at one another. I wondered whether Isaac had been right, and he was beginning to get too old for the job.

'I don't wish to contradict you, chief, but that's impossible,' said Fermín.

'Impossible? You'll have to make yourself a bit clearer . . .'

'David Martín fled the country before the war,' I explained. 'At the start of 1939, towards the end of the conflict, he came back, crossing over the Pyrenees, and was arrested in Puigcerdà a few days later. He was held in prison until well into 1941, when he was most probably murdered.'

Isaac was staring at us in disbelief.

'You must believe him, chief,' Fermín assured him. 'Our sources are reliable.'

'I can assure you that David Martín sat in that same chair you're sitting in, Sempere, and we chatted for a while.'

'Are you quite sure, Isaac?'

'I've never been more certain of anything in all my life,' replied the keeper. 'I remember because I hadn't seen him for years. He was in a bad way and looked ill.'

'Can you remember the date when he came?'

'Perfectly. It was the last night of 1941. New Year's Eve. That was the last time I saw him.'

Fermín and I were lost in our calculations.

'That means that what that jailer, Bebo, told Brians, was true,' I said. 'The night Valls ordered him to be taken to the old mansion near Güell Park to be killed . . . Bebo said he later overheard the gunmen saying that something had happened there, that there was someone else in the house . . . Maybe someone prevented Martín from being killed . . .' I speculated.

Isaac was listening to these musings with concern.

'What are you talking about? Who wanted to murder Martín?'

'It's a long story,' said Fermín. 'With tons of footnotes.'

'Well, I hope to hear it one day . . .'

'Did you think Martín was in his right mind, Isaac?' I asked. Isaac shrugged.

'One never knew with Martín . . . That man had a tormented soul. When he left I asked him to let me walk him as far as the train, but he told me there was a car waiting for him outside.'

'A car?'

'A Mercedes-Benz, no less. Belonging to someone he called the Boss and who, from what he said, was waiting for him by the front door. But when I went out with him there was no car, no boss, there was nothing at all . . .'

'Don't take this the wrong way, chief, but what with it being New Year's Eve, and with the festive spirit of the occasion, couldn't it be that you'd overdone it on the bubbly and, dazed by Christmas carols and the high sugar content of Jijona nougat, you might have imagined all this?' asked Fermín.

'As far as the bubbly is concerned, I only drink fizzy lemonade, and the strongest thing I have here is a bottle of hydrogen per-oxide,' Isaac specified. He didn't seem offended.

'Forgive me for doubting you. It was a mere formality.'

'I understand. But believe me when I say that unless whoever came that night was a ghost, and I don't think he was because one of his ears was bleeding and his hands were shaking with fever – and besides, he polished off all the sugar lumps I had in my kitchen cupboard – Martín was as alive as you or me.'

'And he didn't say what he was coming here for, after so long?'

Isaac nodded.

'He said he'd come to leave something with me and that, when he could, he'd come back for it. Either he'd come or he'd send someone . . .'

'And what did he leave with you?'

'A parcel wrapped in paper and bits of string. I don't know what was inside.'

I swallowed hard.

'Do you still have it?'

# 8

THE PARCEL, PULLED OUT FROM THE BACK OF A CUPBOARD, lay on Isaac's desk. When my fingers brushed the paper, the fine layer of dust covering it rose in a cloud of particles that caught the glow of the oil lamp Isaac held on my left. On my right, Fermín unsheathed his paperknife and handed it to me. The three of us looked at one another.

'God's will be done,' said Fermín.

I slipped the knife under the string binding the parcel and cut it. With the greatest care I removed the wrapping until the content became visible. It was a manuscript. The pages were soiled, covered in stains of wax and blood. The first page bore a title written in diabolical handwriting.

*The Angel's Game*
*By David Martín*

'It's the book he wrote while he was imprisoned in the tower,' I murmured, 'Bebo must have saved it.'

'There's something underneath . . .' said Fermín.

The corner of a piece of parchment peeped out from beneath the manuscript. I gave it a tug and retrieved an envelope. It was sealed with red wax, stamped with the figure of an angel. On the front of the envelope was a single word, written in red ink:

*Daniel*

A cold sensation rose up my arms. Isaac, who was witnessing the scene with a mixture of astonishment and consternation, crept out of the room, followed by Fermín.

'Daniel,' Fermín called out gently. 'We're leaving you alone so you can open the envelope calmly and in private . . .'

I heard their footsteps as they slowly walked away and was only able to catch the start of their conversation.

'Listen, chief, with so many emotions I forgot to mention that earlier, when I came in, I couldn't help overhearing you say that you were thinking of retiring and that there might be an opening soon for the position . . .'

'That's right. I've been here too long. Why?'

'Well, you see, I know we've only just met, so to speak, but I might be interested . . .'

THE VOICES OF ISAAC and Fermín melted into the echoing labyrinth of the Cemetery of Forgotten Books. Left on my own, I sat in the keeper's armchair and removed the sealing wax. The envelope contained a folded sheet of ochre-coloured paper. I opened it and began to read.

Barcelona, 31 December 1941

Dear Daniel,

I write these words in the hope and conviction that one day you'll discover this place, the Cemetery of Forgotten Books, a place that changed my life as I'm sure it will change yours. This same hope leads me to believe that perhaps then, when I'm no longer here, someone will talk to you about me and the friendship that linked me to your mother. I know that if you ever read these words you'll be overwhelmed by questions and doubts. You'll find some of the answers in this manuscript, where I have tried to portray my story as I remember it, knowing that my days of lucidity are numbered and that often I can only recall what never took place.

I also know that when you receive this letter, time will have started to wipe out the traces of those events. I know you will harbour suspicions and that if you discover the truth about your mother's final days you will share my anger and my thirst for revenge. They say it's for the wise and the righteous to forgive, but I know I'll never be able to do so. My soul is already condemned and has no hope of salvation. I know I will devote every drop of breath left in me to try to avenge the death of Isabella. But that is my destiny, not yours.

Your mother would not have wished for you a life like mine, at any price. Your mother would have wished you to have a full life, devoid of hatred and resentment. For her sake, I beg you to read this story and once you have read it, destroy it. Forget everything you might have heard about a past that no longer exists, clean your heart of anger and live the life your mother wanted to give you, always looking ahead.

And if one day, kneeling at her graveside, you feel the fire of anger trying to take hold of you, remember that in my story, as in yours, there was an angel who holds all the answers.

Your friend,
DAVID MARTÍN

Over and over again I read the words David Martín was sending me through time, words that seemed to me suffused with repentance and madness, words I didn't fully understand. I held the letter in my hand for a few more moments and then placed it in the flame of the oil lamp and watched it burn.

I FOUND FERMÍN AND Isaac standing at the foot of the laby-rinth, chatting like old friends. When they saw me their voices hushed and they looked at me expectantly.

'Whatever that letter said only concerns you, Daniel. You don't have to tell us anything.'

I nodded. The echo of church bells resounded faintly through the walls. Isaac looked at us and checked his watch.

'Listen, weren't you two going to a wedding today?'

# 9

THE BRIDE WAS DRESSED IN WHITE, AND THOUGH SHE WORE no dazzling jewellery or ornaments, in the eyes of her groom no woman, in all of history, had ever looked more beautiful than Bernarda did on that early February day, when the sun lit up the square outside the Church of Santa Ana. Don Gustavo Barceló – who must surely have bought all the flowers in Barcelona, for they flooded the entrance to the church – cried like a baby and the priest, the groom's friend, surprised us all with a lucid sermon that brought tears even to Bea's eyes, who was no soft touch.

I almost dropped the rings, but all was forgotten when the priest, once the preliminaries were over, invited Fermín to kiss the bride. Just then, I turned my head for a second and thought I saw a figure in the back row of the church, a stranger who was looking at me and smiling. I couldn't say why, but for a moment I was certain that the unknown man was none other than the Prisoner of Heaven. But when I looked again, he was no longer there. Next to me, Fermín held Bernarda tight and smacked a kiss right on her lips that unleashed an ovation captained by the priest.

When I saw my friend kissing the woman he loved it occurred to me that this moment, this instant stolen from time and from God, was worth all the days of misery that had brought us to this place and the many others that were doubtless waiting for us on our return to life. And that everything that was decent and clean and pure in this world and everything for which it was worth living and breathing was in those lips, in those hands and in the look of that fortunate couple who, I knew, would be together for the rest of their lives.

# Epilogue
## *1960*

A YOUNG MAN, ALREADY SHOWING A FEW GREY HAIRS, walks in the noon sun amongst the gravestones of the cemetery, beneath a sky melting over the blue of the sea.

In his arms he carries a child who barely understands his words but who smiles when their eyes meet. Together they approach a modest grave, set apart on a balcony overlooking the Mediterranean. The man kneels down in front of the grave and, holding his son, lets him stroke the letters engraved on the stone.

ISABELLA SEMPERE

1917–1939

The man remains there for a while, in silence, his eyelids pressed together to hold his tears.

His son's voice brings him back to the present, and when he opens his eyes again he sees that the boy is pointing at a small figure peeping through the petals of some dried flowers, in the shadow of a glass vase at the foot of the tomb. He is certain that it wasn't there the last time he visited the grave. His hand searches among the flowers and picks up a plaster statuette, so small it fits in his fist. An angel. The words he thought he'd forgotten flare up in his memory like an old wound.

*And if one day, kneeling at her graveside, you feel the fire of anger trying to take hold of you, remember that in my story, as in yours, there was an angel who holds all the answers . . .*

The child tries to clutch the angel figure resting in his father's hand and when he touches it with his fingers he accidentally pushes it. The angel falls on the marble and breaks. And that is when the man sees it. A tiny piece of paper hidden inside the plaster. The paper is fine, almost transparent. He unrolls it and instantly recognises the handwriting:

*Mauricio Valls*
*El Pinar*
*Calle de Manuel Arnús*
*Barcelona*

The sea breeze rises through the gravestones and the breath of a curse caresses his face. He puts the piece of paper in his pocket. Shortly afterwards, he places a white rose on the tombstone and then retraces his steps, carrying the boy in his arms, towards the avenue of cypress trees where the mother of his son is waiting. All three melt into an embrace, and when she looks into his eyes she discovers something that was not in them a few moments ago. Something turbulent and dark that frightens her.

'Are you all right, Daniel?'

He looks at her for a long time and smiles.

'I love you,' he says, and kisses her, knowing that the story, his story, has not ended.

It has only just begun.

THE END

# THE PRISONER OF HEAVEN

*Reading Group Notes*

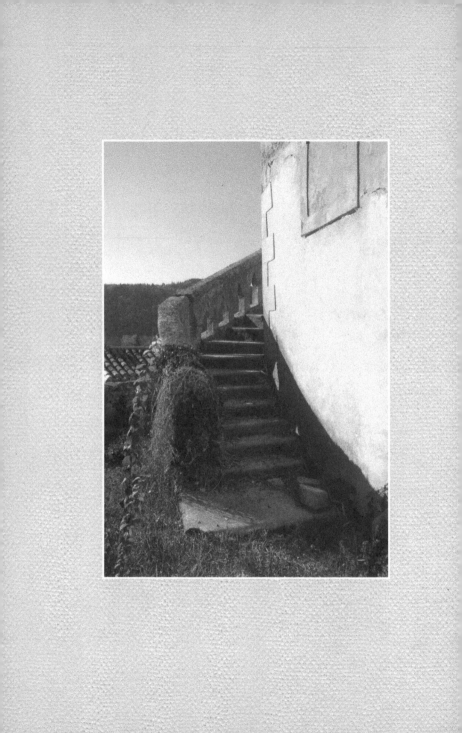

## About the Author

Carlos Ruiz Zafón was born in 1964 in Barcelona and is the author of seven novels, including the international phenomenon *The Shadow of the Wind.* His work has been translated into more than forty languages and has received numerous international awards. His books have sold more than twenty million copies worldwide, and he is the most successful Spanish author since Cervantes. He divides his time between Barcelona and Los Angeles.

The novel's translator, Lucia Graves, is the daughter of the poet Robert Graves.

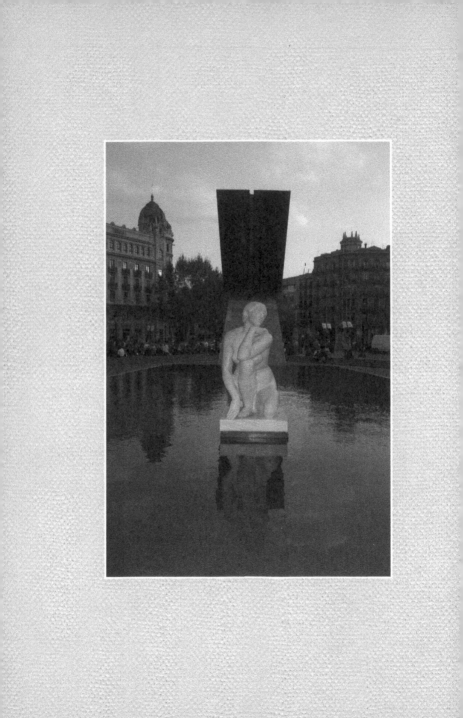

# For Discussion

- If *The Prisoner of Heaven* is your first venture into the Cemetery of Forgotten Books series, how has your experience differed to those who have already read *The Shadow of the Wind* and *The Angel's Game*? Use your discussion to explore your understanding of the various characters who inhabit the world.

- How does the warning in the message from Carax at the start of the novel inform your reading of the subsequent text?

- 'People with a meagre soul always try to make others feel small too.' What is Daniel's rapid judgement of Salgado based upon?

- 'In this world, everything is a fake, young man. Everything except money.' Is there any truth at all in Salgado's words, especially if you take into account what we later learn?

- What techniques does the author use to create the Gothic tone of *The Prisoner of Heaven*? Which classic Gothic novels do you think may have inspired the author?

- 'Everything can be forgiven in this world, save telling the truth.' What do you think of Fermín?

- Daniel has been through much since you first met him. How do you feel about him? Have your feelings changed?

- 'Might it not be that you've seen so much misery and so much evil among men that you want to do something good, even if it's madness?' Is the priest right about Fermín's motives?

- 'There are times and places where not to be anyone is more honourable than to be someone.' What does *The Prisoner of Heaven* say about identity?

- 'Men are like chestnuts they sell in the street: they're all hot and they all smell good when you buy them, but when you take them out of the paper cone you realise that most of them are rotten inside.' Does the plot support this?

- What sense of Franco's Spain do you get from *The Prisoner of Heaven*?

# In Conversation with Carlos Ruiz Zafón

**Which character in *The Prisoner of Heaven* has most of you in them?**

I believe writers tend to split themselves into many of the characters they create. These are your creatures and have a little, or a lot, of you in them. In general when it comes to these stories of the Cemetery of Forgotten Books, the character that I feel resembles me the most is, in the case of *The Prisoner of Heaven*, a temporarily absent one: Julián Carax, the obscure writer whom we met in *The Shadow of the Wind* whose words open the book. Fermín, who is the main lead in *Prisoner*, also has a lot of me, if only because he is a part of my brain articulated as a character and let loose on the page. Daniel has also some of me in him, as does the poor devil David Martín, but I'm afraid I'm much closer to Carax than to any of the others.

**How did you physically write *The Prisoner of Heaven* and why?**

I wrote all of it in my studio in Los Angeles, entirely on the computer and more or less trying to stay put at the desk, or around it. I tend to walk around the room when I am working, talking to myself, roaming around like a caged cat, playing the piano, finding excuses not to write . . . the usual. Writing is essentially rewriting and rewriting everything to death, so

I spend a lot of hours there in the studio trying to make the language work to paint each picture in the reader's mind and generally deploring how lousy my efforts turn out to be. Like most writers, I suppose.

**Are winters 'shadows and ashes' to you?**

It depends. If I am in California, they tend to be more sunshine and electric-blue skies, but to me winters are more of a station of the spirit and sometimes visit you in the middle of the summer or chase you around no matter the time of the year. If I am in Barcelona, winters tend to be more wintery, for some reason. At any rate, I try to avoid winters of discontent and other Shakesperean weather conditions by keeping busy, but I am not always successful. Myself, I am an autumn/fall kind of fellow.

**Silence or music while you write? If music, who do you listen to?**

Both, depending on the day and specific part of a novel I'm working on. The problem with music is that I love it so much that I tend to stop working and start to think about the music, the bass lines, the textures, the orchestration . . . I like almost all kinds of music, but mostly I listen to classical music and jazz. I also listen sometimes to silly little pieces of music I write myself about the characters, the story and the universe of the book I am working on at the moment. These tend to become a sort of musical score to the film in my head and help me sometimes to catch a mood, an atmosphere or an idea.

**'Scars never go away, do they?' Is that your experience?**

Alas, not the ones that really matter, no.

**Which authors do you admire and why?**

How much time and space do you have? I do admire many authors, dead and alive, from the mighty Charles Dickens to the very much alive and kicking Joyce Carol Oates and many, many more. I am terrible at making these kind of lists because unless I was able to include at least 50 names I would feel I wasn't beginning to do justice to the first line of authors whose work I cherish and admire.

**'That's what happens when people reach old age,' said Fermín. 'Nobody remembers they've been bastards too.' Still true?**

I think Fermín is on the money here, as he usually is. Old age likes to inflict many cruelties and indignities to all who reach it, but it also seems to render people into more vulnerable and less threatening versions of themselves, so we tend to forget who they really were and what they did when they didn't appear to

11

be so frail. And maybe that is fair, since we're not the ones to judge them, and life, in all its infinity cruelty, often finds a way to repay the pain we've caused to others.

**What single thing about you would surprise us the most?**

How adorable I am. Knocks people off their socks, really. By the time I say hello you'll want to take me home to meet your mother.

**Does destiny ever make home visits?**

Rarely. These days, it may not even pick up the phone or return your emails either. Maybe destiny just switched to Facebook and Twitter, which may explain its poor judgement and short attention span.

**What's your most vivid memory?**

I have many of those. I have a very strong visual memory. It's like having a little HD camera in my brain that records and replays things in my mind in perfect detail, like small movies. Not always a good thing, but it came with the original equipment. I cannot turn it off.

**Why is the series set when it is?**

I am fascinated by the period between the industrial revolution and the mid twentieth century. I think it is so rich with drama, tragedy, complexity and provides such a fertile field of invention for a writer that I tend to revisit it over and over.

**Any clues about your next book – any snippets for us?**

The fourth and final novel in the Cemetery of Forgotten Books quartet is the grand finale, the place where the labyrinth of stories rearranges itself again and everything is put into yet another perspective. This is when we'll really see the big picture and get to the very essence of the stories, of what is behind each of the books. Even if readers by the end of *Prisoner* feel that now they really know what this chess game is about, they don't. Big surprises await them . . .

# Timelines

## Spain

- **1950:** The Oficina Nacional Permanente de Vigilancia de Espectáculos (Permanent National Office of Film Vigilance) is established as a censorship tool for the Catholic church to limit any 'immoral' content in films
- **1951:** The General Strike begins when thousands of workers walk rather than take trams in a protest against a hike in fare prices. The agitation leads to workers in all industries striking against high living costs and low wages and threatens the Franco regime, who respond with violence

- ☐ Ministry of Information and Tourism is created
- ■ **1952:** Barnaby Conrad published the bestseller *Matador* about the life of Manolete, the great Andalusian bullfighter
- ☐ Food rationing and the *cartilla de racionamiento* (ration card) end
- ☐ Spain enters UNESCO
- ☐ The Junta de Clasificación y Censura de Películas (Film Ratings and Censorship Board) is created
- ■ **1953:** Pact of Madrid between Spain and America lets America use and build military bases on Spanish territory in return for economic and military aid. This essentially ended Spain's isolation from the rest of the world
- ☐ A Concordat with the Vatican ensured the Catholic church officially recognised Franco's regime
- ☐ The Filmoteca Nacional (National Film Archive) is established
- ■ **1954:** First colour edition of *No-Do* (Noticiarios y Documentales: state controlled News and Documentaries often used as a tool of propaganda) airs
- ■ **1955:** Spain enters the UN
- ■ **1956:** Anti-Franco student protests at the University of Madrid; they are violently suppressed and protestors are detained
- ☐ Televisión Española (TVE), Spanish state television, broadcasts for the first time
- ☐ The Gaudí Chair is created at the Polytechnic University of Catalonia to further the study of the Gaudí's works and encourage their conservation
- ■ **1957:** Barcelona Urban Planning Commission plans the construction of residential estates in Bellvitge, La Verneda, Guineueta, Horta, Bon Pastor, Badalona, Baró de Viver and Cornellà in an attempt to house immigrants and shantytown dwellers
- ■ **1958:** Set-designer and pop-artist Eduardo Arroyo left Spain due to his contempt for Franco's regime
- ■ **1959:** The Economic Stabilisation Plan laid the basis for Spain's remarkable economic transformation in the 1960s

- *Serra d'Or* magazine, published in Catalan, is officially started as a form of cultural resistance to Franco's repression of regional cultures
- The Ley de Orden Público (Law of Public Order) is passed, outlawing street demonstrations
- Spain joined the IMF and the World Bank
- **1960:** El Dúo Dinámico had their first original hit with 'Quince Anos Tiene Mi Amor' (My Love Is Fifteen Years Old) http://www.youtube.com/watch?v=ZGRHHdRDLDk

## UK

- **1950:** England competes in its first World Cup, suffering a humiliating defeat by the USA
- The first purpose-built supermarket is opened in Croydon
- Mervyn Peake's *Gormenghast*, Graham Greene's *The Third Man* and C.S. Lewis's *The Lion, The Witch and The Wardrobe* are published
- **1951:** The Festival of Britain on the South Bank in London aims to show that Britain is on the recovery from wartime shortages and austerity by promoting the best of British art, industry and design

- ☐ The first Miss World contest is held at the Lyceum Theatre in London
- ■ **1952:** King George VI dies and Elizabeth becomes queen
- ☐ The Great Smog brings London transport to a standstill
- ■ **1953:** The coronation of Queen Elizabeth II shows TV viewing figures at an all-time high
- ■ **1954:** Roger Bannister breaks the four-minute mile
- ☐ End of food rationing
- ■ **1955:** Mary Quant opens Bazaar, the first boutique, which sparks a fashion and retail revolution and lays the foundations for the 'Swinging London' of the 1960s
- ■ **1956:** The Suez Crisis in Egypt, which eventually leads to an acceleration in decolonisation
- ☐ Clean Air Act is passed as a result of the Great Smog. This introduced smokeless zones in which domestic fuel couldn't be burned
- ■ **1957:** Harold MacMillan becomes prime minister and tells the nation they've 'never had it so good'
- ■ **1958:** The last debutantes are presented at court
- ☐ Hula hoops become a popular pastime

- **1959:** Colin MacInnes publishes *Absolute Beginners* which documents teenage life in west London in the 1950s
- Introduction of the hovercraft makes crossing the channel easier
- **1960:** Largest demonstration of the twentieth century to date sees tens of thousands of people gather to protest the H Bomb
- *Lady Chatterley's Lover* goes on sale and sells out in many bookshops across the country after Penguin win a groundbreaking trial against obscenity charges

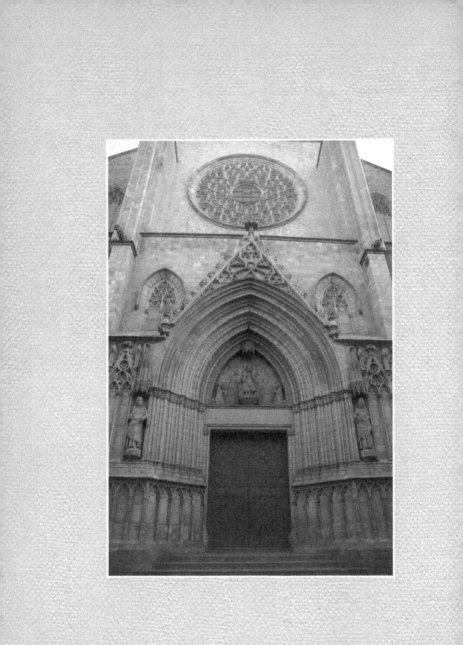

# The Barcelona of Carlos Ruiz Zafon

## Gothic City, Gothic Literature

Ruiz Zafón's writing has been associated with the Gothic novel, a genre that has had very few exponents in Spain. And Barcelona is considered a Gothic city by virtue of its architecture. Is there any relation between these two circumstances?

The writer himself, Barcelona-born, likes to allude to his links with an English-language literary tradition that emerges in the eighteenth century with authors such as Walpole and Beckford and is characterized by the use of medieval settings, a fantastical tone, and psychologically damaged if not downright demonic characters. Gothic, as a creative genre that attracted figures such as Byron, Jane Austen, Melville and Wilkie Collins, has a rich continuation in twentieth-century culture, from the *Rebecca* of Daphne du Maurier and Alfred Hitchcock to the Batman saga in comics and films, by way of Isak Dinesen or Roman Polanski and a good few of the novels of Joyce Carol Oates.

Ruiz Zafón combines this affiliation – the dark scenes, the demonic presences, the tormented characters – with doses of wry humour and observations of ordinary life. His is a nuanced Gothicism.

As for Barcelona, this is a city with more than two thousand years of history, which began its expansion under the Roman Empire. But its first great historic moment is medieval, and there we find the power of the Gothic. As the art critic Robert Hughes affirms in his famous book about the city: 'Today, despite centuries of attrition and destruction, Barcelona's Gothic quarter still contains the most concentrated array of thirteenth- to fifteenth-century buildings in Spain and, not discounting even Venice, the most complete in Europe. They are of all types: parish churches, town houses, government buildings, council halls, guild headquarters, industrial structures, and of course the Cathedral.' The architecture reflected the prosperity of the medieval kingdom of Catalonia and Aragon, when, according to legend, even the fish in the Mediterranean had the four-barred flag on their backs.

Barcelona's Gothic quarter, for a good few years now one of the city's major tourist draws, is one of the elements that contextualize *The Shadow of the Wind*. The quarter is bisected by Calle Fernando, where Gustavo Barceló has his bookshop, between Calle Santa Ana, where the Semperes live, and the Plaza Real, where Clara Barceló plays the piano; Daniel frequently passes to and fro, skirting the Cathedral.

As it appears today, the Gothic quarter is something of an illusion. The whole area was subjected to a process of reconstruction and monumentalization between 1911, when the neo-Gothic façade of the Cathedral was completed, and 1965. Certain parts were rebuilt, such as the Plaza de San Felipe Neri where Nuria Monfort lives in *The Shadow of the Wind* – the square had been badly damaged during the Civil War, and the new buildings were required to be Gothic in style. Other elements were created from scratch, such as the so-called Puente del Obispo, designed by the architect Joan Rubió i Bellver in 1928, which very few people today would put at less than five hundred years old (local legend has it that the head of the Metropolitan Church used the bridge to slip out of his palace unnoticed – there are different explanations of why he should have wanted to).

Barcelona is a city with a lot of very good Gothic architecture, outside the Gothic quarter as well as in, but some of it is reconstructed and stylized, as it is in the Carcasonne of Viollet-le-Duc, who influenced a whole generation of Catalan architects.

The Gothic buildings are a much repeated sign of how in Barcelona the distant past continues to pervade the present with its medieval memory. David Martín, the hero of *The Angel's Game*, moves into a house in Calle Flassaders, in the Ribera district. The neighbourhood lives in the shadow of Santa María del Mar, one of the finest Gothic churches in the world, which has a referential role in the novel similar to that of the Cathedral in *The Shadow of the Wind*.

To all practical purposes, however, Ruiz Zafón is interested not so much in the Gothic as the neo-Gothic, which in Catalonia assumed certain very singular characteristics, and like any 'neo-' is more dramatic and exaggerated than the model it is based on. Neo-Gothic, the reworking of elements of Gothic architecture several centuries after that historical style passed away, is in most cases a nostalgic vision of the past that sees the medieval as the pinnacle of a country's culture. Nineteenth-century Britain saw a revival of the Gothic style, championed by theorists like John Ruskin, with ogee arches, pointed towers and stained glass appearing all over the island, a phenomenon that was understood as a nostalgic reaction to rampant industrialization.

In Catalonia there was also a revival of Gothic in the second half of the nineteenth century, the period of maximum expansion of the local industrial bourgeoisie and the emergence of a movement of nationalist affirmation and recovery of the Catalan language that sought to recreate the glories – real and imagined – of the Middle Ages by way of things like Catalan poetry contests (*Jocs Florals*) and the adoption of a medievalizing aesthetic. This was the background to so-called Modernista architecture, whose prime exponent was Antoni Gaudí, Barcelona's most eccentric and inspired architect (though he was born in Reus). Is it so surprising that the city that produced the finest concentration of Gothic buildings in Europe should also have the most distinguished Gothic revival?

Ruiz Zafón first fell under the hypnotic spell of Catalan neo-

Gothic as a schoolboy at the great college run by the Jesuits in Sarriá. The school – by the architect Joan Martorell, who taught Gaudí and guided his first steps – is a powerful presence in *Marina*, as the boarding school attended by the narrator-hero, and reappears in *The Shadow of the Wind*, transmuted into San Gabriel's School.

Here Carax, Aldaya, Moliner, Ramos and Fumero coincide – the quintet of friends who then diverge, with tragic consequences: 'Its red brick façade dotted with dagger-shaped windows [and] crowned by arches and towers . . . peered over a group of plane trees like a Gothic cathedral.'

As for Gaudí, his febrile spirit pervades many Zafónian pages. The author of *The Shadow of the Wind* grew up in the neighbourhood dominated by the Sagrada Familia, the unfinished 'cathedral of the poor', and the recurring sight of the Expiatory Temple with its spires and bridges and variegated multiform façade contributed, with the Jesuit school, to the neo-Gothic iconography of the writer's childhood, so decisive in his work. For Ruiz Zafón, his Martorell-created school space and Gaudí-dominated home space compose the original sites of imagination, of mystery, of the enigma . . . The dusty zoology museum in the San Ignacio school and the unfinished towers overlooking his home stimulated him – enormously – and shaped his baroque and at times sombre imagination. And here we have the shift from Barcelona's Gothic architecture to the literary Gothic in which our writer soon found the most satisfactory vehicle for his expressive needs.

## The Year of the Games

It is hard to say whether a trilogy like the Cemetery of Forgotten Books could have been written before the 1992 Olympic Games, which placed Barcelona in the spotlight of international attention, made it fashionable, and at the same time led to the biggest urban transformation in its contemporary history.

It is possible that the recent international interest in Barcelona and its history and culture has contributed to *The Shadow of the Wind* being greeted with such well-deserved enthusiasm. We should bear in mind, though, that Carlos Ruiz Zafón's mature fiction is largely a lament for a lost city, the city that disappeared with the Olympic games. As the narrator of *Marina* regretfully observes, 'the Barcelona of my youth no longer exists. Its streets and its light have gone forever and live now only in memory.'

After working in advertising for a while, Carlos Ruiz Zafón (Barcelona, 1964) left the agency to start out as a professional writer and created his first published work, the young adult novel *The Prince of Mist*, in that Olympic summer of 1992. 'I wrote a lot of it at night. The city was all lit up and I would work through till sunrise,' he recalls. *The Prince of Mist*, which won the Edebé prize the following year, is set in a village on the English coast during World War II. His next two novels, *The Midnight Palace* and *The Watcher in the Shadows*, also for young adults, came out in 1994 and 1995, and also have non-Spanish settings: Calcutta in the 1930s and France in the same period.

Meanwhile our author, fascinated since childhood by the world of cinema, moved to Los Angeles, hoping to launch a career in the Seventh Art. It would seem that distance shifted his perception of his home town, because after a few years in the Californian metropolis, for the first time he felt inspired to use the Catalan capital as a literary setting, and has not strayed from it since. *Marina* takes place in Barcelona; he himself calls the book a hybrid between juvenile and adult fiction. *Marina* came out in 1999, followed in 2001 by *The Shadow of the Wind*, and in 2008, after a long wait, by *The Angel's Game*, and all three are set in Barcelona. Meanwhile a number of short stories that had first appeared in diverse publications were collected in the privately circulated *Barcelona Gothic* (2008). In other words, the entire corpus of Carlos Ruiz Zafón's mature fiction is enacted on the same stage.

The post-Olympic Barcelona is an elegant and (mostly) well-kept and interconnected city, famous for its urban design, which has received a Harvard University planning award (although many dissenting voices are now dismissing the city's model of development as moribund). In present-day Barcelona almost everything seems new or recent, even the historic buildings, most of which have been subjected to radical restoration.

By contrast, the city prior to the monumental Olympic face lift and the property speculation that went with it was a lot less looked-after, more ramshackle and labyrinthine, with less efficient transport links. It was not uncommon to find vacant lots and empty apartments, even whole buildings. Much of the outskirts was a no-man's land of dead-end streets where grass and weeds grew, and there were whole neighbourhoods where everything seemed just as it must have been in 1920. Down on the beach you could eat at wooden kiosks, now all bulldozed away. Despite the reforms being introduced by the new democratic administration, many grand official buildings retained their old dark heavy furniture and heinous functionaries who harked back to the Franco era or earlier, to the dictatorship of General Primo de Rivera. It was, in short, a city much more mysterious and full of contrasts, as well as being more sinister and of course more run-down than Barcelona today.

This pre-Olympic city is what captivates Carlos Ruiz Zafón, who has managed to fashion for us an extraordinary synthesis of the many different aspects of the historic Barcelona, its culture, its social life, its crime reports, its palpitations – at times with passionate feeling, at others with ironic detachment, but always with great narrative verve.

One of the most attractive qualities of these books is their point of view. In both *Marina* and *The Shadow of the Wind*, as in much of *The Angel's Game*, the narrator who immerses himself in the city and reveals it to us is a teenager on the threshold of adulthood. His gaze is ours: his ingenuity and his vulnerability, and his insights, too. He is a solitary and far from knowing individual, often defenceless, like those heroes of Dickens's to whom Ruiz Zafón pays tribute in his books, and it is through him we gain access to the secrets of the metropolis and observe with emotion and sadness how the passage of time and life tarnishes friendships, embitters hearts, twists destinies . . . And we also see how truth and love can win through, exercising their redemptive power.

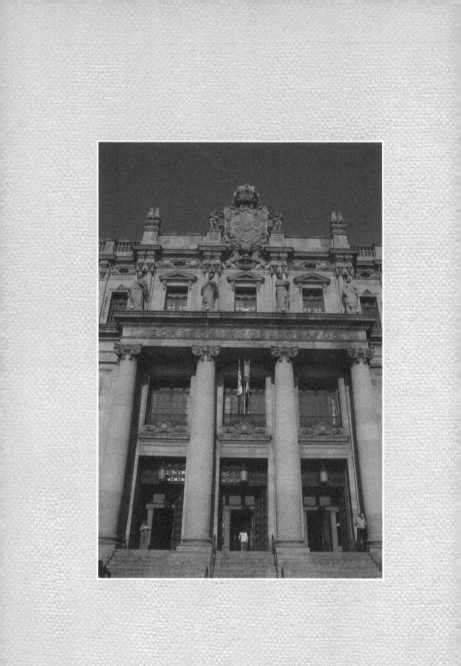

# Suggested Further Reading

*The Count of Monte Cristo*
by Alexandre Dumas

*A Christmas Carol*
by Charles Dickens

*The Turn of the Screw*
by Henry James

*The Strange Case of Dr Jekyll and Mr Hyde*
by Robert Louis Stevenson

*The Mysterious Flame of Queen Loana*
by Umberto Eco

*blog and newsletter*

For literary discussion, author insight,
book news, exclusive content,
recipes and giveaways, visit the
Weidenfeld & Nicolson blog and
sign up for the newsletter at:

## www.wnblog.co.uk

For breaking news, reviews and exclusive competitions
Follow us 🐦 @wnbooks
Find us 📘 facebook.com/WeidenfeldandNicolson